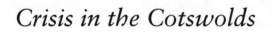

Crisis in the Cotswolds

Crisis in the Cotswolds

REBECCA TOPE

Allison & Busby Limited
12 Fitzroy Mews
London W1T 6DW
allisonandbusby.com

First published in Great Britain by Allison & Busby in 2018.

Copyright © 2018 by REBECCA TOPE

A CIP catalogue record for this book is available from
the British Library.

First Edition

ISBN 978-0-7490-2337-9

Typeset in 12/17.2 pt Sabon by
Allison & Busby Ltd.

The paper used for this Allison & Busby publication
has been produced from trees that have been legally sourced
from well-managed and credibly certified forests.

Printed and bound by
CPI Group (UK) Ltd, Croydon, CR0 4YY

For Tim and Paula Charsley
with thanks for your help with exploring the
Cotswolds

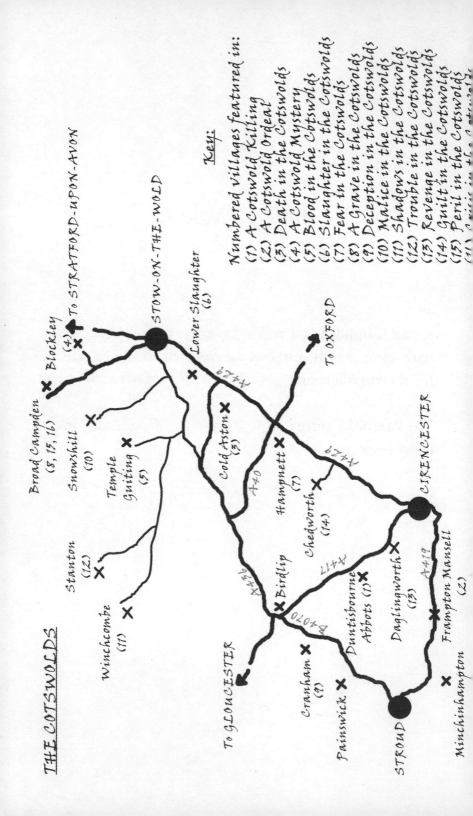

THE COTSWOLDS

To STRATFORD-UPON-AVON

Broad Campden (8, 15, 16)

Blockley (4)

Snowshill (10)

Stanton (12)

Temple Guiting (5)

Winchcombe (11)

STOW-ON-THE-WOLD

Lower Slaughter (6)

Cold Aston (3)

Hampnett (7)

Chedworth (14)

A429

A40

To OXFORD

Birdlip

A417

Cranham (9)

Painswick

Duntisbourne Abbots (1)

Daglingworth (13)

A4070

A436

A419

CIRENCESTER

Frampton Mansell (2)

Minchinhampton

STROUD

To GLOUCESTER

Key:

Numbered villages featured in:

(1) A Cotswold Killing
(2) A Cotswold Ordeal
(3) Death in the Cotswolds
(4) A Cotswold Mystery
(5) Blood in the Cotswolds
(6) Slaughter in the Cotswolds
(7) Fear in the Cotswolds
(8) A Grave in the Cotswolds
(9) Deception in the Cotswolds
(10) Malice in the Cotswolds
(11) Shadows in the Cotswolds
(12) Trouble in the Cotswolds
(13) Revenge in the Cotswolds
(14) Guilt in the Cotswolds
(15) Peril in the Cotswolds
(16) [illegible]

Author's Note

Broad Campden is a real village, but I have tinkered with some details of the layout in order to find a site for the burial ground.

The Paxford Centre is a product of my imagination in every respect.

Chapter One

'That was difficult,' said Drew, clasping and twisting his hands as if holding himself together. 'Worse than difficult, in fact.'

'In what way?' Thea frowned up at him. 'Are they in a terrible hurry or something?'

'No. They want me to pretend the funeral's not happening. They want me to lie, if a particular person phones to enquire. And they will, apparently.'

'Who? Don't they know who they're dealing with? What did you tell them?'

He went to the kettle and made himself a cup of strong instant coffee. His movements were jerky, and Thea could feel his tension from across the room. 'I told them it wasn't something I would generally agree to.'

'Don't make it so strong, Drew. It's bad for your heart.'

'It's not my heart I'm worried about. It's my

conscience. I let money overrule principle. A simple moral dilemma, on the face of it. But who am I to judge the rights and wrongs of it?'

'So – I'm guessing these are nice people, and the person you've got to lie to is a feckless drunken cousin who's going to come and wreck the whole thing.'

'More or less, according to them. But how do I know if I can believe what they say? What if it's the other way round? It's a big thing, to stop somebody coming to a funeral.'

'I could do it,' she offered. 'I'm a better liar than you, after all. You'd just stammer and choke, and they'd know you were fobbing them off.'

She could see he was tempted. 'That would mean you answering every call for the rest of the week. You wouldn't be able to go out.'

'True,' she nodded, with a glance at the clear blue sky outside. 'But I can hear the phone from the garden, and that new lounger hasn't had much use so far.'

'You lazy object,' he sighed. 'What happened to those plans you had for getting a job? That was months ago now.'

'It must have been New-Year-itis. Resolutions and new starts and all that. But Hepzie thinks it wouldn't do. Not to mention Steph and Tim. The whole thing would get impossibly complicated.'

'Other people manage. In fact, as far as I can see, just about every woman in the land has found a way of managing. Look at Maggs.'

'I know they have, but it doesn't look like fun to me. I've never imagined I could compete with Maggs on any level. And I'm not sure it would be sensible economically, either, in our case. We've still got plenty of my house money to fall back on. We'll talk about it again when Tim goes to the big school, okay?'

Drew sighed again. 'That's two and a bit years from now, right?'

'Indeed. No time at all. Now tell me about this dodgy funeral.'

He sat at the table, nursing his mug. 'The deceased is called Stephen Biddulph, aged seventy-nine. The funeral's on Tuesday. There's a wife, Linda, and a son, Lawrence. Second wife. Which is a secret, even from Lawrence. He's always assumed he was a one and only.'

'What? And she told you, just like that?'

'I'm a safe pair of ears. But now that Stephen's dead, she's worried that word will get back to the first wife and her two sons. Secrets have a habit of breaking loose when there's a death. That would rock all sorts of boats. Especially for her precious son, who would be exceedingly upset, apparently.'

Thea gave this some thought. 'He'd be very angry as well, probably. Especially with her for keeping the existence of half-brothers hidden from him. I know I would be.' She scowled at the very idea. 'What a coward she must be.'

'Hey! That's a bit strong. She says Stephen made

her swear never to mention it when Lawrence was born, and she's stuck with it. She's quite proud of herself, I think.'

'So, the man never saw his older sons in all that time?' Her outrage was still all too evident. 'How is that possible in this day and age?'

Drew shrugged. 'Good question.' He finished the coffee and stood up. 'Anyway, can't stop. Mr Fleming tomorrow, nine-thirty sharp.'

'The birdsong one?'

'That's him.'

They had enjoyed this particular customer more than most when it came to planning the funeral. Mr Fleming, deceased, had been avid about birds, and had insisted that his burial take place to the sound of their song. Dying at the beginning of May had been a bonus but, as Thea had pointed out, 'They sing loudest at about 5 a.m. You'll have to be out there pretty early.'

Mrs Fleming, being a woman of pragmatic character, had refused to consider anything sooner than half past nine. 'They won't sing at all if it's raining,' she said. 'These things are clearly impossible to control. If it's a fine day, there'll be very nice early sunshine and most likely some sort of birdsong, even if it's only collared doves.'

Drew, who lived to serve, had worried. 'What if I bring a CD player for backup?' he suggested. 'There are sure to be some discs of birds available.'

'If you like,' the widow agreed. 'But I'm not sure

that's what Dicky had in mind. To be perfectly frank, it's enough for me that he died thinking it would all go as he wanted it to. He imagined the whole thing in advance, and that made him happy. What we actually do on the day isn't terribly relevant, when you stop to think about it.'

Drew was never quite sure how to handle this kind of scepticism. Any lack of consideration for the rituals of death made him uneasy. 'You still think the dead person's hovering over you, watching what goes on,' Thea accused him. 'Don't you?'

'Not exactly,' he prevaricated. 'But it feels wrong to risk it, just in case.'

This elicited a laugh that was more affectionate than mocking. 'You're a one,' she told him.

But they both knew that Drew had a comprehensive understanding of most of the emotional and cultural significances of a funeral. He regularly knew better than the families themselves what were the essential elements that should not be fudged or overlooked. Primary amongst these essentials was a recognition that the person concerned had gone and was not coming back. This was followed closely by a similar recognition that the same thing was going to happen to everybody else in the family, and it therefore behoved them to do as they would be done by. The dead were acutely vulnerable to disrespect and calumny, which explained the taboo against speaking ill of them. Whether grieving the loss or celebrating the life – or, ideally, both – there were certain truths that Drew would not allow to be dodged. He never said 'passed away', never avoided referring directly to 'the body', and never carelessly agreed to any overriding of the dead person's wishes.

And in the case of Mr James Fleming (always known as Dicky), he very much hoped that some obliging birds would sing spectacularly in the trees above the newly dug grave.

But the matter of the Biddulph family – or *families*, to be strictly accurate – was a whole other worry. Thea's offer to shoulder the burden of blatant lying was of very little comfort. Her involvement in the burial business was capricious at the best of times. At the outset, he had assumed that she would step efficiently into the shoes of his first assistant, Maggs Cooper. Arranging the funerals, talking to the relatives, even handling the bodies and attending the burials – it was all there waiting for her when they moved to Broad Campden. But, bit by bit, she had detached herself until her role had reduced to little more than answering the phone and sending out the bills. Her first experience of making arrangements with a young wife and very young son had gone disastrously badly. The family took its business elsewhere and Thea swore never to do that again. 'I'm not Maggs Cooper,' she said repeatedly. 'She's irreplaceable.'

It was true that Maggs was unusual. If ever a person had a vocation, it was her. From her early teens, she knew what she wanted to do and foisted herself on the local undertaker, brooking no arguments. When Drew set up on his own, Maggs went with him. Their success was as much thanks to her as to his own efforts. People loved her. Sensitive but direct, friendly but professional – she struck precisely the right note in her dealings with the bereaved. And now she was in charge of that original business, down in Somerset, with a small child, husband and versatile employee called Pandora, while Drew soldiered on in the Cotswolds, assisted not by his wife but a new employee named Andrew.

'I'll have to think about it,' he said five minutes later. He'd made some toast for himself before pursuing further business in his office.

'Think about what?' Thea had been reading the local paper, forgetting all about Drew and his burials.

'The first Mrs Biddulph,' he reminded her.

'Is that still her name?'

'Good question. Probably not. Look – don't stay by the phone any more than usual. If the call comes through to me, I can handle it. If you do answer it, just be careful what you tell anybody asking about that funeral, okay?'

'No problem.' She smiled at him, her whole face soft and pretty and guileless. His wife, he inwardly repeated, for the thousandth time in nearly a year. His *second* wife. Thea Osborne, née Johnstone, now Slocombe. Stepmother to his children, retired house-sitter and a few years older than him. He had fallen for her within minutes of their first meeting, in the face of disapproval from Maggs and his own anguished conscience, his first wife Karen still being alive at the time.

'Anything in the paper?' he asked.

'Quite a lot, actually. You've got a heartfelt thanks in the obituaries, and somebody's stolen a Labrador bitch and eight puppies, one week old. How is that possible? What foul things people can be. Oh, and they've finally got your plans in the council announcements section. Only a month late, the idiots.'

'It doesn't matter. I can't afford to do it yet, anyway.'

'That's not the point.' Her look was part exasperation and part affection. 'It sends a message that business is growing and you're keen to add more facilities and attract more customers.'

'Yes, I know,' he said, with his customary patience.

Chapter Two

The children came home in two very different moods. Stephanie was moving up to the final year at the primary school the following term and was taking it all very seriously. Shouldering responsibility came naturally to her and she was already positioning herself for the role of Head Girl, despite it being months away. Her rival was a child called Sophie, and the resulting enmity was savage. Most afternoons, Thea was expected to listen to every little skirmish in the never-ending war between them, and today was no exception.

Timmy, by contrast, had no ambitions of any kind beyond basic survival. He strove to avoid attention, especially from other children. Increasingly, Thea had sympathised as she understood him better. Small, colourless, quiet and shy, he was easy to overlook. One of four herself, with a healthy collection of nieces, nephews and a daughter of her own, she had nonetheless never encountered a child quite like

Tim. His fragility endeared him to her, where it often irritated Drew. 'It's the opposite of what might have been expected,' she remarked. 'You being the one with all the patience and so forth.'

Drew never relished discussions concerning his son. 'Just one of those things,' he would say. 'You'll have to put it down to chemistry.' He had moved from guilty to defensive and then to rueful acceptance. Tim was a motherless child and the damage was inescapable. All Thea could do was try to soften the edges of his woe.

Now, the little boy was contentedly sitting at the big kitchen table with his juice, biscuit and latest electronic device, ignoring his sister's complaints about Sophie. Even his palpable relief at the end of every school day made Thea wince for him. It was as if he mentally ticked one more box off the thousands he would have to endure until he could find freedom. The previous summer had been a whirl of getting married, moving to Broad Campden, entertaining the bewildered children and generally adjusting to the new life for them all. Now they were more firmly settled, with Drew often busy to the point of discomfort, and the future more easy to see. Thea's spaniel had her routines, pottering up and down the quiet lane where they lived, often unsupervised. A middle-aged Labrador four houses along had made her acquaintance, and the two would get together, somewhat against Cotswolds protocol, which much preferred its animals to be kept under rigid control. Hepzibah was a familiar figure, the

Labrador unambitious and, compared to the sudden appearance of an undertaker in their midst, the dogs gave no grounds for neighbourhood objection.

'And she *deliberately* broke my pencil,' Stephanie whined. 'She dropped it on its point while she was pretending to give it back to me. And then Mrs French told me not to make wild accusations.'

Thea had to hide a smile at the outrage on the child's face. 'Sounds as if you had a fairly normal day, then,' she said. 'How about you, Tim?'

He shrugged, as he always did, but then looked up. 'Daniel Oakhurst's big brother is going to die. I think they're going to call Dad about it. I forgot to tell you.'

'Really? How old is he?'

'Dunno. Year Twelve or something. He's got cancer in his head. Mrs Carroll told us not to talk about it, but Daniel says that's silly. They talk about it all the time at their house, he says. He's okay, Daniel.'

This was a major breakthrough, and Thea took care not to overreact. Implications swarmed through her mind – first of which was a probable improved status for Timmy, as the son of the man who handled such a high-profile funeral. The hint of a friend made at school at long last came close second. She wondered how a Year Four teacher might approach the fact of a young death with her class. 'We'd better tell him about it now, then,' she said. 'Where do the Oakhurst family live?'

'Right near the school,' said Stephanie. 'Jemima

Oakhurst is in my class. The brother's called Curtis.'

Timmy and Thea both looked at her with less than admiring expressions. 'Is she your friend?' asked Thea.

'No,' said Stephanie. 'She's horrible.'

'Okay. So let's leave it to Timmy, shall we? He can be the go-between.'

Stephanie gave a hesitant shrug. All her life she had been expected to yield to her little brother's needs, and mostly she went along with the expectations. In the big things – the very biggest thing, anyway – she had had her way, and that left her feeling somehow in Timmy's debt. Drew had broken a promise to his son because he and Stephanie had cravenly chosen to bury his mother in another field than their own. The betrayal was stark and permanent. Nobody thought the debt would ever be fully paid off.

The prospect of another funeral, this time of a teenage boy, gave rise to mixed feelings. Thea had long since grown accustomed to the flash of relief, even a momentary excitement, at the knowledge that the council tax could be paid for another month, or the freezer restocked. Only after that did she find space for sympathy and fellow feeling for those who had suffered the loss. Then came the story, every one of them different. Drew had great skill in eliciting the smaller details, the near-forgotten facts that made this person unique. 'Mrs Taylor was a rally driver in her twenties' or 'William Collins mined opals in Australia until he was forty-five. He made a fortune and then lost the whole lot in three years, gambling on greyhounds. Isn't that incredible?' He nearly always added those final words, his eyes shining at the strange ways of the world.

'Do you think Dad should phone the Oakhursts?' Thea asked Timmy. 'What did Daniel say exactly?'

'We should wait for them to call us,' interposed Stephanie with total authority. 'That's the way it works.'

'Yes, I know, but . . .' Thea floundered, aware that this young girl had a much more natural grasp of the business than she ever would.

'You lot are quiet,' said Drew, looking round the door. 'What's going on?'

'Tim's got a message for you,' said Thea.

'Has he indeed? And I've got one for you. All of you. Guess who's coming to visit us tomorrow night?'

Stephanie studied his face for two seconds. 'Maggs,' she said with total certainty.

'And Den?' shouted Tim.

'And Meredith?' Thea added, adopting a smile that was just a trifle broader than the feelings lying behind it.

'All of them,' Drew confirmed. 'They're staying the weekend.' He sighed contentedly. 'Won't that be wonderful.'

Friday was mainly dedicated to housework, thanks to the imminent arrival of three guests. There was a spare room for them, kept available for visitations that seldom happened. Thea's siblings had not once come to see the Broad Campden set-up, but her mother had stayed a few days at Easter. The only other person was Thea's daughter, Jessica, who had recently taken to making monthly overnight stays, belatedly eager to get to know her stepbrother and -sister. 'It's brilliant to have more relatives,' she enthused. 'And they're such great kids, aren't they?'

'Drew's not so bad, either,' Thea had laughed.

'He's a catch,' the girl agreed.

Now there was dusting, washing and shopping for food, all on a bright sunny day that had been scheduled for idling about in the garden. The school half-term holiday was rapidly approaching, bringing demands for entertainment from the children. When she suggested to Drew that he clear some days for himself so they could go out as a family, he'd raised his eyebrows and said people didn't die to order, unfortunately.

'No, but you could put the funerals back a couple of days, couldn't you?'

'I'll do what I can,' was the closest she got to agreement.

The phone call came at half past ten next morning. The dog barked up the stairs to inform her mistress that she was wanted. Drew was not yet back from burying Mr Fleming. If the landline wasn't answered, the call would be redirected to his mobile, but he preferred that not to happen, and if it was during a funeral, it would go unheeded. Thea had been schooled in the procedures for handling reports of a death, as well as enquiries. Only as she reached the final stair, two strides away from the phone, did she remember the Biddulph business.

'Hello? Drew Slocombe Undertaker,' she said briskly.

'Ah. Yes. Hello. I understand that you're handling the funeral of a Mr Stephen Biddulph. I wonder if you could tell me the day and the time?'

She took a deep breath. 'Oh, let me see.' She rustled a piece of paper, probably very unconvincingly. 'No, I'm sorry. I don't think we've got anybody of that name in the diary. You did say "Biddulph", didn't you?'

'That's right. And please don't play games with me. I know for a fact that you're burying him sometime next week. That's not in question at all. All I'm asking is for a civilised response to a perfectly normal enquiry.'

Her heart was thumping, mostly with shame at her own behaviour. 'Well, I really am sorry, but I can't help you any more than I have. I've got no more information for you.'

'I see.' Anger filled her ear, along with distress and frustration. 'So I have to camp out in your benighted little village for a week, then, do I? Because there is no way in the world my family and I are going to miss it, you see. I don't know who you are, but I can tell you, you've got yourself drawn into something pretty unsavoury.'

'I'm Thea Slocombe, actually. My husband runs the business. And I might add that I don't know who *you* are, either.'

'My name, if it matters, is Clovis Biddulph. Stephen was my father. But it's perfectly clear that your husband has been told to make bloody sure no unwanted relatives show up to ruin the nice natural little burial they've got planned. I get it. Well, Mrs Thea Slocombe, you can tell the lot of them it's not going to work. It beats me how they ever thought it could. Even if they bury him at midnight, I'm going to be there. And it's not just me, either. Tell them that, and see what they do then.'

She made a wordless sound and put the phone back on its stand. 'Dear me,' she said to the spaniel. 'Looks like trouble.'

'I did your lying for you,' she told Drew when he came in at lunchtime. 'Except I made rather a poor job of it. That man knows perfectly well you're doing the funeral. Somebody probably Facebooked it. Nobody can keep secrets any more.' The whole business had made her irritable. 'Honestly, Drew, it's all wrong. How can people let themselves get into such messes?'

He was twisting his hands together, as he had the day before. It made him look like a very worried undertaker.

'I wish you wouldn't do that,' she said. 'It's starting to be a habit.'

'What?'

'Wringing your hands. I didn't know anybody actually did that, but now you are. What are you so scared of?'

'I'm not *scared*. I just don't know what I should do about it. It takes me back to when I was at Plant's and reputation was crucial. Daphne used to give us little lectures about being seen to be absolutely reliable and straight. Which she wasn't, really, when it came to the crunch. That was why I left. I didn't like the way everything was stitched up with the nursing homes and the coroner's officer.'

'I thought it was because you disapproved of the overcharging?'

'That too. I always felt the families were being quietly exploited, and I wanted to be on their side.'

'And you *are*. But sometimes people make things impossible. It's not your fault.'

'It is, though. I should have told them straight yesterday. What did the man on the phone say?'

'He said there was no way he was going to miss the funeral and, if he had to, he'd camp here. He thinks you've planned a secret midnight burial.'

He laughed. 'We never thought of that.' Then his features straightened again. 'But who would be idiotic enough to put it on Facebook? After everything Mrs Biddulph said to me?'

She thought for a moment. 'Could be somebody secretly sympathises with the first family and wanted to alert them. How many are there in the second family?'

'Wife. Lawrence. He's got a wife and a little daughter.'

'Has he? I thought he sounded too young for that, the way you were talking yesterday. How old is his mother, then?'

'She must be fifty or so. Stephen was only twenty when he married the first time. He was probably well under forty when Lawrence was born. He's had plenty of time to marry and have children.'

'Hang on, Drew. This isn't adding up.' She looked at him with a frown. 'It's not like you to get in that sort of muddle. If Stephen was forty, that was nearly forty years ago, which makes this wife only ten when she had Lawrence, if she's fifty now. You've got it wrong somewhere.'

He bowed his head in mock misery. 'I'm losing it,' he moaned. 'Midlife crisis or something. Let's start again. Stephen was seventy-nine. Linda – that's the second wife's name – looks about fifty. She didn't say how long they've been married, but she could have been only eighteen at the time. So Lawrence could be thirty. That works, doesn't it?'

'Just about. Did you meet him? Or his wife and child?'

Drew shook his head. 'Just Linda. All I know is what she told me.'

'But Lawrence has got a wife – right?'

'Yes. She's very upset about the old man dying, apparently. Got on wonderfully well with him. And he was a devoted granddad to the little one. She's called Modestine, which is a source of some disagreement, I gather.'

'So I should think. Poor little thing. What would you call her for short?'

He shrugged. 'History doesn't relate that detail.'

She gave him an admiring look. 'I know I've said it before, but it's miraculous, the way you get all this information from one short session. I can't imagine how that works.'

'It all comes easily enough. Talking about flowers, for example. People go through all the friends and relations who might be sending some. And when it's my sort of funeral, you get all the different opinions about burial and cremation, and ecology and religion. It's a serious business. It makes everybody focus on the important stuff.'

'It's a special talent, and you know it. You and Maggs are the only people I've ever met who could do it.' She sighed. 'I know because I tried, and failed. Although I can tell you that the son who phoned me is called Clovis. I don't think I can entirely dislike someone with such a wonderful name.'

'You didn't give yourself a chance with that funeral I asked you to arrange. It was my fault for throwing you in at the deep end.'

She let it drop there, a conversation they'd had

27

many times before. 'So, are they local? The Biddulphs, I mean. I suppose they must be if he wants to be buried here. But Clovis and Modestine both sound rather French. Has somebody got an exotic Parisian grandmother, do you think?'

'Quite possibly,' he said vaguely. 'Linda and Lawrence are more or less local. The first lot aren't very far away, from the sound of it. Stephen saw that piece about us in the paper last year. He put it into his will and told his family. All much as usual.'

'What's the matter?' she asked. 'You've gone all distant.'

'I was thinking about Maggs,' he said. 'It sounds as if she wants to tell me something.'

'It'll be another baby,' said Thea with confidence. 'She knows that'll make things complicated back at North Staverton.'

Drew winced. 'It certainly would. I couldn't believe how much harder it was with two than one. But it didn't really sound like that. Surely she'd have just told me on the phone and said she wanted to come and discuss the implications if it was only that?'

'You think it's more serious? Like what? I bet you it's a baby and she wants to watch your face when she tells you.'

'I'm trying not to think about it until they get here. Once I'd got to Den having a life-threatening illness, or them suddenly deciding to emigrate to Tasmania, I thought I should just wait and see.'

'Such self-control!' she applauded. 'But I doubt they fancy Tasmania, all the same.'

They were eating bread, pâté and salad, and drinking fruit juice. Thea was keen to put a permanent table outside, but most of the suitable space had been set aside for Drew's hearse. Bodies had to be collected from wherever they'd died, and for that he used a medium-sized van, which also had to be parked somewhere. The house, left to him by an impressed client, was on a narrow lane with houses set at various angles, built before anyone dreamt of owning two cars. People coming to arrange a funeral were advised to park further away and walk the final distance. The inconvenience was permanent and insoluble. After a year of conducting the business there, frustration was, if anything, increasing.

'Someone's coming to the door,' Drew said suddenly. 'I saw a head.' He pointed out of the kitchen window. From the front room, Hepzie gave a single bark of confirmation, two seconds before the doorbell rang.

'You're not expecting anybody, are you?' said Thea.

But Drew was already in the hallway, opening the door.

Chapter Three

'You *told* them!' came a loud, accusing female voice. 'After you *promised* not to. I've just heard from the only person who knows both families, saying they've found out about the funeral.'

'Mrs Biddulph. Come on in and we can talk about it,' he said calmly.

Thea was hovering at her husband's shoulder before she had time to think. 'That was quick,' she said, realising a moment later that she should have known better. The obvious implication that she had spoken to the forbidden stepson hung in the air for all to hear. 'Oh, sorry,' she went on. 'It's none of my business. Sorry. I'll just . . .' she flapped a hand towards the kitchen. 'Come on, Heps. We've got work to do.' It was a dreadful parody of a busy housewife that would have shamed any amateur theatre company.

'Come through,' said Drew, ignoring Thea completely.

'What did she mean?' the woman asked suspiciously as they vanished into the back room.

Thea sank onto a kitchen chair and tried to persuade herself that it had not been obvious after all that she had dropped Drew into boiling water. There were several steps between her refusing to tell a downright lie to the man on the phone and the second Mrs Biddulph accusing Drew of treachery. But it was a mess, however one looked at it.

She cleared the table and put the kettle on, thinking Drew might offer his visitor some tea. It was not his usual practice to do so, but this funeral was in no way usual. The bereaved could frequently be irrational, argumentative and quite often intoxicated, but they very seldom made wild accusations.

The tea was not required, in the event. After twenty minutes, the two emerged from the sanctum, grim-faced but civil. 'I hope I've made my position clear,' said Drew, sounding very unlike himself.

'It's not *your* position that matters, though, is it?' She sounded as if she'd said the same thing a few times already. 'I just can't have that woman putting in an appearance, telling Lawrence who he is, perhaps bringing all sorts of others with her.'

Drew sighed. 'I've given you my suggestions,' he said. 'Perhaps you could have a think about them and let me know tomorrow what you've decided. It's completely up to you, as I said. You're under no obligation to me at all.'

31

They had somehow drifted to the front door, which Drew opened. 'Goodbye, Mrs Biddulph, and please let me say I really am extremely sorry it's come to this.'

She turned to face him, her features softening. 'You don't have to be sorry. I know it's not your fault.' She peered into the living room, where Thea was visible, plumping cushions. 'I'm still not sure what your wife meant when she said "That was quick",' she said. 'I suppose everything's quick these days, with everybody texting and messaging and so forth. Nobody gets a moment to *think* any more. But I suppose we'll have to go ahead on Tuesday. I don't seem to have much choice, do I? I wouldn't know what to say to Lawrence if we postponed it.'

She went at last, Drew standing in the doorway as she walked up the lane.

'Sorry,' said Thea abjectly. 'I was such a fool.'

'It didn't matter. I'd already decided not to play any more games. I turned it round on her and said I was very unhappy that my wife was being dragged into their problems, and that what she'd asked of me was unacceptable. I suggested she makes contact with the first wife and try to have a civilised discussion. The thing is, absolutely *nobody* knows that this is the second Mrs Biddulph. 'But one person knows. She said so when she first got here just now.'

'But she told you almost as soon as she met you.'

'She did. Probably because I asked about death notices and letting people know when we were having

32

the burial. That seemed to open the floodgates. She emphatically rejected any sort of public notice and asked me not to tell anyone if they phoned. When I must have seemed to find that odd, she explained the reason. With a whole mass of family history for good measure.'

'It sounded as if there was some doubt about the funeral going ahead, just now.'

'That's right. It's on hold until she tells me otherwise. She's got until Monday morning. Mr B. is going to be okay at the hospital mortuary until then, anyway.' He heaved a deep breath and exhaled slowly. 'So, let's forget all about them and enjoy seeing Maggs again. She said they should get here about six. We'll have to kill a fatted calf for them.'

Thea had somehow overlooked the expected time of arrival and the need to provide a full-scale meal for seven people. Plus two more meals on the following day and, doubtless, a Sunday lunch as well. Catering was never her strong point. 'Could we take them to the pub, do you think?' she asked hopefully.

'Certainly not. Maybe tomorrow for lunch, but it would be ludicrous to take them out the moment they get here. Don't forget Meredith. She probably goes to bed at seven.'

'Remind me how old she is? I've lost track.'

'She was born two Septembers ago, which makes her twenty months. A toddler. Probably saying quite a lot by now. Still having a daytime sleep.' His gaze lost focus. 'I remember it all as if it was yesterday.'

'Well, I don't. Jessica's first ten years are a complete blank. I *thought* I was being a fully committed hands-on mother, but now I wonder whether I was even there much of the time.'

'Doesn't Stephanie ever remind you of Jess? Doing little girl things? They seem to have a lot of the same interests.'

'Now and then, I suppose. Jessica never watched films the way Stephanie does. She collected things. For years it was leaves. She pressed them, stuck them into books, and made pictures out of them. Carl taught her what they all were, and she labelled them. Like stamps, really. She must still have them somewhere.'

'Hasn't she told Steph about that? She'd probably love to have a go. I rather like leaves myself,' he added wistfully.

'Everyone does.' Thea was impatient. 'But that doesn't mean you have to make a *fetish* of them.'

'It's nearly two o'clock. Do you need to go and get food? I'm here for the kids, if so. I've got plenty to get on with.'

'I suppose I should. Is chicken all right? Then pasta or something tomorrow and a big pot of chilli on Sunday? I don't have to do a Sunday roast, do I?'

'It's up to you. I could do Sunday, if you like. What about a barbecue?'

She stared at him. 'You're joking, aren't you? The thing's on the point of collapse, for a start. And it'll probably rain. And we haven't got any charcoal.'

'Pity,' he said mildly. 'We should get a new one, and make sure we use it this summer. I love a nice barbie.'

All men do, she wanted to say, but bit the words back. She could already hear herself sounding like an irritating know-all.

'Chicken's perfect,' he told her. 'And I will do Sunday. It's only fair. They're really my guests, after all. You hardly know Den.'

'We did that antique stall together last year. It'll be nice to see him again. Is he still going to car boot sales or whatever it was?'

'No idea. You'll have to ask him.'

She watched his face and saw a return of the anxiety as to what it might be that Maggs had to say. Thea felt a surge of irritation in his defence. Why make him wait instead of saying it over the phone? It was unkind. 'I bet it's another baby,' she said with a smile.

'It probably is.' He reached out for her. 'Thanks, love. You don't have to worry about entertaining them, you know. It's only Maggs. They're practically family. Let's just make sure we enjoy ourselves, okay?'

'Okay,' she answered bravely.

The children's excitement blossomed as six o'clock approached. 'Can we stay up late to talk to them?' Stephanie pleaded. 'It is Friday, after all.'

'Just for a bit,' said Thea. 'You've got all weekend to talk. They'll just want to settle in and put Meredith to bed.'

'Where will she sleep?' Timmy gazed wide-eyed from face to face. 'There's no bed for her.'

'They're bringing one with them. It's a fold-up cot. I've actually no idea what it's like,' Thea admitted with a laugh. 'They might want you to help them put it up.'

The boy frowned as if burdened with an unfair responsibility. 'Only if you want to,' Thea assured him.

'Where will they *park*?' Stephanie wondered. 'There's no room for another car.'

'Yes there is, because I've moved ours,' said Drew. 'It's up by the church.'

'I'm hungry,' Tim complained, at five o'clock. 'Why aren't we having tea?'

'We're waiting to have it all together with Maggs and Den. I've done a great big chicken stew, and we're having rice with it.'

'Oh,' said Tim. 'Well, I hope they won't be late, then.'

'So do I,' said Drew. 'But if they are, we can have a few crisps or something to stop us from starving.'

At five to six, a car pulled up outside and Hepzie yapped. Both children hurtled to open the front door, deliberately jostling each other in the race to be first. Thea and Drew stayed in the living room, instinctively composing themselves into a united couple, lord and lady of the manor, welcoming the travellers. At least, that was how Thea fancied they might appear. It could just be that there would no space for them in the hallway once three more people entered it.

'Oh! Who are *you*?' came Stephanie's loud enquiry, in place of the expected salutations.

'That's no way to greet a visitor,' came a familiar Geordie accent. 'My name is Sonia Gladwin, as a matter of fact.'

Before the sentence was finished, Thea had rushed out to investigate. 'Sonia,' she gasped, unable to find anything to add that wouldn't be at least as impertinent as Stephanie's greeting had been.

The detective superintendent looked at the family gathered round her, including Drew in the doorway. 'Is this a bad time?' she said.

Chapter Four

'Well, it is a bit,' said Thea. 'We've got people coming at any moment, and apart from anything else, your car's going to be in their way.'

'Right. Okay. Sorry about that. Funeral people, are they?' Her brow creased. 'Funny time for it – but then you exist to break the rules, don't you?'

'No, no. They're friends. Colleagues. Not customers, anyway. What do you *want*?' The question burst out, the constraints of polite protocol cast to the winds.

'I want your help. A woman has gone missing not far from here and we're very concerned for her safety. I think she's someone you know from a while back. The thing is, it's complicated. Delicate.' She looked round again at the four faces. 'I wouldn't ask if it could be avoided, but it really would be a help if you could just hear the story and see what you think.'

'Sonia – I *can't*. I've got to feed seven people, and help get a toddler to bed, and—'

Drew stepped up. 'Go into the study,' he ordered. 'We can manage for a bit. They might not even be here for another half an hour. Go and be a good citizen.'

'Well keep an eye on the dinner, then. Don't let it dry out. I was going to add more water to it. And the wine needs to be opened. And I didn't finish laying the table.'

Gladwin was heading for the study – a room she already knew well. 'Come on,' she said. 'Let's get on with it.'

Thea bit her lip at the tone. She was no stranger to murder enquiries, some of which had been Gladwin's cases. She had moved all around the Cotswolds on a series of house-sitting jobs, encountering trouble, malice and fear along the way. At one point she had been in a relationship with another senior detective, involving herself quite directly in one or two investigations by his side. When DS Gladwin moved into the area and took up the reins, there was an immediate rapport. Slender, dark and energetic, she had moved with her husband and twin sons from the urban jungles of Tyneside to the comparatively sedate goings-on in Gloucestershire. 'It's a whole different class of murder,' she said. 'Which doesn't mean people don't behave every bit as badly – just in other ways from what I'm used to.'

'Right, then,' said the detective now, without pausing to sit down. 'Do you remember a woman called Juliet Wilson, in Stanton?'

'Juliet? Gosh, yes. That seems a long time ago now. Those pet rats. And the *horses*. What a palaver that was! You're not telling me it's Juliet who's gone missing? Her mother must be frantic.'

'You do remember her. Good. You'll understand why we're worried. She moved out of her mother's house, some time ago. Mrs Wilson broke her hip and all sorts of complications set in, which nobody realised until a neighbour reported screams.'

'Screams?'

'Yes – well, that's not important now. Juliet moved to a shared house in Blockley, with two other women, and got herself a little job in a boarding kennel. It was all going really well. It's always hard to admit, but the general view seems to be that she was in a much better state once she got away from her mother.'

'How long has she been missing?'

'Three days. She was last seen on Tuesday afternoon, when she left work.'

'Blockley's no distance from here. I'm surprised I haven't bumped into her if she's been living there.'

'Well, she knew you were here, apparently. She's got all the cuttings about the burial ground in her room. She talked about you to her housemates. They think she intended to come and visit you, if she could get up the courage.'

'She was never shy before. She kept walking into the house I was looking after, without even knocking.'

'It's different now. You're married, for one thing.'

'And she had a thing about men – I remember. It all came out at the end, didn't it? She'd good reason to be wary.'

'Which is one good reason for doing everything we can to find her. I have to say I've got a very bad feeling about it.'

'But she always did go off on her own. We saw her roaming in some woods in the freezing cold, one time. She insisted she was all right and knew what she was doing.'

Gladwin sighed. 'We think something must have happened to scare her. She could be hiding, of course. There's a lot of wide open space out there. But she'd need food, and the nights are still bloody cold.'

'So what can *I* do?'

'Think back to what you knew of her.'

'She was very sweet. We parted on good terms. But then I went off for Christmas with Drew, and I don't think I've even been to Stanton again. I haven't seen her at all since then. Does she drive?'

'No. Never got as far as that.'

'I really hope she's all right.'

'So do we all. So – if you've got time, have a scout around, between Blockley and here. You've always been good at that.'

'At finding dead bodies, you mean?' Thea's voice was harsh. 'Thanks very much.'

'I just wanted you to know. Juliet obviously had some special feeling for you. She might have been coming here when something happened to her. She goes everywhere on foot, just as she always did. She knows the footpaths and tracks. I just wanted you to know,' she repeated.

'Okay. Yes. I'm glad you told me. I'll see if I can think of anything useful – but I don't imagine I'll come up with anything.'

Squeals, voices and a yapping spaniel announced that the Coopers had finally arrived. 'Bathroom – quick!' came a loud female voice. 'This nappy's about to explode.'

'You'd better go and see to your visitors,' said Gladwin. 'Sorry about the terrible timing. I'll phone you if there's any news.'

'Thanks,' said Thea with minimal enthusiasm. 'I hope Juliet shows up safe, anyway.'

There followed a brief skirmish outside involving cars, Den and Gladwin managing it between them, having refused Drew's offer to direct the manoeuvres. Nobody had made any introductions and Den came back looking puzzled. 'Who was that?' he asked.

Thea cocked her head teasingly. 'Couldn't you tell? Didn't you get any vibes?'

'Don't tell me she's a cop.' He looked to Drew for rescue. 'Why didn't you tell me?'

'There wasn't time. She's a detective superintendent with the Gloucestershire force. She and Thea are old mates. Don't worry – she's got no idea who you are, either. As if it mattered.' Drew was sounding tetchy, with the collapse into near-chaos caused by Gladwin's presence, Meredith's overflowing nappy and Hepzibah's rampant enthusiasm for the newcomers.

'Okay. So – what's cooking? I can smell something

fabulous. Should I lay the table or something? Pour drinks? Entertain the young people? I'm at your disposal. Maggs and Merry won't be long. I can't tell you what torment the last ten miles have been. I'm not sure the car will be useable for a while.' Somehow, everybody had drifted into the kitchen, in an instinctive expectation of food, and were standing around awkwardly.

Drew and Thea gave their guest identical fond looks. Den Cooper was a man in a million, they both agreed. Six feet four inches tall, in his mid-thirties, calm, insightful and seemingly contented – he showed every sign of having found his place in life. Stephanie clung to his arm, gazing up at him in wonder.

'You're ever so tall, aren't you,' she said. 'Is it weird?'

'Sometimes. I bang my head quite a lot, and my feet stick out of the end of most beds.'

'I'll put the rice on,' said Thea. 'And that means dinner is served in precisely sixteen minutes from now. If anybody wants gin or something, they'll have to get it for themselves, or ask Drew.'

Maggs and her daughter made a less dramatic entrance the second time. 'Me pooed nappy,' the child announced, superfluously. She looked round proudly, taking her time in examining each face. In turn, the Slocombes all met her gaze. A well-built little body, with her father's long face, topped with dark-brown hair, she could pass as a native of anywhere between India and Brazil, taking in North Africa, Mexico and much of Europe. Her unknown maternal grandfather was assumed to be African, giving

Maggs black kinky hair and skin the colour of stained oak. Den's West Country genes had greatly modified the colouring and outline of his wife's, producing a robust offspring of immense character, if not actual beauty.

'That's nothing to be proud of,' Tim told her severely.

Meredith paused, understanding the tone but not the words. 'Me want drink,' she responded in defiance.

'Twelve minutes,' said Thea. 'It's too soon to sit up. Could you all go into the other room for a bit. It's getting crowded, and I don't want to drop boiling water on anybody.'

Meredith violently objected to this move, which seemed to threaten acute disappointment. Maggs extracted a spouted cup from a bag, and Drew nudged Stephanie to lead the way across the hall. 'I'll do some gin and tonic, shall I?' he asked of nobody in particular. 'Maggs? Are you drinking?'

She turned to stare at him. 'Why wouldn't I be?'

'No reason. You never used to like gin.'

'You're right. I don't. What else have you got?'

With considerable inefficiency, Drew managed to provide everyone with a drink, only to have them all summoned back to the table before they could swallow much of it. He and Thea had silently shared the certain knowledge that Maggs was not pregnant, as suspected.

The meal came to order, the children enjoying the occasion and the adults exchanging news. Nothing of any great import was disclosed, leaving Thea apprehensive as to what it was Maggs wanted to impart that clearly required a period of privacy away from all the others. The sense of something ominous hanging over them became stronger as the meal proceeded. The chicken stew was judged a success, with a stack of licked-clean plates to prove it. Ice cream followed, which she admitted was a cop-out. 'But I'm doing a proper pudding tomorrow,' she promised.

It was almost nine before the four adults finally slumped into the chairs and sofa in the living room. 'It's great to be here,' said Den. 'It must be a major disruption to your routine.'

'We thrive on disruption,' said Drew. 'We wouldn't know ourselves without it.'

Maggs sat straighter, leaning forward slightly. 'That sounds like my cue, then,' she said. 'I won't leave you in suspense any longer – I can see you're desperate to know what we've come to tell you. And no – I'm not pregnant, Drew. I could have told you that over the phone.'

Thea saw Den trying to catch Drew's eye. When he finally did, it was to signal something that looked like apology. Something sheepish and embarrassed, too.

'Uh-oh,' said Drew.

'It isn't good. I can't pretend it is. In a nutshell, I want to give up Peaceful Repose. I don't want to be an undertaker any more.'

Chapter Five

Drew's mouth appeared to be malfunctioning. It opened and closed, and opened again, while the colour drained from his cheeks. Thea felt a prickling of tears, watching his shock and distress. 'But you can't,' she said, as if stating a plain fact. 'I thought it was your life's work. Vocation – isn't that what you always said?'

Maggs was watching Drew, waiting for him to regain composure. She merely shook her head in response to Thea's question. 'It doesn't have to be a disaster,' she said. 'You can find someone else to run it for you. Pandora would be more than happy to stay on, and even do a bit more than she does already. You know how fond she is of you.'

'But *why*?' he blurted. 'What happened? It's only a couple of weeks since I was there. You never gave me a hint of this then.'

'I know. I hadn't decided then. But something you said – it just all fell apart.' She grimaced at the pain she was causing. 'Or maybe it came together. I twisted my ankle the next day and couldn't walk. I just sat on the sofa all day, thinking.'

'Never a good idea,' said Den, reminding them all that he could occasionally be quite remarkably crass, for all his fine qualities. Everybody ignored him.

'So what on earth did I say to have such an effect?' Drew wanted to know.

'It sounds ridiculous now. But we were walking round the graves, and you admired my paths as usual. Then you said, "Room for another five hundred at least. That should see us through the next two or three years, unless there's a sudden boom in business." And I thought, "Well, that's not very long, is it? What's going to happen after that?" I'm only twenty-eight, Drew. And we're so short of cash all the time. I sat on that sofa, working out the sums – with Den juggling work and Merry, and helping with the funerals it all seemed rather pointless.'

'But . . .' Drew protested helplessly.

'Five hundred burials over three years at present charges comes to less than fifteen thousand pounds a year actual income once we've paid Pandora. Den earns about sixteen a year, after tax and everything. That's barely a living wage. We can't afford to send Merry to nursery until she's three and we get some benefit money towards it. And I do want another one. Maybe two more. We need a bigger house. I want a dog and holidays and a proper garden. And a real future.'

'But . . .' said Drew again. 'We can find ways of raising your share. The North Staverton house – you could live there instead of where you are. I've said so before. You can have it rent free. The garden's huge.'

'No thanks,' said Den stiffly. 'I know it's pathetic, but we can't take charity on that scale.'

'It wouldn't be charity, you fool. It would be payment in kind. A tied cottage that goes with the job. It's perfectly normal procedure.'

'That's not his real reason,' said Maggs, with a complicated glance at her husband. 'He doesn't want to live beside a cemetery. And he doesn't want his daughter to, either. It's a thing with him.'

'And that's not *your* real reason, either, so don't put it onto me,' said her husband with mild reproachfulness. 'We're dodging around, talking about practicalities, when it's all much more *visceral* than that.'

'I know,' said Maggs. 'The thing is, basically, I'm sick of death and dead people. It's all got out of balance since we had Merry. We've done our best to live like normal people – which is why we've stayed in that little house – but there's always one ear out for the phone, and a worry that people might think we're frivolous if we start behaving like everybody else. I've done it for ten years now, if you count going in to Plant's at weekends when I was still at school. It's taken all that time to get it out of my system. But now I have, and I don't want to do it any more.'

'Well, that's plain enough,' said Thea, losing patience with the whole conversation. 'Nobody can force you to stay, after all. But you must see how impossible you've made it for Drew.'

Maggs lifted her chin and fixed Thea with a very direct look. 'It's not at all impossible. He can sell the whole thing as a going concern, and concentrate exclusively on this place. It's not as if Peaceful Repose was bringing in any money for you. I was keeping everything it earned. As a business plan, it was never very sensible.'

'But . . .' moaned Drew yet again. 'I don't want to sell it. I *created* it. And who on earth would want to buy it?'

'There's no rush—' Den started to say, but Thea interrupted him.

'You can't ever get away from death, you know. Don't you think it rather *diminishes* you to just escape to some rosy future like this?'

The room crackled. Three faces looked at her, making it clear that she was the misfit here. They had all known each other for much longer than they'd known her. They had history, which included Karen, Daphne Plant and a farmer's daughter called Lilah. Den had wanted to marry Lilah, before he met Maggs. They were mere names to Thea, subjects of old anecdotes conveyed by Drew bit by bit during cosy morning chats in bed, or late-night snuggles on the sofa.

'Okay. Sorry,' she muttered. 'But it's a valid point, all the same.'

'Nobody's trying to escape anything,' said Maggs. 'I'm not saying I *regret* anything about working for Drew. It's been a privilege. I know I've helped hundreds of people. I know I've got a talent for it. But I'm not getting anywhere at Peaceful Repose. I've done all I can. Now it's just the same old routines, saying the same things every time. The *people* change, I know. They're all different in the details. But basically it's all a bit too easy. I want to be *stretched*.'

Den gave a snort, and seemed about to make another of his slightly too obvious jokes. Maggs and Drew both repressed him with a look.

'You don't know *what* you want,' Thea accused her. 'You're contradicting yourself. All I can hear is that you want more money. And I seem to remember you insisting loud and clear, only a year ago, that you didn't care about that side of it at all.'

'Thea!' Drew's voice contained a rare warning. 'You're not helping.'

'No, I don't suppose I am. Because I can't see how anybody can help if it's got to this stage. All I can see is that we've got a bloody awful weekend ahead of us, trying to stay cheerful for the children and pretending everything's all right when it's not. Well, luckily for me I've got something else to think about.' She turned to Drew. 'Do you remember a woman called Juliet Wilson, in Stanton? The one who took that white Alsatian with the torn ear?' She didn't wait for a reply, but stormed on, 'Well, she's gone missing.

Gladwin wants me – us, even – to help look for her. They're almost sure something terrible's happened to her. So, I'm going out tomorrow to see if I can help. You obviously don't need me here.'

Again the room hummed with the unaccustomed emotion. The knowledge that of the four she was being the most immature and uncontrolled only made Thea want to shout and accuse even more vigorously.

Den, the former policeman, witness to enough unpleasant crimes to recognise the signs, was the first to speak. 'What's this? Is that what the detective woman came to tell you? And you've been letting us carry on as if nothing was happening? Who is it that's missing? Where do they want us to search? Is she a friend of yours? How old is she?' He stood up, looming tall and urgent over the others. 'Well?' he demanded.

Thea was struck momentarily silent. 'Well . . . Um . . . There's nothing we can do about it tonight. She's in her thirties, and has some problems. Learning difficulties, I suppose. Nothing too major, really. She's extremely good with dogs.'

'I remember her very well,' said Drew. 'In fact, I saw her this week. It must have been Wednesday afternoon. She was in my burial field looking at the graves.'

'For heaven's sake,' said Thea unfairly, 'why on earth didn't you say something?'

'Why on earth should I? We only spoke for a couple of minutes and then I forgot all about it. There was nothing peculiar about her that I could see. When did Gladwin say she went missing?'

'Tuesday. Nobody's seen her since Tuesday.'

'Well, I have. And she looked fine. She's probably just . . . I don't know . . . gone off for a long walk on the wolds.'

'For three days?' It was Den who made this incredulous remark. 'You mean, sleeping in the open? In the middle of May? It must have been about five degrees last night.'

'She does do that sort of thing,' said Thea. 'Well, maybe not sleeping out, but roaming around the countryside.'

'Except this must be different, for the police to be involved,' Den pointed out. 'She sounds pretty vulnerable to me.'

'Once a cop, always a cop,' sighed Maggs fondly. 'He'll be out at first light tomorrow, volunteering to join the search. And dawn's about five o'clock at this time of year.'

Thea felt sidelined, not for the first time. There had been occasions when she had been the first to discover a dead body, only to be pushed away by bustling paramedics or uniformed police. She was, in the final analysis, only an amateur. She had no proper qualifications, no special talents – just curiosity, raw intelligence and a low threshold for boredom.

'Drew, you'll have to tell them, right away,' she

said. 'If nothing else, it'll give them a better idea about where to look for her.'

'It's half past ten,' he objected. 'They won't be searching any more tonight, surely? It'll wait till morning, won't it?' He was looking to Den for professional advice.

The former policeman pursed his lips and looked dubious. 'Well, it's not a child that's missing,' he said. 'I very much doubt they've got twenty-four-hour search teams out there. Unless there's been a very obvious threat of violence, I'd think tomorrow would be soon enough.'

'Good. So now we should all go to bed,' said Drew. 'Looks like an early start tomorrow, one way or another. What time does Meredith usually wake up?'

'Six,' said Maggs. 'She likes the birds. I swear she talks to blackbirds in their own language.'

'We've got a blackbird, right outside her window,' said Thea. 'It starts before six, though.'

'Oh joy,' said Maggs, and everyone laughed.

Saturday morning turned out to be grey and cool, the blackbird rising late for once. Nobody in the house stirred until almost seven o'clock, and then it was Timmy who first emerged. The spaniel in her basket in the kitchen had been on the alert for movement, and once the little boy opened the door, she rushed up the stairs to find her new friend Meredith. Timmy poured himself a glass of milk, drank it, and then went upstairs as noisily as he could. Between them, he and

Hepzie effectively roused everybody in the house.

But there was no sociable communal breakfast. Awkwardness prevailed, much to the confusion of the three children. 'Where should we go to help with the search?' asked Den, with determination.

'You're not serious?' Maggs demanded. 'You'd leave me with the kid all day, just like that?'

'What search?' asked Stephanie. 'Is something lost?'

Thea aimed for a tone of calm good sense. 'Drew's got to call Gladwin anyway, so she'll tell us all that sort of thing.'

'I'll leave it until half past eight,' he said. 'And then we can see if we can make some plans for the day.' He went to the kitchen door and looked out. 'Not raining, anyway,' he reported.

Stephanie was not satisfied with any of this. 'What's happening? Why are you all being so funny? What do we have to search for?'

'There's a woman who's got lost somewhere near here,' Drew told her. 'The police think she might have got hurt or something, so we thought it would be helpful if we went out to look for her. Thea knows her, and I do a bit, so we could recognise her.'

'But what about us? And Meredith? You can't *all* go, can you?' She looked at Maggs. 'You're not going, are you?'

'No way. If you ask me, it'll end up with nobody going. The woman's probably been found by now. It sounds to me as if she's just gone off for a long walk, and there's no sense in worrying about her in the first place.'

'Hasn't she got a phone? Couldn't she just call someone if she got hurt?' The child's face was genuinely puzzled. Like everyone in her generation, she had been schooled in what to do if she got into difficulties, the central element in any emergency being quite obviously the mobile phone.

'I think it's quite likely she hasn't got one,' said Thea. 'Some people haven't, you know.'

'Like me,' said Timmy.

'Next birthday, Tim,' said Drew. 'Not long now.'

'I thought we were all going on an outing,' Stephanie persisted. 'You *said* we were. The farm park, you said. Meredith would love that. Or the model village. We've only been there once.'

'Or the Roman villa,' teased Drew, having discovered that his offspring had yet to perceive much of interest in the details of Roman Britain. Even the excellent Cirencester museum had failed to significantly engage either of them, despite efforts from both Drew and Thea. The only aspect of local history that had really fired their imaginations was the canal system, thanks to Thea's own passion for them.

'Erghh!' groaned Timmy.

It was all going to work out fine, Thea assured herself. The normal bickering over how to spend the day that went on in any weekend group was something she was well used to. Her own family had been experts at it. If a decision had been made by half past ten, that would be seen as a major triumph. But this time there was the lurking image of Juliet Wilson adrift in the deceptively tame-looking countryside. There was also the echoing voice of Mr Clovis Biddulph, promising her that he was not going to go away. All was not well, even before Maggs dropped her own special bombshell. A threefold crisis was developing before her very eyes, and there was little hope that any of it would be acceptably resolved by bedtime.

She sighed. 'We don't know what we're doing until Drew's spoken to Gladwin,' she said. 'I've got a direct number for her. You could call it now. It's gone eight.'

She was surprised and slightly amused to realise that he was mildly nervous about making the call. He had met Gladwin a number of times, but seldom been directly involved in her investigations. The only exception was when he himself had been under a cloud of suspicion – which Thea supposed might be the cause of his hesitation now. 'She'll be really grateful,' she encouraged.

'Why don't you do it?' he said, nudging the phone towards her. Their mobiles sat side by side on the kitchen worktop, one of the few areas of their domestic life that had clear rules and routines. 'Use yours, if the number's in the memory already.'

It made sense, so she willingly obliged. The detective answered almost instantly. 'Gladwin,' she said briskly.

'Hey, it's Thea. Listen – Drew says he saw Juliet Wilson in our burial ground on Wednesday. We would have called you last night, but we thought you would most likely have suspended the search until this morning.' She stopped, afraid she might be prattling.

'Hold on.' Gladwin's voice was tight and strange, Thea finally noticed. 'You're telling me she was seen on Wednesday? Somewhere near Broad Campden?'

Before Thea could agree, there was another voice, apparently speaking close to Gladwin. 'What? Oh . . . can you wait a minute? Hello . . . Thea? Are you still there? The thing is, I'm about two hundred yards away from your burial ground at the moment. And we've just found Juliet's body. She's only been dead a few hours at most.'

Chapter Six

The argument was muted, thanks to the presence of the children. Den was the least controlled, bursting out repeatedly with accusations, recriminations and general anguish. After a while, Maggs took hold of his arm and shook it. She was at least ten inches shorter than him, which did nothing to diminish her authority. 'That's enough,' she said. 'Everyone feels guilty already without you going on about it. We can't change it, and it's not our fault. There's no guarantee that she would have been found, even if Drew *had* phoned last night. Stop saying she would. We've got no idea where she was between Wednesday and now.'

Her grasp of the whole picture had impressed Thea, who was still grappling with her own sense of responsibility and disabling grief. Juliet had been such a loveable person, with her lack of guile and perpetual wish to make friends. And Rosa! That poor bereft mother, whose entire adult life had been devoted to her needy daughter – what would be her future now? The fact that Juliet had moved to a degree of independent living might have left some space for Rosa to develop other interests, but they were unlikely to have any effect in filling this sudden void.

Maggs had taken everything in at a glance. Her own role in distracting Drew had been considerable. She had plunged him into a crisis from which he was not easily diverted, playing down a somewhat vague and distant search for a missing woman. Maggs knew Drew extremely well. She knew that he would now be accusing himself of a lack of due concern. And yet the postponement had seemed entirely sensible to all four of them, at the time – except possibly for Thea, until she had been persuaded by Den that it could wait.

But only Drew had heard what Gladwin said when Thea handed him the phone. 'Why the hell didn't you tell me that last night? We could have saved her. She was killed *this morning*, don't you understand? A quarter of a mile from where you saw her two days ago.' And then she had made a sound rich with exasperation and growing rage. Drew reported most of it to the others, apparently in full agreement with the detective.

Den had quickly drawn the same conclusion, his face pale with remorse. 'We should have phoned,' he said over and over. 'Why didn't we phone?'

'If we had,' Maggs said now, 'we can't be at all sure they'd have done anything at all. They'd have relaxed the worry about her, and phoned her mother, and said everything would come right in the morning. They'd have assumed Juliet was doing her own thing, in no danger at all. She's an adult, after all, and not completely helpless.'

'Was,' said Drew. 'She *was* an adult. Now she's a corpse.'

Both his children looked at him on hearing the final word. He *never* used it to describe the people he was employed to bury. They were 'the deceased' or, more usually, given their actual names. Once in a while he might refer to 'the body'. Timmy had once started making facetious remarks about corpses, only to find himself reprimanded. 'It's disrespectful,' said Drew.

'That's not respectful, Dad,' Stephanie said now. 'Who are you talking about, anyway?'

Thea answered her. 'We told you – a woman has been missing. Now they've found her dead body. Nobody knows what happened to her. She might have got too cold, staying out all night.'

The young girl eyed her reproachfully. 'It's not winter, is it?' she said with due scepticism. 'How could she die of cold?'

'Then maybe she hurt herself somehow, or got poorly. We don't know, Steph, but it's very sad. Lots of people knew her and liked her, and it's going to come as a shock to all of them.'

'Right,' said Stephanie. She knew a lot about the consequences of death, especially when it was a woman in the first half of her life. 'Did she have any children?'

'No. No she didn't. She might have had a dog, though. She was very fond of dogs. And other animals.' Thea turned her head away, feeling a rush of tears. Poor sweet Juliet! How in the world could she be dead?

Timmy was watching and listening just as keenly as his sister, uneasy at the strange atmosphere, so different from the sociable fun the weekend had promised to be. 'You said she was killed,' he said to Drew. 'You said that's what the police person told you. That means murder, doesn't it?'

His father met his worried gaze. 'I'm afraid that's right, Tim. That is what she said. And that makes it all a whole big lot worse.'

'You don't say "a whole big lot", Dad. That's not good English.'

'It's right, though,' said Den. 'There's really nothing in the world worse than murder. Everybody knows that, don't they?'

'Thea knows it, anyway,' said Stephanie 'She's been around lots of them. There was one in Winchcombe, and one in Blockley, and one in Snowshill, and one in—'

'Stop it, Steph,' ordered Drew. 'Just stop it.'

'Okay,' shrugged the child, unrepentant. 'So what happens now? Are we going out anywhere?'

Meredith, who had been diligently munching through a mixture of banana, toast and raisins, raised her head at this encouraging new tone. The foregoing conversation had struck her as much too adult and dull to warrant her attention. But Stephanie's question seemed to carry the promise of some interesting action at last. 'Out, out, out,' she said supportively.

'Some of us probably are,' said Maggs. 'We might not all go to the same place, though.' She looked round the crowded room. 'My guess is that Thea and Drew might have to be somewhere else. But Den and I can take you kids somewhere nice. I expect,' she finished.

'Does Gladwin want to see you?' Thea asked Drew. 'What did she say about that?'

'She said she'd call back when things had got a bit clearer. She was in the middle of all that police doctor stuff. Photographer and so forth. You know more about all that than I do. I only get called when they're ready for a removal – and then it's hardly ever me they call, is it?' As an alternative undertaker, conducting natural green burials, his clientele was a small proportion of the whole, and almost never were they victims of sudden attack or accident. Mainstream undertakers had the resources for rapid collection of bodies from a wide range of situations, which Drew did not.

'You did Mr Fleming's funeral yesterday,' Thea remembered. 'The field must have been full of people. Do you think Juliet was hanging round, watching, for some reason? Maybe she knew him?'

Drew flipped his head to indicate confusion. 'What? What are you talking about? The field wasn't "full of people". I think there might have been seven of us, in total, including me and Andrew. If Juliet knew him, she could have come and joined in. She'd have been welcomed.'

In the same instant, they both remembered another funeral where certain people would be far from welcome. 'Not like the Biddulphs,' Thea said.

'Stop!' Maggs ordered. 'This isn't getting us anywhere. You two can go somewhere else to talk about people we don't know. Unless you want me and Den to leave you in peace, of course, and just drive off home again.'

For two seconds, Thea found herself wanting precisely that. The sheer number of people was adding to the sense that everything was out of control. But a glance at the faces of Drew and his children was enough to change her mind. 'No, of course we don't want that. We're being ridiculous. You need to talk to Drew, for one thing. And it's lovely to get to know Merry now she's so grown-up. I don't think I'll be wanted by the police at all. I haven't got anything whatsoever to tell them. So why don't we leave Drew to get all that side of things settled, and then all of us get together for lunch somewhere? That was the original plan, after all. We don't have to change it.' She waited for a thunderbolt that never came. Surely she couldn't simply abandon Gladwin, Rosa and even the alarming Clovis Biddulph, and simply go out for the day with family and friends? Apparently she could.

'That sounds like sense to me,' said Maggs. 'We can't stand round like this all day.'

'Right. Come on, kids – let's find shoes and things, and see if we can make a proper plan. Den – maybe you should have a look at the map. You don't know the area as well as the rest of us.'

Meredith squawked warningly, prompting her father to release her from her seat and wipe her sticky face.

Maggs and Drew were suddenly left alone in the kitchen. 'Are you going too?' she asked him.

'It depends what DS Gladwin wants me to do. I expect I can get away once I've shown her where I saw Juliet.'

'What happens if a new funeral comes in this morning? Nobody's going to be here for the phone.'

'It gets diverted to my mobile – the same as it does for you, if anyone wants a burial at Peaceful Repose. It doesn't happen very often at a weekend, for either of us, does it? The hospice knows my limitations – but there's nobody there just now wanting my services. The most likely thing is general enquiries, and I can usually handle them wherever I happen to be.'

'Does Andrew ever take the calls?'

'He never has, but we should probably think about changing that. He's still a bit hazy about the paperwork.' Drew gave her a long thoughtful look. 'You surely know all this? Have we got so out of touch you have to ask? Is that part of the problem?'

'We haven't had a real discussion about procedures since well before last Christmas. We know basically what goes on, but we don't talk like we used to. It's lonely, Drew – even with Den and Pandora, it's not the same. I knew it wouldn't be, and I can cope with the big stuff. It's all the little stories, mistakes and funny moments I can't really share with anybody but you. I bet you know what I mean.'

He could not deny it. Thea would never fully grasp the unique undertaker's witticisms, which ranged from the many sounds a dead body could make to the barely avoided disasters during a funeral that could cause a person's heart to stop with terror, but which sounded trivial to someone not involved. The necessary balance between respect, sympathy, professionalism and trustworthiness could not fail to produce comic moments that only someone else in the business could understand. The small deceptions and sudden shocking truths could both be funny at times. 'Well, however tedious they are, you're bound to miss them,' was a favourite quote from a new widow, acknowledging frankly what a trial her demented husband had been. It made Drew laugh every time he thought of it.

'I know what you mean,' he said. 'But we'll have to leave all that for another time. This police thing is going to trump everything else for a while. She was really sweet, you know – Juliet Wilson. I only met her briefly in Stanton, but she was one of those people you don't forget. If somebody really has killed her, they deserve every punishment there is.'

'It could turn out to be an accident,' said Maggs optimistically. 'It doesn't sound as if anyone could possibly be vile enough to deliberately murder her.'

'Let's hope so,' he said, with little conviction. 'Apart from anything else, a murder so close to my burial ground would give us all the wrong sort of publicity.'

'It wouldn't be the first time,' Maggs said, reminding him of events that happened long before he met Thea. 'And I notice you still haven't given the burial ground here a name. Not even "Peaceful Repose Two".'

'Very funny,' he groaned. 'Somehow, none of us seem to be able to think of anything.'

'Peaceful Repose is fairly awful,' she said. 'I keep wanting to shorten it, but you can't say "PR" or "Pea-Rep". You have to say the whole thing.'

Drew shook off the elegiac mood that was threatening to engulf him in this talk with Maggs. Her announcement of the night before still seemed unreal to him. The implications had him wavering between panic and real sadness. It was the end of an era, a crisis for his whole enterprise, and he was filled with nostalgia for the early days. He had dreamt, the previous night, that he was back at Plant's, where funerals conformed to established norms and people were discouraged from diverging from standard practice. In the dream, he had been shouting at Daphne Plant, only to find Maggs standing beside her, giving her support to entirely the wrong side of the argument.

'Come on,' he said. 'We can't stand around chatting. I've got to go.'

'And I need to find my husband and daughter. Listen – we're happy to take charge of your two if that helps. Just for this morning, anyway. It looks to me as if Thea needs to be with you, while this police business is going on.'

'You don't have to do that. What about car seats?'

'What about them? They can all fit in the back easily enough. We'll take them to that farm park place, and see you back here sometime this afternoon. That still gives us loads of time to talk. We don't have to leave here until about three tomorrow. That's if you can stand us for that long.'

'Thanks, Maggs,' he said. 'If you're sure. Let me give you some money. That place costs a fair bit to go in.'

'I hoped you'd say that,' she laughed.

Chapter Seven

Drew and Thea walked the quarter-mile to the burial ground, apprehensive as to what they would have to face. Gladwin had been imprecise as to the exact place where Juliet's body had been found, but there was no difficulty in locating it. 'Oh, God,' groaned Drew. 'It's even worse than I thought.'

In the field that was now the second Slocombe natural burial ground, there were police vehicles, two large dogs with handlers, people in white coveralls and a group of individuals clearly the focal point of the proceedings. 'At least they're not walking over the graves,' said Thea.

There were sixty-six graves, nearly half of them very obviously dug within the past six months or so. They were in two and a half well-spaced rows, starting from the southern edge of the field, stretching from hedge to hedge. Many in the first row had young saplings growing at their head, some were marked with natural stone, none in the traditional headstone shape. Boulders, cairns, even a hand-carved wooden abstract roughly in the form of a large fish. A far greater proportion of the ground was as yet undisturbed, other than by a path running from the road gate to the graves. In the north-western corner was a neglected gateway leading to an adjacent field. Drew and Andrew had fortified the existing wooden gate with lengths of timber, although the prospect of farm animals finding their way in was not especially disconcerting. Drew had done his best to trace the owner of the neighbouring land, only to be passed around by vague officials who admitted it had not been properly registered and the owner could not be identified. Beyond it was an expanse of woodland measuring perhaps twelve or fifteen acres.

The gate had been removed from its hinges and was leaning drunkenly against the hedge. Another larger vehicle could be glimpsed on the far side of the next field, on the edge of the woods. Something white was also visible.

'That's where she was found,' said Gladwin, who had detached herself from the group of police personnel. 'She's still there, under that gazebo.'

'But *how*?' wondered Thea. 'Nobody goes over there. There's no footpath or anything.'

'Good question. It was a birdwatcher, believe it or not. He saw some sort of hawk or buzzard – several of them, actually – hovering over the place. He'd seen them doing it before when a lamb was dead or dying, so he decided to go for a look. Six o'clock this morning.'

'That's the best time for birds at the moment,' said Drew, looking at his most recent grave.

Thea was quicker. 'Er . . . isn't that a bit of a coincidence? I mean, Mr Fleming and his birdsong – and then this birdwatcher person? Surely there must be a connection?'

Gladwin put a hand to her stomach as if in pain. 'Please, Thea – don't do this. Just explain what the hell you're talking about.'

Thea pointed to the newest grave. 'That's Mr Fleming. Drew buried him yesterday morning, early. When the birds were doing their dawn chorus, only a bit later, because it's May and they start about five in the morning. It was a request, you see. He got as close as was reasonable. And now, today, this person who found Juliet must have been after the same thing. But why *here*? The best guess is that it's a relation of Mr Fleming, come back to commune with him and the birds, and all that sort of thing.'

She had every confidence that her explanation was crystal clear, but Gladwin still looked perplexed, and Drew was showing signs of exasperation. 'Why bring the Flemings into it?' he asked her crossly.

'Why not?' she flashed back.

'Now, now,' said Gladwin. 'The birdwatcher's name is Anthony Spiller. Does that mean anything to you?'

'Nephew,' said Drew promptly. 'Sister's son. Thea's absolutely right, as usual. He'll have come for a quiet moment with his uncle, while the birds were singing. Poor chap – he must have been horrified by what he found.'

'Excited. Overwhelmed. All the usual reactions,' said Gladwin wearily. 'He'll have told someone in the team about his uncle, I expect. It just wasn't in the notes that came through to me. It gives him a convincing reason for being here, anyway.' Then she threw a thoughtful glance at Thea. 'You were quick,' she commended. 'Do you know how often you think just like a police detective? Quicker than most, in fact. And all without a day of training.' She sighed. 'Some people are born that way, I guess.'

'It helps to be part of a large family, always trying to work out what the others are up to,' said Thea modestly. 'But I admit I was born nosy. I always think people are keeping something from me that I'd really like to know about.'

'That'll be the big family again,' smiled Gladwin.

'Probably.'

Drew was looking harassed. Thea had followed him as he'd walked a little way towards his rows of graves, as if to check they were all present and correct. The ground was open to the public, for families to come and go as they liked, and prospective inmates were encouraged to have a look. In North Staverton, with the field only yards from the house, he had been able to supervise visitors. In Broad Campden, with a distance of a quarter of a mile separating house from cemetery, he had to be content with daily visits to check that all was well. 'At least she wasn't actually on my land,' he muttered.

'Not this time,' Thea muttered back.

He gave her a look full of anguished recollection. 'They won't think it was me, will they?' It was intended as a joke, but neither of them smiled.

'Well, let's get on with it, shall we?' Gladwin was striding after them. 'I need exact time, place and every detail of your encounter with Miss Wilson on Wednesday. That's why you're here, after all. I've got a recorder, if that's okay? We can get it all printed out and ready for signature later on. But, just for now, it's going to be very useful to be on the actual spot. She was here in your field, was she?'

Before he could reply, she held up a finger. 'Sorry – let me turn this on first. Right. For the record, this is DS Gladwin interviewing Mr Drew Slocombe at' – she glanced at her watch – '9.57 a.m., Saturday 16th May. Now, sir, could you please tell me in your own words where and when you saw Miss Juliet Wilson earlier this week.' The sudden formality in the familiar setting, with people coming and going all around them, made Thea think of early outside broadcasts on television. She could hear birds singing, a plane overhead, and the regular swishing of passing cars. Gladwin held her device under Drew's nose, adding to the sense of something slightly old-fashioned and amateurish.

'Well,' Drew began. 'It must have been about four o'clock. I'd gone to mark the Fleming grave for Andrew, and there she was. She didn't see me at first, and I tried not to disturb her in case she was a relative on a visit. But she was close to where I had to put the marker, so I had to go up to her. I said something like, "I hope I'm not bothering you" and she laughed. "You don't remember me, do you?" she said, and I must admit I didn't. I was trying to think whose relative she was, you see. I think I asked her which grave she'd come to visit, and she said, "All of them." I thought that was a bit funny, but we do get people who are just curious to see the place, so I told her that was fine with me, and that I was sorry, I still didn't remember who she was. "I'm Juliet. We were in Stanton. You only saw me for a few minutes. It was Christmas time." She spoke like a young girl, her head on one side, and that was when I knew who she was. "Oh, yes, of course," I said. "You were really helpful, when Thea needed to leave the house she was looking after. There was that dog . . ." Anyway, that's about it as far as I can remember. I was glad to see her looking well and confident.'

'No sign that she was sleeping rough?'

'I don't think so. She was very direct – it was obvious that she still wasn't too good at social situations.'

'Direct? How?'

'Questions. She asked me quite a few. Something about the people I buried and the families. Wanted names, seeing that there aren't any headstones, and I had to tell her that sort of thing was a bit confidential sometimes.'

'And she understood that?' Gladwin hesitated. 'Is that even true?'

'Only very occasionally. I shouldn't have said it really. It was just that she was being a bit annoying and I had to say something. To be honest, I was trying to get away – just saying whatever I thought would satisfy her. I feel bad about that now,' he admitted, rubbing his forehead.

'She was like that with me in Stanton,' said Thea. 'She didn't know when to stop.'

'So then what?' Gladwin asked Drew.

'I marked the plot for Mr Fleming and walked back home.'

'You left her there? Knowing she was someone with learning difficulties? Weren't you concerned about her?' Gladwin eyed him reproachfully.

'It was a warm summer afternoon. She looked to be perfectly in control of herself. It didn't occur to me to worry about her. And what could I have done, even if I had been?'

'You could ask her if her mother or friends knew where she was. Whether she needed a lift somewhere.'

'I didn't have the car. I walked there. It never crossed my mind to worry about her.'

'Why did you think she was looking at the graves in the first place?'

He shook his head. 'People often look at graves. It's normal behaviour. We're fairly high profile, as you must realise, so we get visitors who are curious about us. She wasn't doing anything unusual, just slowly walking along the path, looking at the young trees and things.'

'All right,' said Gladwin. 'So when you left her, it was – what? – four-fifteen? Something like that? On Wednesday 13th May.'

'Yes. Possibly a bit later than that. I got home about half past, and it's only a five-minute walk.'

She turned the recorder off and looked at Thea, who had quietly listened to the whole conversation. 'And he didn't tell you he'd seen Juliet, when he got home?'

'No. It was the usual bedlam, getting tea, feeding the dog, listening to the kids telling us about school. Drew mostly escapes into his office when all that's going on, sorting out the schedule for the next day. He catches up with it after supper usually.'

'And by the time the kids were in bed, I'd completely forgotten about Juliet,' he added.

'That was three nights ago,' said Gladwin. 'Did she spend all that time around here somewhere? If she did, she must have stayed well hidden. You did a funeral here yesterday, right? What about Thursday?'

'Andrew was here in the afternoon digging the new grave. We can ask him if he saw her. But there was certainly not a sign of her yesterday when we did the Fleming funeral. I can't believe she'd be here for three nights. She must have gone away and come back – or been brought back, because it's a quiet place . . .'

'To dump a body,' Gladwin finished his sentence heartlessly. 'Right.'

Thea cleared her throat. 'I hate to ask, but how exactly did she die?'

'You know I'm not supposed to tell you. Let's just say it wasn't very subtle. And no, there was no sign of any . . . *interference*, as they used to say.'

'Poor, *poor* Rosa,' Thea moaned. 'How will she ever be able to bear it?' Images from earlier episodes came to mind: a dead child and its crazed mother; a young man hanging from a beam in a barn; a local eccentric dead in the snow. Death in so many guises, inflicted in so many ways.

'She was starting to feel her work was almost done. After thirty years of constant worry and vigilance, she was finally letting go. I spent an hour with her late on Thursday, when it was becoming clear that Juliet really had gone missing.'

Thea frowned. 'But why were *you* involved? I mean – it couldn't have been serious enough at that stage, surely? Nobody could have imagined she'd been *murdered*.'

'It's that magic word, "vulnerable" that set everything ringing. Rosa knew enough to use it to extremely good effect. She's been around the system long enough, after all.'

'But Juliet's gone missing before,' Thea remembered. 'I mean – she was constantly going off on her own when I knew her in Stanton.'

'She hadn't done it recently. Everything was so *settled*, at least in Rosa's mind. Job, independent living, even a dog of her own.'

Thea shivered. 'Who's got it now?'

'Rosa, of course. She's carrying it around with her, as if it was a piece of Juliet.'

'So she went off without it on Tuesday?'

Gladwin hesitated. 'That's a good question. I'll have to check. I didn't see the housemates – one of the uniforms went round for a chat with them. They didn't have a lot to say, other than that Juliet never came home on Tuesday, and by the end of Wednesday they were getting seriously worried and contacted Rosa, who came to us. I don't recall any mention of the dog at that point.'

'So she was out for *four* nights,' said Drew.

'Right.'

'But it is the merry month of May, after all,' he went on. 'People do funny things in May, even these days. Especially country people. Not just the birds, but the early sunrise and the new flowers – all that business. They sleep out, to watch the wildlife. Foxes and badgers and rabbits and hares. I would guess that Juliet might have been into that kind of thing.'

The two women looked at him blankly. 'I have no idea,' said Gladwin.

'Nor me,' said Thea. 'Where did you get all that stuff from, anyway?'

'Simple observation,' he shrugged. 'And I think I read something about rough camping in France. You can't really do it here any more, which seems rather a shame.'

The word *camping* rang a bell with Thea. Somebody had told her he was going to camp out. A second later she recalled Clovis Biddulph's assurance that he was absolutely not going to miss his father's burial, even if he had to camp out in Drew's field. She opened her mouth to mention it, and then changed her mind. No need for that sort of complication.

Gladwin squared her narrow shoulders. 'So, that's about it for now. You've got visitors, haven't you? You'll be wanting to get back to them. The timing's never good when this kind of thing happens, is it?'

'They've gone out for the morning. We'll probably go and meet them somewhere for lunch,' said Thea, feeling no enthusiasm for renewed socialisation with the Coopers. She knew perfectly well where her real interest lay, and that was here with the police detective, trying to understand the who and the why and the how and the when of Juliet Wilson's murder.

'What a mess,' moaned Drew as they walked back to the house. 'I forgot to ask whether all that police activity would be gone by Tuesday. I've got Mr Biddulph then – I hope. Linda still hasn't said for certain whether we can go ahead. But the complications are going to be bad enough, without blue tape and forensic chaps in white overalls.'

'It's three days away. They're sure to be gone well before then. But what *about* the Biddulphs? There couldn't be any connection with Juliet, could there? All these people are fairly local, after all. We don't know who knows who.'

'Oh, stop!' he begged. 'First you've got the Flemings involved, and now the Biddulphs. You're always so obsessed with making connections, when there usually aren't any. Mr Fleming lived in Stow. The nephew is local, admittedly. Nice chap, from what I saw of him. He was very good yesterday, carrying, lowering and being nice to his aunt. Linda and Lawrence Biddulph are from Ebrington. Clovis and his mother and brother apparently live over towards Oxford, according to Linda. She might be out of date about that, though. She says she's had no contact with them for fifteen or twenty years.

'They all live in three different places, I suppose. The sons must be well over forty by now. They won't still be at home with their mother.'

'He said he was going to camp out, so as to be sure not to miss the funeral,' she said in a small voice. 'I presume he knows enough to find the field and keep watch over it, even if not literally in a tent.'

'He? You mean Clovis?'

'Yes.'

'So you're thinking he came here yesterday, or early this morning, and murdered Juliet – for what reason? Misplaced rage about his father? Or what?'

'I didn't say that at all. I'm just pointing out what he said to me, and how it might actually be a relevant detail. I do have to remind you that quite often the connections I make actually do turn out to be important. *Very* often, in fact.'

'I'll take your word for it. Gladwin obviously thinks

you're a born detective, anyway. Maybe you are. But I'm *not*. I hate the whole business, and wish I never had to see a person from the CID ever again.'

'And you an undertaker,' she teased, hoping to lighten the mood. 'How's that going to work, then?'

He said nothing until they were in their lane, the house only half a minute's walk away. 'I was thinking in the night that maybe Maggs has got a point,' he then said. 'That maybe this line of work isn't very wholesome, in the long run. I mean – undertakers are undeniably strange. It has to have an effect, doing it over a lifetime. What does it do to the kids? Stephanie made it perfectly clear that she couldn't bear to have her mother's grave right outside her window. There was a message there, which I chose not to hear.'

Thea went cold, and silently cursed Maggs Cooper. 'What else would you do?' she asked him.

'No idea. Don't panic. I expect I'll settle down again soon enough. It's just a midlife wobble. I'll be forty next year. Forty!'

'Shut up. You're just a baby. It's fifty that's worrying me.'

They both laughed, and squashed together in an awkward side-by-side hug. Back indoors, they enjoyed ten whole minutes before the gathering crises on all sides intruded yet again.

Chapter Eight

Three things happened in rapid succession. First, Anthony Spiller phoned to talk about his discovery of a body close to Drew's burial ground. He seemed to feel he'd inadvertently got the undertaker into trouble. 'I'm so sorry,' he repeated. 'I just wanted to go and sit with Uncle Dicky for a bit, and listen to the birds with him. That's all. I never *dreamt* . . .'

'It must have been a horrible shock,' Drew sympathised.

'It was *unreal*. I mean – there was me, sitting by a grave, and suddenly there was this other body, just a hundred yards away. I still can't believe it.'

'No,' said Drew. 'I can imagine.'

And so it went on for another minute or two.

Secondly, Maggs called to arrange where they should meet for lunch. 'Make it about one,' she suggested. 'We've got lots still to see here. And it took longer to get to than we expected. Do you know any good eating places?'

Thea and Drew consulted briefly. 'They're mostly rather pricey,' Drew said. 'Gastro-pubs.'

Maggs snorted. 'Well, it is the Cotswolds,' she said, with a hint of a sneer. 'But there must be somewhere that'd give us sausage and chips, preferably in a garden. It's quite warm.'

'The trouble is, they change all the time. What's cheap and cheerful one minute goes all upmarket and fancy-schmantcy the next. We can't keep up with it. I think the best idea is for you to come back here when you're done and we can go to our local.'

'Okay,' said Maggs slowly. 'Seems a shame, though. We thought it'd be nice to explore a bit.'

'We'll take you to Chipping Campden this afternoon,' Drew promised. 'And we might go to Cirencester or Winchcombe tomorrow. I'll drive.'

'Rash promises,' Thea remarked, when he'd finished. 'You don't know what else you might be doing by tomorrow.'

He blinked at her. 'Like what?'

'Like applying for a training course in helicopter flying. Or signing up for the army. Or even teaching. Who knows?'

'Yeah, yeah. The trouble is, I'm too old for any of those.'

'I think they'd still consider you for teaching.'

'Stop it, okay? I wish I'd never said anything now.'

'I wish you hadn't, too,' she said sourly.

Thirdly, there was a knock on the door that took

them by surprise. Hepzie barked, as usual too late to be of any use. She had been left alone in the house while her people went to meet Gladwin, and was feeling neglected. 'Shut up,' Thea told her.

Drew opened the door. A man was standing there, his handsome face shadowed by a mixture of dark emotions. 'You're the man who does the burials,' he told Drew. 'Don't try to deny it. I can see the hearse.'

'Why would I deny it?'

'Because that's what you people do. Liars and cheats, the lot of you.'

Thea came forward, having recognised the voice. 'You must be Mr Biddulph,' she said. 'Mr Clovis Biddulph, right?'

She met his gaze, and was astonished at the effect it had. He was of middle height, with black hair and blue eyes fringed with long lashes. He was of roughly her own age. And when he stared into her face, holding the connection for several long seconds, she felt that never before had she really seen another person so completely.

'Do you two know each other? Have you met before?' asked Drew, conscious of something troubling in the air.

'Oh – no, I don't think so,' said Thea. 'Just spoken on the phone. You *are* Clovis, aren't you?' she asked again.

'That's right.' His initial rage was already less apparent.

Thea had always been pretty, and men had always looked twice at her. She was so used to it that she barely even noticed by the time she reached her thirties. She knew it gave her an advantage in social situations, with even other women showing due appreciation. While aware that it was nothing more than a superficial accident of proportion and bone structure, she also understood that it was an inescapable part of her person. Small and pretty trumped every other permutation when it came to sex appeal and interactions with other people.

And this man had the same fortunate mixture and he knew how to use it. She knew already that he was not vain, or unintelligent, or self-obsessed. He probably wasn't as good a man as Drew, nor as controlled in his emotions. There was something Latin about him. No English man had ever given her a look like the one she'd just experienced.

'You'd better come in,' said Drew. 'Now you've found us.'

The words echoed in Thea's head and she was seized with terror. *No!* she wanted to cry out. *Send him away before he destroys us.*

It was ridiculous, overwrought, adolescent nonsense, she told herself wildly as she let Drew lead the man into his office. She held back and hoped she could remain hidden away in the kitchen, or even perhaps the garden shed, until he'd gone. Except they didn't have a garden shed, because the hearse and van took up too much of the available space.

It was approaching twelve o'clock. An hour before they were due to meet the others at the Bakers Arms. Would Clovis Biddulph stay talking to Drew for all that time? What, after all, did he have to say? Drew wasn't a family therapist, even if he did listen to a great many accounts of domestic dysfunction. Realistically, his only role was to give the man's father a dignified burial – and if family conflict made that impossible, he would be well within his rights to simply walk away and wash his hands of them. The only reason she could think of for the man to be here at all was to force Drew to admit that the burial was to be in Broad Campden, and to supply the day and time appointed for the funeral. But newly bereaved people did not always need reasons for what they did. They acted out of extreme emotion, often assisted by alcohol and a sense of high drama. She had also been made aware of a frequent sense of urgency – an atavistic knowledge that dead bodies were acutely time-limited and that their disposal could not be unduly delayed. Especially where alternative undertakers who abjured embalming were involved.

All this went through her mind as she lurked in the kitchen with the spaniel. 'I suppose we could go for a walk,' she muttered, to the dog's great delight. But before she could put the idea into practice, the door opened and Drew looked in.

'Oh, there you are. Do you think you could join

us for a minute? Mr Biddulph thinks you ought to be included.'

'What? Why? Didn't you tell him it was nothing to do with me?'

Drew had a look of a man out of his depth. He came further into the room. 'He says that since you were the person who spoke to him when he phoned, you have a responsibility towards him. Something like that. He's very insistent.'

'Has he calmed down at all?'

They were speaking in whispers, but still Thea worried that they could be overheard. Drew had not closed the door of the office.

'Oh yes. You needn't worry about that. Why – were you scared of him?' He looked almost hopeful, as if this would be one of the easier scenarios to cope with.

Yes! she wanted to shout. 'Of course not,' she said. 'Well, come on, then. Let's get it over with.' Her heart pounding, she followed her husband along to the room at the back of the house.

Clovis Biddulph was sitting in one of the padded chairs Drew provided for his clients. His legs were crossed at the ankles and he looked outrageously comfortable. No wonder poor Drew didn't know what to make of him, thought Thea.

'Ah – Mrs Slocombe. I'm sorry to drag you here, but it seemed quite wrong to leave you out of the picture. I should probably mention that I spent some considerable time yesterday in tracking you down

86

online. There's a surprising quantity of material – nearly all of it concerning murder investigations. You were a house-sitter, I gather, until recently. I have to say I was most intrigued to meet you.'

She did her best to avoid looking directly at him, but there was no possibility of succeeding. 'Well, here I am,' she said faintly. She and Drew sat down awkwardly. The strange man was so completely in charge, it almost felt as if he had a gun pointing at them.

'Yes,' he agreed pleasantly.

Drew jumped into the awkward pause. 'The thing is, there really isn't anything I – or my wife – can do about your family issues. I can't give or withhold permission for you to attend the burial. At most, I can make a plea that you don't cause any trouble. My first loyalty is to your . . . the current Mrs Biddulph. She's your father's next of kin, and she gave me my instructions for the funeral.'

'She and her precious son,' said Clovis, with an unnatural lack of bitterness. His easy manner was far more unnerving than anger would have been. 'I dare say she told you that my little half-brother has no idea that I exist. Nor our other brother, Luc. And the misguided woman apparently wishes to keep it that way.' His laugh was every bit as relaxed as his words. 'We've always known about *him*, of course. My mother made sure of that. She would have been delighted if we'd approached the brat and made our existence known to him – but we never did. Couldn't really see the point, I suppose. And Luc's . . . well, you might not be aware that Luc has problems.'

'Oh?' said Drew, apparently more than happy to let the man talk, as was Thea.

'He smashed himself up in a car five years ago. In and out of hospital ever since. They don't think he'll ever manage to walk again.' Finally, a flash of anger crossed his face. 'We contacted my father about it, and got no response whatsoever. Not a word. How do you think we felt about that?'

'Not good,' Drew suggested. 'So – when did you last see him? Your father, I mean.'

'Thirty-six years ago,' came the prompt reply. 'I was ten and Luc was seven. He just walked out one day. It turned out, of course, that he'd been seeing Linda for a while, and just went off with her. My mother didn't tell us the whole story until we were older. She had a sort of breakdown at the time, from the shock. She made him wait five years for the divorce. The moment it came through, he married Linda. They'd already got a son by then – Lawrence.'

Drew made a wordless sound, expressing sympathetic interest. Clovis went on, 'So you're right when you say she's his next of kin. We don't dispute that for a moment. But there's Luc to consider, you see. I don't mean financially, but he's been trying to sort himself out emotionally, and a lot of stuff's been coming to the surface. We're not claiming that some of the old man's estate should come to us. He never paid a penny in child maintenance, you know. But by the time we were old enough to think of confronting him about it, we were both past needing it, quite honestly. Luc was only just out of school, but he'd got a good job at British Aerospace – training scheme and so forth.'

Drew gave him an enquiring look, and Clovis smiled. 'Yes, I've done all right for myself as well.' He stroked a hand down his expensive-looking shirt.

Thea was wondering whether she might manage to slip out again, while the man was in full spate. But he seemed to read her mind, abruptly stopping his monologue and giving her a searching look. Her knees trembled, but she returned his look steadily. 'I really don't think I need to be here,' she said. 'What you're telling us is all very interesting, but as Drew says, it doesn't actually change anything, does it? Your father seems to have behaved badly towards you, and now he's died before you can confront him, that must be frustrating. But none of it is Lawrence's fault, is it? Can't you just let them have the funeral, before you . . . well, shatter his illusions?'

Drew inhaled noisily, letting it be understood that her plain-speaking was not the way he would have done things. 'Er . . . well . . .' he stammered. 'Perhaps we ought to leave that side of things up to you. It's not for us to dictate . . .'

'Mrs Slocombe obviously has a perfect grasp of how things stand,' purred Clovis Biddulph. 'And she's not afraid to say so. That's very impressive. I am extremely impressed.' He beamed his approval from his clear blue eyes, and smiled with his sensuous lips, and Thea's knees almost melted.

He's just a smarmy . . . she couldn't think of anything that quite served the purpose. Smarmy, ingratiating, far too good-looking to be genuine . . . she feverishly listed all the reasons why she could not possibly be stupid enough to actually *respond* to his efforts.

'Are you married, Mr Biddulph?' she asked in desperation.

He jerked back as if she'd slapped him. 'What? Oh – no, actually. Never quite got to that point. What does that have to do with anything?'

Drew loyally picked up the baton. 'Well, your wife might have had a view about things,' he said feebly, with a puzzled glance at Thea.

'Why have you come here?' Thea demanded, throwing every last shred of protocol out of the window. 'What are you trying to do? It's the weekend. We've got to go out in a minute. Drew's given you everything he can. There's no sense in it.'

'All right, then.' The man got up from his chair without any further argument. 'Thank you for listening. That's all I really wanted, you see. Just someone to hear it from the other side. *We* – my mother and brother and me - have nothing to apologise for. We've got the moral high ground, when all's said and done. We were abandoned, left to fend for ourselves, badly damaged by the sudden loss of husband, father and provider. It's a bit rich, now, to try and keep us away from the funeral.'

He looked intently from one to the other. 'It isn't nice to be treated as a dirty shameful secret. You've met Linda – which is more than we have. I hope you saw her for what she is. A cowardly social climber, afraid of what people would think if they knew the full story. I ask you – can you honestly live with yourselves if you let her have her way?'

He blinked his long lashes and rubbed his shapely nose. Thea felt a mirroring lump in her throat. 'That's what I *said*. Isn't it, Drew? I said it was cowardly and unfair.'

'Unfair to Lawrence, if I remember rightly,' said Drew, who appeared to have had more than enough.

'Unfair to everybody,' she insisted. 'And rather ridiculous, in this day and age. How could she think she'd ever keep the secret?'

'Well . . .' said Drew, before Clovis interrupted.

'She kept it for thirty years,' he said. 'It's only because my father's dead that she's got to spill the beans now.'

'And she will,' pleaded Drew. 'As soon as the funeral's over. Just give her a few days, and it'll all look very different.'

'Sorry, but we're all going to be there – whenever it is. We all need it in our different ways – Luc most of all. I'm going now to locate the burial ground, which I don't imagine will be very difficult. And I'll be watching for a new grave being prepared. As a detective job, it's all going to be pretty elementary. Just as finding you two has been. Things have changed a lot in the past thirty years, you know. Nobody gets to keep a secret any more.'

Drew heaved a heartfelt sigh. 'Well, I can't stop you. But I should perhaps warn you that just at the moment the burial ground is crawling with police. There's been a murder just a field away.'

Chapter Nine

They walked to the Bakers Arms in an awkward silence. The spaniel followed them, off the lead, knowing to keep out of the path of any vehicles. On a mild Saturday in May, there was only sporadic passing traffic. Thea had watched Clovis Biddulph leave, still struggling to focus on anything there might be to dislike about him. There was nothing. He was intelligent; handsome; direct; honest; handsome; sensitive; dignified; hopelessly, disgracefully handsome . . . But hadn't he been dreadfully angry and rude on the phone? He'd made threats, snarled and sneered and been altogether horrible. Yes, but he'd had good reason to be. He'd come to explain himself – although he had made no attempt to apologise.

It wasn't important, she assured herself. After Tuesday, the whole Biddulph business would be filed away and forgotten. Except there was actually Tuesday to get through. He, his mother and the disabled Luc would show up and confront Linda and

Lawrence, and there would be tears and shouting and a wholesale loss of dignity. And the man at the core of it, the man who was obviously to blame for the whole mess, would be lying quietly in one of Drew's simple beech-veneered boxes, smugly oblivious to it all.

'He doesn't really deserve a dignified funeral, when you think about it,' she said aloud.

'What? Who?'

'Stephen Biddulph. He must have forced Linda to keep quiet about his former family. And look where it's got her. Everybody angry and scared. The wretched Lawrence with no idea what's coming.'

'Scared? Nobody's scared, as far as I can see.'

'Linda must be,' she said quickly. 'She doesn't know how Lawrence will react, does she?'

'At least I don't have to tell any more lies,' said Drew, clearly thinking about something else. 'We'd better try and get a table outside, so the kids can run around – don't you think?'

'It's not very suitable for Meredith. It might be better indoors, if there's any space left.'

It was good, she told herself, that Drew was barely showing an interest in the Biddulphs. Good that he hadn't properly noticed her peculiar reaction to Clovis. It would make it so much easier to forget the whole silly business if he never said a word about it.

Her confidence increased over lunch. Maggs and Den were fifteen minutes late, but there was no difficulty in holding onto the biggest table in the bar.

For some reason, business was slow, and the landlord was more than happy to accommodate them. The children tumbled in, Stephanie and Timmy each holding one of Meredith's hands, almost dragging her down the passageway from the entrance at the back of the building. Hepzie rushed to greet them, as if deprived of their company for a month.

'We saw a *tapir*,' said Timmy. 'It's got a little trunk like an elephant.'

'Effylant,' said Meredith, looking round as if hoping to see one in the other bar.

Stephanie was the first to subside. 'Are zoos cruel, do you think?' she asked worriedly.

'That's a big question,' said Drew. 'I think some of them are, yes. But a lot of animals don't mind the shortage of space, and hardly notice they're inside a cage.'

'Hey, don't start that now,' ordered Maggs. 'I'm starving. Can we get something that can be brought quickly, do you think?'

Drew laughed at her. 'Are you sure you're not pregnant?' he said.

Den rolled his eyes. 'Don't start that again,' he warned. 'It's turning into a touchy subject.'

'She'll be *three* at this rate,' Maggs grumbled. 'And I wanted another one by the time she was two.'

'Can't order these things,' said Drew comfortably.

All three of the other adults looked at him disgustedly. 'He's too good for this world,' said Thea, thinking the same thing could definitely not be said of her.

'Makes you sick,' said Maggs. 'So – how was your morning down amongst the corpses?'

Timmy straightened and stared at her in disbelief. 'She said it as well!' he gasped, as if unable to credit the evidence of his ears. 'Dad – *Maggs* said it as well.'

'I heard her,' said Drew. 'The thing is, people say things like that when they're with friends, and that's okay. But you have to be more careful when there are families around. Didn't I already explain that?' he concluded tiredly.

'You can be as politically incorrect as you like between friends,' said Maggs.

'Don't be too sure,' Thea corrected her. 'Before you know it, Merry will have reported you at her nursery, and the thought police'll be at your door. That's what happened in East Germany, you know.'

Thea's tendency to see sinister implications in every CCTV camera, and to view Twitter and the rest as far too intrusive for anybody's good, might have gone into abeyance recently, but it was far from abandoned.

'So, Tim – don't tell anybody at school that I said "corpse" – right?' said Maggs. 'Not that anyone's likely to think there's much wrong with it. It's only a silly convention, after all.'

'It's not, though,' said Drew. 'It's disrespectful. You know it is.'

'So how was your morning?' asked Den loudly. 'If it's not an indiscreet question.'

'Mmm, it is a bit,' said Drew with a small frown.

'Not suitable subject matter for the dinner table, as my mother might have said.'

'Tell us about the zoo,' Thea suggested. 'That's much more interesting.'

It was well past two when they left the pub, Meredith drooping sleepily and Hepzie getting restless. The tall former police officer carried his chunky little girl over his shoulder, and Stephanie raced the spaniel down the short length of village road to the church. Timmy watched them critically. 'If a big lorry came now . . .' he said.

'We'd hear it in plenty of time,' Thea reassured him. 'But I do sometimes wish there were pavements, even so.' Broad Campden was a typical stop-start Cotswolds settlement. The pub was a distance from the church, which in turn was removed from the cluster of houses that formed the apparent centre of the village. There were fields and hedges in between; a quiet looping lane and a modest little stream added to the picture. The Slocombes lived down another meandering lane, which petered out into a field. 'The very definition of leading nowhere,' Thea said.

A small group of people stood on the wide grassy knoll opposite the church, reading a plaque attached to the huge cherry tree that grew there. They resolved themselves into a man, woman and young girl, and as Stephanie approached them she slowed, eyeing the child with interest. The strangers turned to face them, apparently eager to speak. Hepzie performed immediate introductions, jumping up and wagging her feathery tail.

'Can you get her down, please?' came the woman's strained voice. 'Modestine is allergic to dogs.'

'Come here, Heps,' Thea ordered, with a sigh. Her tolerance of allergies was notoriously thin.

'Modestine?' repeated Drew. 'Then you must be . . . Mr and Mrs Biddulph. Are you looking for me? I'm Drew Slocombe.'

'Ah – that's lucky. We were sort of hoping to find you,' said the man. 'We've been to your house, but got no response. We really came to have a look at the burial ground, but we haven't found it yet.'

'That's right,' interrupted the woman. 'We thought we should show Modestine where Granpaps was going to be laid to rest. It helps to talk them through these things in advance, don't you find? We were all so terribly fond of him, you know. He was such a devoted family man. We want the funeral to go *perfectly*. He deserves that.'

This stark contrast with the characterisation that Clovis had given the man made Thea's head buzz. Two such different experiences seemed somehow dreadful. The buzzing got worse when she realised the half-brothers could have met in the field.

'Oh – absolutely,' gushed Drew. 'The burial ground is down that way. Just a few minutes' walk. And you already know our house is down *here*,' he indicated the opposite direction. 'If you need me for anything, just come and knock. I'm not going out again today.'

Thea gave him a reproachful look, hoping to remind him that he had virtually promised Maggs a walk to Chipping Campden. He ignored her, keeping his attention on his clients.

'Can we drive to the field?' The woman pointed to a black car tucked beside the church.

'Yes. That is – you can usually. But there's been a bit of an incident there today, so you might not find a space. I'm not sure how things stand just at the moment. It's really no distance. Down that road, and it's the first thing you come to on the right, once you're past all the houses.'

'Incident?' repeated the man, who Thea had readily identified as Lawrence, even without any help from Drew. He was taller than his older half-brother, darker, with thick black eyebrows and not the least bit handsome. There were grooves on his face that suggested acute emotional distress. His voice contained a kind of whine, and his wife was obviously a bit of a nag.

'I'm afraid so,' said Drew. 'But there's no need for you to worry. Everything's going to be fine for Tuesday. It really doesn't concern us, other than being so close by. Just that there could be a bit of trouble parking.'

'Hmm,' said the wife suspiciously.

Thea was also having doubts. As she understood it, Lawrence's mother still had not finally agreed to hold the funeral on the coming Tuesday. Yet Drew gave no hint of this uncertainty. The children had been conducting their own introductions. Modestine looked to be about four, which was young enough for Stephanie to feel maternal towards her. Meredith struggled for release from Den, having decided things were far too interesting for her to proceed with the planned nap. Timmy was kicking stones from the edge of the patch of grass and throwing glances at the newcomer.

'What's your name?' he asked her, having missed the introductions.

'Modestine,' she announced defiantly. Thea, hearing this, concluded the child was still too young for the inevitable teasing the name would incur. Although, maybe it wouldn't. Outlandish names were ubiquitous these days, after all. But wasn't it a name from a book, she kept wondering. Where had she heard it before?

Stephanie, miraculously, had the answer. 'That's a donkey's name,' she said with a little laugh. 'A bad-tempered donkey in a story about a long walk.'

'How do you know that?' Thea interrupted. 'Can you remember who wrote the book?'

'Robert Louis Stevenson,' came the prompt reply.

'I don't believe you. He wrote *Treasure Island* and *Kidnapped*. Adventure stories. Nothing about going for walks with a donkey.'

Stephanie drew herself up. 'It *is*,' she insisted. 'It's in the library at school.'

'She's right,' said Lawrence. 'What a clever girl!'

So why name your kid after a donkey? Thea wanted to demand. *Why not?* would probably be the swift reply.

Unexpectedly, a reply to the silent question was soon forthcoming. 'My grandmother was French. She suggested the name, and we liked it well enough to go along with it.'

And she must have suggested Clovis as well, Thea realised. Stephen Biddulph's mother, married to an Englishman, and not long dead, it seemed, if she had influence over this little girl's name. 'I see,' she said with a smile.

'I don't imagine you do,' Lawrence argued. 'But it doesn't matter.' He sighed and looked round for his wife, like a child for its mother.

'Well . . .' said Drew, supported by Maggs, who was looking impatient. 'As I say – any trouble, just come and find me down this way.'

'I'm sure that won't be necessary,' said Mrs Lawrence Biddulph. 'Let's get on with it, shall we? It's taken me all day to get you this far.' She looked at her husband with a mixture of impatience and solicitude. 'You shouldn't have taken those sedatives last night. It's thrown your sleeping patterns into chaos.'

'Sorry,' he mumbled.

The woman looked to Thea for support. 'Honestly! He didn't wake up until nearly eleven. I put him in the spare room, so we didn't disturb each other, and he slept like a dead thing.'

'It does that to people,' said Thea. 'Grief, I mean.'

'Well, let's hope he pulls out of it after the funeral, then. He's meant to be going back to work on Monday week.'

Thea watched the little family straggle down to the burial field, thinking *Well, at least I'm not as much of a cow as that.*

Back in the house, the remains of the afternoon felt ominously unplanned to Thea. It was doubtless down to her, as hostess, to produce tea, biscuits, entertainment and a generally comfortable atmosphere. 'We could play a game,' she suggested, thinking of her own family weekends of thirty years ago, where one or other of them would insist on Monopoly or Pictionary. *Thirty years?* she caught herself asking. Could it really be that long since she was fifteen and Jocelyn twelve and the older ones in and out of the house at random times? Her father had kept his weekends sacrosanct for the family and was permanently eager for a game of cards or something with a board. He had always done his best to win, as well. Not like Drew, who deliberately lost to Timmy as often as was humanly possible in the misguided assumption that this would make the child feel good about himself.

But a game would exclude young Meredith and make conversation difficult. 'What do you want to do?' she asked helplessly.

Den Cooper took over. 'Merry needs a nap, for a start,' he said. 'And Maggs and Drew have things to talk about. It's lovely out there – and I notice there's a footpath that goes right into Chipping Campden. Why don't we take Stephanie, Timmy and Hepzibah for a good long walk? You can show me the local sights. I've never been here before, remember.'

He made it sound blessedly simple. Stephanie and Tim were delighted at the prospect of a second outing in one day, and Thea was just glad not to have to make decisions. The evening meal would have to take care of itself – she could manage an acceptable spaghetti bolognese at fairly short notice, and nobody was likely to be hungry after the filling pub lunch.

Den's role as rescuer continued as they set out down the unpaved lane and into the first field. The footpath kinked around an uninhabited house, which Thea had become increasingly intrigued by. It had a large grapevine growing against the front wall, and tall dark conifers close by that still loomed like giants, despite having been lopped some months earlier. The path followed a narrow alleyway at the back of the house, before returning to the same big field they had started in. There were then choices to be made. A favourite with Thea and her dog for short strolls, was to turn left past a small fenced-off field often containing odd-looking sheep, opposite an ancient house that had been renovated and embellished until it had to be worth an astronomical sum. There was then the handsome old Quaker Meeting House, just a few steps further, before coming back to the church, and pub. The whole area was an indecisive mixture of natural countryside and human interventions: alternating extravagantly expensive houses with patches of neglect, interspersed with evidence of genuine agriculture. Thea had embarked on some research into it all over the winter but, apart from identifying some very engaging characters from the Arts and Crafts Movement, she had not got very far.

She pointed some of this out to Den, before indicating their way, straight across the field towards the church tower in the distance. 'It's really no distance at all,' she said. 'That's the lower end of Chipping Campden.' The children and dog went ahead, familiar with the route. Den waited until they were out of earshot and then said, 'I'm not sure Maggs really understands what the consequences will be for Drew – her giving up the business.'

'I'm not sure anybody does, including Drew himself. It's a big shock. I can see her point of view, I suppose. I mean – I wouldn't do it. But she's not me. She's always seemed so *right* for the work.'

'She is. But people don't stay in the same job for life any more. Look at me. I was so mad keen on the police when I was a kid. Fifteen, sixteen – it was all I could think about. And then one day it just turned to ashes. I can't describe it, but I knew I didn't want to keep on doing it. I doubt if I'll carry on doing what I'm doing now, either. And look at Drew. He was a nurse, for heaven's sake.'

'And I've never really been anything. We're all just floating through life, aren't we? My sister's boy, Noel, says he's going to be a lawyer for twenty years, then retire and open his own museum. That sounds rather splendid, don't you think?'

'It does,' he agreed. Then, with a slight clearing of his throat, he went on, 'So – what exactly is your involvement in this murder? What happened this morning, and why did that DS woman come here yesterday? We saw all the vehicles gathered at Drew's field this morning as we went past.'

'Didn't you itch to join them? Isn't it a case of once a policeman always a policeman?'

'Not in my case. I was perfectly happy to let them get on with it. I was never a very good detective, really. It always felt much too personal. I let my emotions get tangled up in them, every time.'

'Hmm. Maybe that's the difference between us, then. I mean – I do have feelings for the victims, and I get very angry at the way some people behave, but it doesn't often get under my skin. Only a few times . . .' Her voice faltered as she recalled Hampnett, Snowshill and a shocking episode more recently, just a short way from her present home. 'Well, there have been some nasty moments,' she concluded.

'But you love the quest, the drama of it all. You enjoy being asked to help, and the element of danger. Don't you?'

'I do seem to, I suppose. I like meeting new people, learning about them and working out what they want. It *is* a quest, in a way, you're right. You start from a casual meeting, knowing nothing at all about them, and a week later you've got their family background, past career, who they hold a grudge against. It's often very satisfying.'

'So,' he said again, 'tell me about the body down the road.'

'Juliet Wilson. A very sweet young woman with some mental health issues. Or learning difficulties. She was just a bit simple, as they used to say. I have no idea what the current label for her would be, other than "vulnerable", which was obviously horribly accurate. I met her a year or two ago in Stanton. The Christmas before last. She was living with her mother at that point, but then moved to a shared house in Blockley. She was actually holding down a job, apparently. She was really good with animals. But rather nervous around men. Something traumatic happened to her, I think. I never quite got to the bottom of that. It does upset me that she's dead. I don't think I really believe it yet. How anybody could kill such an innocent person is beyond understanding.'

'I still don't entirely grasp why the DS came to you about it.'

'She's called Gladwin. Sonia Gladwin. She knew that I'd met Juliet, and came to tell me she'd gone missing.'

He paused in his slow walk and looked at her. 'That's not it, though, is it? She's the senior investigating officer, I presume. She's not going to drive round the Cotswolds interviewing everybody who ever knew the missing woman. So why you?'

'We're friends. She likes to chew things over with me. Blockley's only a couple of miles from here. Last night, nobody knew Juliet was dead at that point, so it wasn't hugely urgent. I guess she just used it as an excuse to come for a chat.'

'Still not convinced. She sees you as a kind of unpaid consultant, it seems to me. Rather like I was myself, for a bit. When Drew's Karen was hurt, I was involved in the investigation on an ad hoc sort of basis, because I knew the people and the place. If I were you, I'd get put on a more official footing. They might pay you some expenses.'

Thea returned his look, with a thoughtful smile. 'That's clever of you. I think there is something like that going on, but we've never really put it into words. I've been useful quite a few times, but I've also got in the way, and put myself in danger and been generally annoying. I think she's just got into the habit of including me when there's something going on.'

'And now there is something going on – again. And Maggs and I are the ones getting in the way. Drew's got funerals to attend to, as well. It must be troublesome for him, having a murder so close to the field. Will they be gone before he needs to use it? When's the next burial?'

'Tuesday. And it's a tricky one.' She gave him a brief summary of the Biddulph complications. 'That was the son of the second wife just now. He doesn't know his father was married before, and he's got two half-brothers. His mother wants to get the funeral out of the way before she tells him.'

'But he's a grown man! How've they kept the secret all this time?'

'It's not *they*, is it? Just his mother. Presumably he never asked, and it just went along like that, year after year. It must have been easier before the Internet, though. Everybody's so easy to trace now. If he'd ever suspected, he'd have found out without much trouble.'

'Maybe he did, but couldn't bring himself to tell his mother he knew about it all along. He's got a wife and child. She could have done some research. When people have kids, they generally want to know more about themselves.'

'That's true. But he probably thought he *did* know all about himself. Why would he even think there was a mystery?'

'Because his father's twenties – or whatever – must have been a blank, unless he made something up. He was married with two sons – for how long? That's a pretty big secret to keep.'

Thea sighed, thinking of Clovis. 'I met one of them. He certainly doesn't seem easy to keep hidden.'

Den noticed the change of tone. 'What? Is there something special about him?'

'You could say that. He's incredibly handsome, for a start. And *nice*. There's a *look* about him – goes right into you, somehow. He came here this morning, just before we met you at the pub. I'm still shivering inside. Don't tell Drew,' she added girlishly.

'Don't tell him what?' He seemed genuinely bewildered.

'Oh, nothing. A moment of total madness. Hormones, I suppose. I don't know what came over me.'

They had reached the far side of the second field on their walk, the path then taking them across two more, in a curve, before delivering them into Chipping Campden. The children knew the way, and had run ahead almost out of sight. 'Will they wait for us?' asked Den.

'Oh yes. We've got them pretty well trained. We might have to let them go into one or two shops, though.' She was glad of the abandonment of the tricky topic of Clovis Biddulph. Den wouldn't understand, and it had been idiotic of her to mention it. He could not be relied on to refrain from saying something to Maggs, and she might well decide to inform Drew. Until the previous evening, nobody had doubted where Maggs's strongest loyalties lay. Drew had taken a gamble on her, giving her responsibility far beyond her years, trusting her to conduct half of his business with minimal intervention from him.

But her relief was premature. 'And then there's Lawrence,' he said slowly. 'Who isn't handsome or sexy or even very nice. And because of him, you and Drew were expected to tell outright lies. Is that right?'

'Absolutely. Drew was in a state about it, so it was

lucky in a way that I took the phone call from Clovis. But in the end, we had to own up. He knew, anyway, that we were doing the funeral. So it all fell apart, and Drew had to explain to Linda that it wasn't easy to keep a funeral secret.'

'How did Clovis find out?'

'Good question. Somebody must have tweeted or Facebooked or something. And then Linda heard that the secret was out.'

'Who told her? It sounds like quite a small, closed family.'

'There must be sisters or cousins or neighbours. Linda lives quite locally. Stephen – the man who's died – probably told people he'd decided to have a natural burial. It wasn't a sudden death. He'd been to have a look at our field, a few months ago. He's sure to have talked about it to people other than Linda and Lawrence.'

'But he didn't mention a first wife and two older sons?'

'Of course he didn't. I imagine it was his own guilty feelings that forced Linda to keep it all quiet.'

'Not necessarily. Some women, even now, feel there's a bit of a stigma to being a second wife. It might have come as much from her – or more.'

'I'm a second wife,' Thea said, as if only just noticing. 'And I don't feel any stigma.'

'It's different when the first one dies. You didn't steal him away, as Linda might have done.'

'Oh.' Privately, she thought he was oversimplifying the reality of how she met Drew while Karen was still alive, and how it could very possibly have turned out much messier than it did.

Stephanie and Timmy had stopped on the pavement at an opening to a small arcade, on the left. 'Can we go to the bookshop?' Stephanie called.

'Go on, then.' Thea waved her consent. 'Ten minutes.' She turned to Den. 'At least half the stock is children's books. It's tucked away down there with no natural light, but the kids love it.'

'Are they going to buy anything?'

'I doubt it. I've got enough cash for one little paperback, if they insist. I left the card at home.'

Den laughed. 'I can make a contribution, if necessary. Now, can we go back to dead people? I take it there's no connection between the Biddulph funeral and the murder of Juliet Wilson?'

'Hard to see what. The birdsong man's more likely, and even that's extremely tenuous.'

Den groaned. 'Birdsong man?'

She explained, finishing by saying, 'I mean – his funeral was on Friday, and Juliet was still alive then. Probably hanging about somewhere near the burial field. And his nephew found her body this morning. That connects them, if nothing else.' She had another thought. 'And it's very likely that Juliet loved birdsong as well. She might have known the man. She knew a lot of people.'

'And any one of them could have killed her.'

'Presumably, yes.'

'And DS Gladwin wants you to help her sift through who they all were, and what the motive might have been, and why Juliet was out in the open for three days. That makes sense,' he nodded. 'It makes perfect sense, actually.'

She looked up at him, standing a foot taller than her. 'Does it?'

'You're an asset, Thea Slocombe. I didn't realise before how useful you must be to the police. The way your mind works. Your lack of sentimentality. Your quick grasp of people you've only known for five minutes. You should hear yourself. Better than any computer can ever hope to be. You've got talent – don't waste it.'

'Oh shucks,' she giggled. 'That's taking it much too far.'

'It's not, though,' he said seriously. 'And you should put it on a more formal footing. At least claim for expenses.'

'I would, if there were any. To be honest, I think *I* should pay *them*. They've saved me from terminal boredom many a time.'

He laughed. 'Come on. Those poor children will be wondering where we've got to.'

They went down the chilly little arcade to the shop at the end, where Stephanie and Tim were conducting a fierce but muted argument. 'She won't buy *two* books,' Stephanie hissed. 'We have to find one we both like.'

'I want this one,' the little boy insisted.

'And I don't.'

'Hey, hey!' admonished Thea. 'Den says he'll help if we haven't got enough money. What is it, Tim?'

He held out a large volume about the development of tools in former times. 'Good Lord, that must cost a fortune. We can't buy that, darling. You'll have to order it from the library. Remember the title, and we'll do that on Tuesday after school. Choose something smaller, okay?'

Mutinously, Timmy replaced the book, and almost randomly took a small paperback from the shelf. 'Never heard of it,' said Thea, having given it a quick glance. 'Looks okay, though. What about you, Steph?'

'I've got the new Malorie Blackman.' The smugness in her tone made Thea feel for Timmy. 'Well, bully for you,' she said, before pulling the younger child to her for a quick hug. 'I promise we can go to the library. If not Tuesday, then one day next week.' She had remembered, with a lurch, that life might be uncomfortably unpredictable, come Tuesday.

Chapter Ten

They didn't linger any longer in the small town, but quickly took a different path back to Broad Campden. It was straighter and shorter, and much less fun. Stephanie was mildly reproachful at being ignored throughout the walk. 'I wanted to talk to Den,' she complained.

'So talk to him now,' said Thea. She'd captured her dog and put it on a lead, what with a road running close by. 'I'll talk to Timmy.'

But she and Timmy could think of little to say to each other, so ambled along in an amiable silence, each content with his or her own thoughts.

The house was quiet when they got in. Maggs was in the garden with Meredith, and Drew was in his office. It was impossible to tell whether they'd said all they needed to and amicably gone separate ways, or whether things had become so fractious they had to get away from each other. Thea and Den sought out their respective spouses to learn which it was.

Listening first at the door, to ensure there was no unexpected visitor, Thea tapped and waited for a response. The office was treated as if it were a separate building, with none of the family allowed to simply walk in uninvited. 'Yes?' came Drew's voice.

'Is everything okay?' she asked, once in the room.

'Not really. No, not at all, actually. I can't think what I should do.'

'Surely there are plenty of options?'

'Two or three at most, and none of them even remotely appealing. I'll have to speak to Andrew,' he sighed.

This was an ominous leap of logic. 'Why? What are you going to say to him?' She imagined Drew offering his assistant the North Staverton business to operate instead of Maggs. Or telling him they were closing down and he was out of a job. Or that he'd be running the Broad Campden end while Drew went back to Somerset. Anything seemed possible.

'I don't know. I want to keep him in the picture, that's all. He's a much better businessman than I'll ever be. He's been asking me about the footing he's on here, and I haven't known what to say. Now I can see how sloppy and amateurish I've been with Maggs. We've never put anything in writing, you know. I've never even had an accountant, which Andrew says is barely legal. I've never made enough profit for HMRC to take much notice of me. Now it's all crashing down and I have no idea where to start to get it straight.'

'Okay.' Perversely, his despair came as something of a relief to Thea. Problems with tax and legalities seemed to her very much preferable to sudden drastic decisions about their way of life. Although, she reminded herself, the two probably went together in the long run. 'Well, we can sit down and go through it all, like grown-ups. Andrew as well, of course. You haven't broken any laws, surely?'

'Not wittingly, no.'

'And you've kept meticulous records of the graves, and everything to do with the burials. Including the money you've been paid. I can't see there's much to worry about.'

'I hope you're right.' He reached for her hand. 'Maggs says I should sell Peaceful Repose, but I'm not sure I can, if it's not properly registered as a business.'

She had been standing since entering the room. Now she pulled a chair close to his and sat facing him, shaking the proffered hand in an effort to reassure. 'That sounds like a technicality to me. You own the house and land outright. No mortgages on it. The burial ground can never be changed or disturbed, even if nobody wants to carry on with new burials there. Which is unlikely, given how people like the idea.'

'I'd have to give Maggs half the proceeds.'

'Would you?' She paused. 'I suppose that's fair. I think.' The justice of the suggestion felt fragile to her.

If there had been sloppy practice, wasn't Maggs as much to blame for that as Drew? And it was certainly his house, fair and square. A great-aunt had left it to him when he and Karen were first married. 'What's it worth, anyway?'

'I haven't a clue. There's not much of a market for burial grounds.'

'But the *house*, Drew. That could go as a separate entity. Detached country cottage, three bedrooms, big garden. It has to be three hundred thousand, surely?'

'With hundreds of dead people right outside the window. That probably cuts the value by about half.'

'They could put up a fence.'

Drew groaned. 'I can't bear to think of it. I had such *dreams*. Karen and I both did.'

Thea went cold. Jealousy of Karen had not troubled her very much at all, right from her first meeting with Drew. It would be ridiculous to start feeling it now. But who could ignore the passion behind his words, and the clear implication that his present life fell short of those dreams?

'Haven't we got dreams as well?' she asked, dropping his hand. 'You left North Staverton a year ago. It's in the past. I don't much like what you're saying. It's as if that was your real love, and all this is second best.'

He met her gaze with utter frankness. 'I know. And I'm trying not to lie to myself or to pretend I feel something when I don't. I was forced to come here, remember, by Greta Simmonds. She meant it kindly, of course. But there was definitely coercion in there somewhere. I never felt I had much of a choice. I thought it suited Maggs, and you, and even the children once they settled down. But it hasn't felt as right as Peaceful Repose always did.'

'I can see that,' she said bravely, a lump rising in her throat. 'It's funny, really, the way women keep leaving houses to you. Most people don't even have it happen once, let alone twice. It is a sort of power beyond the grave, I suppose.'

'It was with this place. The woman was so zealous about alternative funerals, she deprived her own family to ensure it happened. It always felt wrong, you know. Right from the first day.'

'But you've made it *right*. You know you have. You've got a steady supply of customers, all wildly enthusiastic about what you're doing here. We've got this lovely big house in a hugely sought-after part of the country. The kids like it. We can tackle the paperwork easily enough. Nothing has to change. Let Maggs go, with your blessing. She's earned it. Life moves on, and if you can sell North Staverton, there'll be some cash for improvements here. A new building, better fences, a proper parking area. All the things the council wants you to do.'

'Mm,' he said dubiously. 'And all our eggs in one not-very-sturdy basket. No safety net if things go sour.'

'They won't go sour. And we'll still have this

house – without a field of corpses outside the window. Worth double what the other one is, at least. That feels like a pretty good safety net to me.'

'Don't call them corpses,' he said automatically.

It was past five o'clock, and people were milling about, aware of an evening ahead for which there were no plans. The children were conscious of strain between the four adults, glancing from face to face in an attempt to work out the source. Maggs was the first to confront their worries. 'Hey, kids, let's go and watch a DVD for a bit. Or is that too old-fashioned for you these days?'

Stephanie hesitated. 'We've only got a few,' she warned.

'That's okay. Den and I brought some with us. Have you seen *Totoro*?'

Stephanie rolled her eyes. 'Of course. We've seen *all* the Ghibli ones.'

'Ah. That's a shame. Well, I've got one or two others. Good old classics. *The Railway Children* for one. How about that?'

'Blimey!' said Thea. 'I used to watch that when I was six. It's great, Steph. Give it a try.'

Both children shrugged compliantly and Thea threw Maggs a grateful look. 'I'll have supper all done by the time it's finished, then,' she said. 'It's going to be the best bolognese you've ever tasted. *And* there'll be pudding.'

For a full two minutes, Meredith resisted these sensible plans as a matter of principle, but finding herself ignored, opted to go with the consensus and settled onto her mother's lap. Thea and the two men were left in the kitchen, along with the dog whose dinner was already late.

'Leave me to get on with it,' she ordered Den and Drew. 'Have a couple of beers outside or something.'

'I want to watch the movie,' said Den.

'And I need to speak to Andrew,' said Drew. 'I have to get that out of the way. He might have heard about the business with Juliet and be wondering what's going on.'

It was as if a wicked demon had been listening for an opening. No sooner had the word 'Juliet' left his lips than the doorbell rang.

'Who the hell is that?' Thea demanded angrily. 'Just as we've got everything sorted.'

'Who do you think?' said Drew, who could see a silhouette through the small frosted window beside the door. 'I'll go and let her in.'

'Sorry, sorry,' said Gladwin, all in a rush. 'Terrible time to come, I know. You've got people, haven't you. I won't be long. Thea? Where's Thea?'

'Here. In the kitchen, where I belong.' Thea wished she was wearing an apron to reinforce the point. 'Feeding the five thousand.'

'Carry on, then. I'll talk as you chop carrots or whatever you're doing.'

'I'm actually chopping carrots. You must be psychic.'

'I could do some, if you like.'

'You can do the onions. Serves you right if they make you cry.'

'Okay.'

They both laughed, Thea thinking it was always so easy where Gladwin was concerned. None of the usual protocols operated. There had been a number of occasions like this, where the detective dropped all the accoutrements of her professional status and became an ordinary normal human being. They both understood that it made no difference to the investigation, whatever it was at the time. In fact, they believed it helped. 'Let's cut through the crap,' Gladwin might say. 'What's your take on who's most likely to have done it?' Or words to that effect.

'So – can Drew get back into his field yet?' Thea asked. 'Have all those vehicles gone?'

'One or two left, but they'll be away before dark. It's been a big forensic job. We've had a dozen bods combing the grass all day. Didn't find much.'

'How've you got time to be here, then? Isn't it madly busy?'

'It is. But they all know what they've got to do. And you Slocombes are part of it, don't forget. Several points of contact, in fact. Drew's the last person we've found to see Juliet alive. That puts him right in there, for a start.'

'Do you want to talk to him again?'

Drew had gone into his office, the moment Gladwin had followed Thea into the kitchen, closing the door loudly enough to make a point.

'No, not really. Although, now I think about it, I should probably have a list of all the funerals he's done in the past . . . say a month or so. And forthcoming ones. There has to be a reason why she was hanging around your field like that.' She shook her head. 'That's quite important. I nearly forgot. My head's not working properly these days. Must be hormones.'

'Where would we be without hormones to blame?' Thea agreed, giving rise to a questioning look from the other woman. Quickly, Thea went back to the main subject. 'You think we've buried somebody Juliet knows, and she wanted to stay near the grave?' Thinking about it, Thea concluded this was quite a probable explanation. She remembered how Juliet had been in Stanton, a cousin of hers recently buried in a country churchyard. She had seemed to find the process far from alarming, even comforting, with the flowers and the soothing words spoken over the grave.

'It seems possible, although her mother insists that nobody they know has died lately.'

'Rosa would know, surely?'

'Presumably – although Juliet's been meeting new people at work. And she's done some volunteering at a rehab centre near Paxford. Apparently one of her housemates used to go there, and suggested Juliet go along as well. It was working very nicely, from what we can gather. I've sent a couple of uniforms over there to ask how she fitted in.'

'Volunteering as what, exactly?' Thea had finished the carrots, and was extracting her largest cooking pot from the back of a cupboard. 'Let me get this going, okay?' She peered into the pot. 'Haven't used this since we moved here. Looks as if it might need a wipe.'

'Funny the way they're never as clean as you think,' agreed Gladwin. 'I really don't know what Juliet did at the centre.'

'I think a spider's been living in it. Gosh, I am a slut, aren't I.'

'Join the club.'

'I still can't really believe she's dead. I mean – Juliet! Such a totally harmless person.'

'I know. It's brutal, senseless, disgusting. We can only think she must have seen something she shouldn't. Or knew something about somebody.'

'Yes, but . . . what on earth could be worth *killing* her for?'

'That's what we've got to find out.'

Thea remembered her afternoon chat with Den. 'Um . . . Sonia,' she began. 'Do you want me to really help with this? Like, actually going out there and talking to people, in a casual sort of way – but also semi-official?'

'You mean you're offering to be a police informer?' Gladwin's eyes sparkled. 'Like on the telly?'

'Not exactly. Sort of. I could go and chat to people

at that centre, for example. Or . . . I don't know. Ask some of our funeral families whether they knew her.'

Gladwin shook her head firmly. 'No, not that. That's got to be official-official. In fact, I guess I should go and ask Drew for the list now. It's the last thing I'm doing today. That cooking's making me feel hungry.'

Thea had cleaned her pot, set it on the hob and put a large quantity of minced beef into it. The carrots were next, followed by garlic, onions, tomatoes and herbs. 'I'd ask you to stay, but . . .'

'Don't even think it. The idea's outrageous – much as I'd like to meet your visitors. That tall bloke – what's his name?'

'Den Cooper. He used to be in the police, actually. Now he's a security officer at Bristol airport.'

'Interesting.' Then the detective shook herself. 'Well, better get on. Thanks for the suggestion about the semi-official stuff. I hope you're not going to ask us to pay you as well?'

Thea opened her mouth to reply, but couldn't find the right words. Gladwin laughed. 'It's not for me to decide about that sort of thing, anyway. It's been so far from normal procedure up to now, I'd be scared to try to get things on a formal footing. The money men might have something to say if we tried to get you onto the payroll.'

'Go and talk to Drew,' said Thea. 'I've got to cook.' She opened a cupboard and began to root about amongst packets and jars. 'Oh, God!' she groaned.

'What?'

'There's no spaghetti. I used it all up last time, I remember now. What on earth am I going to do? Seven people have been promised spag bol.'

'Use macaroni and blame it on the hormones,' said Gladwin.

Chapter Eleven

The meal was well received by all except Timmy, who took great exception to the pasta substitution. 'I can't wind *macaroni* round my fork,' he objected. 'It's completely different.'

'Just as nice, though,' said his father with a warning look. 'Thea's done a great job.'

'At least there's parmesan,' said Stephanie. 'That's the best part.'

'Not for me, it isn't. I don't like it,' persisted her brother.

'Well, Meredith's enjoying it, look,' Maggs pointed out. 'And macaroni's much easier for her than spaghetti would be. She's doing it all by herself.' The toddler had orange tomato stains all over her face and was beaming delightedly.

The bottle of Rioja that Drew had bought earlier in the week was drained within five minutes. 'I should have bought two,' he apologised. 'But we've got some rosé for tomorrow.'

'And I won't have any because I'll be driving,' said Den.

The promised pudding turned out to be pancakes with lemon juice and sugar. It was rapturously received by all, and by seven o'clock the whole meal was a distant memory. At seven-fifteen the doorbell rang again, and Drew's face flushed with annoyance. 'It had better not be Gladwin again,' he said. He had not taken kindly to her request for recent burials, with contact details of the families.

Thea went to the door and took several seconds to recognise the small woman standing on the step, clutching a fluffy white dog. 'Rosa!' she realised at last. The transformation from the bustling competent person she had met in Stanton to the shrunken old husk before her now was horrifying. 'Gosh! Come in. Oh dear. This is so dreadful, isn't it? Come in,' she repeated, gabbling desperately.

'I expect I'm intruding.' Even the voice had faded to a whisper.

'Of course you're not. We have got some people here – but we could go and sit in the garden, perhaps? It's a nice evening. Is that Juliet's dog? Shall we take him outside, so he can potter around?' There was over an hour of daylight left, and the kitchen felt all wrong for the situation.

Juliet Wilson's mother followed silently as she was led through to the back door. Thea wondered whether Drew's office might be more appropriate than the cramped garden, even though it was much too soon to be thinking about Juliet's funeral, and that room would inevitably carry implications to that effect. The main thing was to find a spot where they wouldn't be disturbed. Raw emotion was to be expected, to an unpredictable extent. She remembered that Rosa was at least half Italian, which could turn out to be a factor.

'Can I get you a drink?' she asked, having placed the woman on a rather mossy garden bench that had come with the house. The dog, released from Rosa's arms, sat gazing around pathetically. 'Tea or something?'

'Oh, no. I shouldn't have come, really, but the policewoman said Juliet was close to your new place, and it was somebody you knew who found her – and, well, we liked you, back in Stanton. You seemed sort of . . . special.' A feeble smile crossed her face. 'Not the way they mean that nowadays – they called Juliet "special" sometimes – but clever and sensible. Unusual.'

'Juliet *was* special, in the old-fashioned sense. I can't *imagine* . . .' She choked on the rest of the sentence. 'It's the most awful thing,' she managed.

'It is,' Rosa nodded. 'It's going to be the death of me. I can feel it already, the life just leaking out of me. I knew right away, when they told me. It isn't just living without my girl. It's living in a world where this sort of thing can happen. Who would want to? What's the point?'

Thea made no attempt to answer. She remembered similar feelings when her husband had died so needlessly. People had assured her that life went on, that she would find purpose again, and they'd been right. But it hadn't helped at the time. She could barely even hear them.

'I wasn't even surprised when they came to tell me. She'd been gone since Tuesday, not telling anybody where she was going, and not taking Buster with her. That meant trouble.'

'Do you think somebody *took* her? Kept her somewhere without a phone or anything?'

Rosa raised her ravaged face. 'Who would do that? *Why?* No, I can't think that would be it. I think she might have found a badger sett or maybe even a red squirrel drey. Something she thought needed protecting and watching. A mistle thrush nested in the woods near our house, when she was sixteen. One of the local cats was determined to steal the babies, so Juliet camped out all night for ten days, to guard it. That's the sort of thing she did.'

'But wouldn't she have told somebody about it? And why not take the dog as well?'

'If she could find anyone to listen,' said Rosa bitterly. 'Or who she could trust. They're culling the badgers around here, you know. She wouldn't dare reveal a sett, even to someone she knew well. And then one of those bastard culling men would have tried to move her, maybe hitting her too hard. She was big, remember. And strong. She'd take some subduing. Maybe she thought Buster would get hurt.' Tears stood silvery on the grey cheeks, but the expression was fierce and proud.

The image of a masked and garbed badger-killer lashing out in furious frustration at a large female protester gripped Thea. 'There'd be signs of recent culling, though,' she realised. 'I don't think that could have been it.' She gave the sad little dog a considering look. 'It does make you wonder whether she had a definite plan in mind. Something that Buster would have got in the way of.'

Rosa waved this away with a sniff. 'They say somebody must have swung at her with a heavy object. I forced them to tell me, but you're never sure you can believe what they say, are you? They always tell the families the person didn't suffer, and it was all over in a second. It's hardly ever true.'

'It might be.' Thea remembered Gladwin saying *It wasn't very subtle*. 'I don't know any details, either, but I did get the impression it was quite quick.'

'I can't bear to think about it, but I can't *not* think about it. I have to know exactly what happened, even though I don't want to. You can't stop yourself. She was my *baby*. My own flesh.'

'Yes,' said Thea, pushing away thoughts of her own daughter. Jessica was twenty-four and very far from a baby. You lost them, whatever happened. That chuckling bundle of dependency disappeared in one way or another, and turned into a person you were never quite sure you properly understood.

'Well . . .' the woman hesitated. 'I should go. But I can't just sit at home, can I? It might be weeks before they catch the man who did it. They might *never* catch him. They might never know where she was, and what she was doing, all those days.'

'Haven't they told you that Drew saw her on Wednesday?'

'What? Who's Drew?' Rosa stared blankly at her.

'My husband. The undertaker. Drew Slocombe. He was in the burial field on Wednesday afternoon, and Juliet went up to him. He thinks she was looking at the graves. They don't all have names on them,' she added inconsequentially.

'Oh.' Rosa shook her head. 'What does that mean? I can't make it *mean* anything.' Despair returned tenfold to her face, and she covered it with her hands. 'I can't do this.' The words filtered thickly through her fingers. 'How do people do it?'

'They just keep on breathing,' said Thea, again thinking of her own experience. 'People bring food and drink, and the sun keeps on rising, and that's about it. You feed the dog and take it out now and then. It goes on like that for months. I didn't even wash my hair for three weeks, until my sister did it for me.'

Rosa seemed oblivious to this disclosure. She wasn't ready for empathy or other people's sharings. Thea reproached herself for letting her own memories intrude. *Me, me, me*, she told herself crossly.

'Do you want to speak to Drew?' she asked, after

131

some silent moments. 'He could tell you how she seemed on Wednesday.'

Slowly the face was uncovered. 'I don't know. I suppose he's told the police, and they'll make something of it if they can. I can't see that it makes any difference. Wednesday's too long ago. What did she do on Thursday and Friday – where *was* she? She didn't go to work. She loved that job. She was absolutely dedicated to it. Why did she stop going? Something must have happened.'

'The police will have asked them, I expect.'

'Yes.' She grimaced. 'There's a woman who wants to stay in my house with me. A family something officer. She's meant to keep me informed of what they find out.'

'Liaison. Family liaison officer,' said Thea automatically. 'They're usually very helpful.'

'It feels like being supervised. It must be a horrible job.'

'Is she nice?'

'Not very,' said Rosa, with a hint of her former self. 'She tries too hard and she overdoes the sympathy.'

'Does she know you're here?'

'No, she doesn't. I don't have to answer to her. Unless they think *I* killed Juliet, of course.'

Thea didn't smile. Mothers had been known to kill their offspring, she supposed. 'They don't think that,' she said.

'Juliet's like her father, you know. He was big and fair like her. His mother was Polish, and Juliet looks like her. I wonder where he is now.'

132

'Is he called Wilson?'

Rosa blinked. 'Jan Wilson, yes. He said the J as the English do, but really it should be Yan. Nice man. I treated him very badly.' She sighed. 'Somebody should tell him his daughter's dead. If they can find him.'

'Do the police know about him?'

Rosa sighed. 'Oh yes,' she said.

'Well, they'll probably tell him when they find him. It's all part of their job.'

A silence ensued, with both women conscious that there was little more to be said. The image of poor Juliet remained powerfully present, the sheer outrageousness of her murder still too large to fully confront.

'They'll find out who did it,' said Thea, finally. 'Which probably won't make anybody feel any better.'

'I would like to understand the reason, though. That might help a little bit. If there was even a tiny scrap of sense to it . . . well, that would be easier. At least, it *might* be.' Rosa heaved another profound sigh. 'That sounds silly, doesn't it?'

'Not at all. It sounds very wise, actually.'

They parted with watery smiles, each feeling they'd formed a bond. The forces of evil, just beyond the gate, had brought them together. Thea felt a cloudy sense of obligation to maintain something good and innocent, in Juliet's memory. 'I'm glad you came,' she said.

'So am I. Thank you.'

The dumpy woman made her way back up the lane, as Thea watched. The light had almost gone beneath the big leafy trees, making it seem as if Rosa was being swallowed up in a grey mist. Drew came to stand behind her, on the doorstep. 'I kept everybody out of the way,' he said. 'Was that right?'

'Absolutely. And very noble. Did we finish supper? What about coffee? Where is everybody?'

'Den's putting Merry to bed. The film didn't appeal so Maggs is playing Monopoly with our two. Timmy's in heaven. I mean – he's very happy indeed,' he corrected with a grimace when he heard his own words.

'Oh Lord. Not Monopoly. It'll go on till midnight.'

'I know. Lucky it's Sunday tomorrow. We can all sleep in.'

'Stephanie hates Monopoly,' Thea remembered. 'How did they persuade her?'

'Maggs did it. Some promise about tomorrow morning. I didn't catch what it was, but I expect we'll have to go along with whatever it is.'

Thea groaned. 'Do you think they'd notice if I went off to bed now?'

'Probably. It's only half past seven. They'll think you're ill.'

'I will be if things go on like this,' she warned him. 'I'll have a flaming nervous breakdown.'

He gave her a worried look. 'Don't say that,' he pleaded. 'Things can't be as awful as all that, can they?'

She chewed her lip. 'You have to admit they are pretty awful. Everywhere I look there's some sort of crisis. I can't begin to imagine the future. Even next week seems like a whole different world.'

'By this time next week, we'll have everything sorted,' he assured her. 'And that's a promise.'

Chapter Twelve

Sunday began by exceeding Thea's hopes by some margin. She woke shortly before eight to the soaring sound of blackbirds challenging each other across the fields, other birds joining in as well. It was better than any opera, she reflected drowsily. Then she detected a warbling human voice closer to hand, identified as Meredith serenading the morning. 'She's got a great sense of rhythm,' mumbled Drew. 'And she can hold a tune.'

'They all can at that age,' said Thea, thinking of some programme she'd seen or heard. 'But adults knock it out of them, more often than not.'

'That seems to be true of nearly everything.'

'It probably is. Something about original sin, or the human condition.'

'The opposite of original sin, surely? Original innocence, tainted and corrupted by the wicked world.'

'Don't,' said Thea. But it was too late. Already the fate of Juliet Wilson had thumped back at her, along with all the worries and troubles of the past few days.

He quickly changed the subject. 'Guess what Maggs promised the kids for today?'

'I have no idea. But I hope it's not going to include lunch, after I got that huge piece of pork.' She had had second thoughts about the Sunday roast, deciding it was quicker and easier than most of the alternatives.

'Well, actually, it might. It's Snowshill Manor, and the website says it doesn't open until midday. But they could be back here by two, so a late lunch would work.'

Thea passionately resented the way social life always seemed to centre around meals. She also nursed an irrational animosity towards Snowshill Manor, for no better reason than the gardens refused admittance to dogs. 'Honestly!' she said. 'What a silly plan.'

'It's not really,' he argued. 'Stephanie's been wanting to see it for weeks now, and she's got Timmy on her side. I wouldn't mind seeing it myself, come to that.'

'And Merry? Will they let her in? She's liable to go toddling round knocking everything over, if it's how I imagine it.' He gave her a look, the implications of which were instantly evident. 'Oh, I see. You're all intending to go off for hours, leaving me with the cooking and the kid. I'm sure I remember a promise that you'd take charge of at least one meal. What happened to that?'

'I would, but since you don't want to go to Snowshill . . .'

'All right. Point taken. Leave me to get on with it. Merry can peel the potatoes.'

'Very funny. And you'll have the dog. But Den says he'll stay as well, if you need him to. He's pretty lukewarm about the whole idea.'

'You surprise me. What about his new hobby, buying and selling antiques? I'd have thought Snowshill was right up his street.'

'Wrong sort of antiques, apparently.'

'And when was all this decided, anyway?'

'Last night. After you went to bed. For the record, Stephanie won at Monopoly, and Timmy was awake until quarter past ten. He ran out of money at about nine, but insisted the others keep going to the bitter end, with him being the bank. He really is remarkably good at that, you know,' he concluded thoughtfully.

'Well, I can see it's all fixed. I suppose it's quite a good idea, in some ways. If you get there early, you can be first in. It can't take more than an hour, surely? So I'll have everything ready for two. They'll be leaving right after lunch, I presume?'

'They want to be away by half past three, yes. Amazing what can happen over one little weekend, isn't it?'

She gave no reply to that, thinking his words were a definite understatement. She could tell that he was not thinking about Juliet, or the Biddulphs, or anything to do with past and present funerals. All he meant was Maggs and her announcement, and the various activities his children had been enjoying.

At that point, Den wandered into the room carrying

138

his daughter. 'We decided to take Meredith as well,' he said. 'She likes an outing.'

'Fine,' said Thea, feeling more relief than she dared express. 'You can all go, and I'll take the dog out for an hour. Then I'll come back and prepare a full-scale feast for everybody. It's not particularly arduous. Meat, potatoes, broccoli and peas. I can manage that. And I can do a big fruit salad for pudding with all those bananas we bought last week.'

'And the pineapple. Don't forget the pineapple. It must be ripe by now.' The pineapple had been a rash impulse on Thea's part four days earlier, which Drew had judged to be unready for consumption.

'There's some tinned peaches somewhere as well,' she said.

It was a game she knew he had played with Karen, who had been very much more interested in food than was the second Mrs Slocombe. Discussions about forthcoming meals, often first thing in the morning, were irritating to Thea. She was much happier helping the children with homework, listening to their accounts of classroom feuds, or planning weekend outings than she was trying to feed them. She understood that fresh vegetables, good cuts of meat, sugar-free drinks were all obligatory, but secretly she hankered for the funds that would cover Waitrose ready meals and regular Indian takeaways.

By ten o'clock Thea was impatient for everybody to leave the house. When they objected that they'd have far too much time to kill before even the Snowshill garden would open its gates, she whistled for her dog, and left them all to sort themselves out. 'You don't need me,' she said, three times.

Outside, the world suddenly opened up invitingly. She could go in any of half a dozen directions. Fields, lanes, footpaths were all laid on in abundance. The hedgerows were frothy with spring blossom, insisting that Thea inspect the different plants and remind herself of their identities. Carl, her first husband, had taken her and Jessica for many a long nature ramble on which he would teach them to distinguish between Queen Anne's lace and meadowsweet, hemlock and hogweed. She had loved the names and been perpetually impressed by his knowledge.

'Let's go down to the burial field,' she suggested to the dog, surprising them both. Hepzie preferred the walk they had taken the day before with Den or, even better, the Monarchs Way path that took them on rising ground to wide open spaces where she could run and run. When she realised they were heading for the modest five acres where Drew's friend Andrew dug deep holes and then covered them in again, she sighed.

'I just want to have another little look,' Thea muttered. 'We might be missing something.' Listening to herself, she had to admit that she felt a foolish sense of having already missed a piece of highly important action in letting Juliet Wilson loiter so close by for so many days. She was also bothered by Rosa's mention of badger culling. She had been culpably ignorant if she'd failed to observe such goings-on on her very doorstep. Did Drew have badgers living on his land without knowing it? Maybe the spaniel could answer that, given half a chance.

Hepzie ran ahead, keeping tightly into the minimal verge, for fear of passing traffic. Now well into her middle years, she had developed into a reliably sensible animal. Having suffered a broken leg less than six months earlier, she had a slight limp, which nobody but Thea would admit to being able to see. At the entrance to the burial ground, she automatically turned in.

'Just run about,' Thea told her. 'See if you can smell out a badger.'

The words were unfamiliar and Hepzie ignored them. She could smell old meat, faintly but definitely, coming from some of Andrew's holes. Her ancient wolfish genes prompted her to attempt to dig for it, but she knew that was forbidden. The conflict made her uneasy and recalcitrant. Better to run off into the next field, and then the woods, where there might be a rabbit or squirrel to chase. Setting off tentatively, she sped up when her mistress showed no sign of stopping her.

Instead, Thea followed slowly, after pausing to inspect the row of graves. There was something forlorn about them, she thought, taking up such a small proportion of the whole field as they did. The baby trees planted over some of them were barely visible, in spite of their tender spring leaves. A potential customer had once characterised the whole ground as *bleak*, and Thea had been unable to forget the word ever since.

Was it all a huge mistake, then? Would Drew ordain that they dispose of this entire property and go back to North Staverton? The children would slip effortlessly back into their former school, the house would welcome them like the old friends they were. Only Thea would be displaced, transplanted yet again, with no social network and no definable role. Not that her social network in the Cotswolds was particularly robust. She bumped into people she had known for a week or two during various house-sitting jobs, and she counted Sonia Gladwin as a friend. Nine months after abandoning her career as a house-sitter, she had yet to replace it with anything else. Cooking meals for a man and two children did not count as a valid occupation. The ever-present threat of boredom, which had explained so much of her intrusive behaviour towards the inhabitants of numerous villages while in charge of empty houses, returned tenfold. Repeatedly, she had announced to Drew that she was going to get a job. She needed to be occupied and they were in sore need of extra money. Den Cooper had listened sympathetically to her complaints, which only served to fortify them. Now, she was really going to do it. She'd broached the subject with Gladwin and was determined to press her case. Nothing was going to distract her this time.

Thoughts of Gladwin recalled the very recent events

on this exact spot. There had been a murder, less than two days earlier. That, obviously, was the real reason she had brought the dog over here, instead of letting her have her head on the higher wolds. She wanted to see for herself just where it had all happened. She might find a clue overlooked by the SOCOs. She might remember some detail about Juliet that everybody else had forgotten. Or failing that, she could simply accord the victim a few minutes of reflection – which some people might almost have characterised as prayer. She would think warmly of the life that had ended and resolve to do anything she could to assuage the suffering of Juliet's mother.

Walking around the field, and then following her dog through the gateway into the adjacent one, she gave her thoughts full rein. The police had driven back and forth through the gap in the hedge, not troubling to drag the ancient gate back into position. There were never any animals in the second field but, even so, the gate ought to have been put back as it had been originally. Wasn't that the first rule of the Country Code? And what gave the police the right to flout it?

She pushed away such observations, bringing her attention back to Juliet and her ghastly fate. She could see the feathery tip of Hepzie's tail amongst tangles of bramble and nettle at the edge of the strip of woodland on the other side of the field. There would normally be police tape closing off the scene of the crime but, for some reason, they appeared not to have bothered on this occasion. Presumably, they had found all they hoped to and judged it unprofitable to maintain any sort of presence. Over recent years, Thea had witnessed every permutation of police response, which varied more than the strict book of rules might suggest. Finances, manpower, weather and the personality of the senior investigating officer all created diversity.

'Poor, poor Juliet,' she murmured. There seemed to be little else to say. She hoped her suffering had been minimal, fear completely absent. Had she known her attacker, and felt the searing pain of betrayal? Had she been simply bewildered, unable to believe what was happening? These same thoughts were inevitably going through Rosa's mind, over and over. The urgent need for answers could only be satisfied by finding who did it and persuading him or her to give an account of what had really happened.

It was time to go home and cook a roast dinner. 'Come on, Heps,' she called. The dog obediently materialised at her side and they walked back towards the road. Halfway across the burial field they both saw a large figure coming through the gate. A very big man, with short brown hair and clothes that looked too warm for the season, was walking towards them.

Chapter Thirteen

Thea's instant assumption was that here was the killer, revisiting the scene. He *looked* like a murderer, and her heart thudded insistently. Hepzie gave an alarmed yap at the sight of him. He did not smile at her as he walked towards her.

'Um . . . Hello,' she said, when they were close enough to speak.

'Hello,' he replied in a much lighter voice than his bulk suggested. 'My name is Adam Rogers. I wanted to see where poor Juliet died.'

He spoke with careful deliberation, the words sounding rehearsed. Cautiously, Thea diagnosed something awry with him. Something akin to Juliet's condition. Something that would very probably bring them together in the care system.

'Ah,' she said. 'Well, this is it. You knew her, then?'

'I did. She was my girlfriend.' He finally produced a self-conscious smile. 'Sort of, anyway.'

'Oh dear. Then I am terribly sorry about what happened. You must be dreadfully upset.' Instinctively, she was speaking as if to a child. Very much the same way as she had spoken to Juliet, she realised. Short words. No metaphors or idioms or ironic asides.

'The police talked to me.' He frowned. 'They asked me twenty-seven questions. I counted them.'

'Gosh! Did you have answers for all of them?'

'Oh yes. I'm not sure they were all the right ones, though. Some were a bit hard to understand.'

'Where do you live?'

He smiled again. 'How many are you going to ask me?'

'Oh, I'm sorry. It's none of my business. My name is Thea Slocombe. My husband runs this burial ground. See the graves.' She pointed. 'I came here for the same reason as you, probably. Just to think about Juliet and wonder what happened to her.'

'I live in Blockley, with some people called Dunsford. They get paid to look after me and two others. They've got Down's syndrome, but I haven't. We've all got learning difficulties. Like Juliet. But she's got a job.' Reflected pride at this achievement shone brightly. 'Most of us just go to the workshop at the day centre and do some weaving or pottery.'

'I see. And that's how you knew Juliet – when she was going there?'

'Exactly.'

She looked at his huge meaty hands and the very

broad shoulders. He must be strong, she thought. And perhaps unpredictable, with little self-control. Or was she being outrageously unfair, stereotyping him without any justification? She recalled discussions and documentaries on the subject of relationships between people of restricted capacity. Quite where things currently stood, she had no idea. The social services changed their rules constantly, encouraging and enabling one minute, and enforcing draconian limitations the next. She regularly arrived at the conclusion that the way villagers in Victorian times handled such dilemmas were probably a lot less damaging than present-day practices.

'But didn't Juliet go to a different centre, somewhere near here?'

He did not appear to have a direct answer to this, but went on, 'She stopped going, just after Easter. She was a success story,' he said proudly. 'They paid her proper wages, and she went there all on her own on the bus. Every day.'

'I knew her, too. She was a lovely person.'

'They all say that.' He nodded to himself. 'She shouldn't be dead.'

'No,' Thea agreed emphatically. Then she shook herself. 'Well, I've got to go home now. I'll leave you to it. Maybe I'll see you again.'

He twitched in naked astonishment. 'You're not taking me home? Or phoning somebody?'

'No. Why should I?'

'Well, people usually do. Like I'm a lost child or something.'

'Do you think you're a lost child? Did you walk here from Blockley? Will people be looking for you?'

'No. I mean, yes.' He shook his head. 'Too many questions. I did walk here, because I'm clever with maps.' He waved a folded copy of the large-scale Ordnance Survey for the area. 'And I did tell Philip where I was going. He's my house-father. That's what I call them. My house-father and mother. He said it was no problem because of the tracker. I felt very sad about Juliet, and wanted to think about her.'

'Who told you this is where she was killed?'

'It was on the news,' he said, frowning as if suspecting a hidden intent behind the question. 'Philip said I should be careful not to annoy anybody, and if there were police people about, then to do anything they told me. But there's only you.'

'That's right.'

'Is Juliet going to be buried here?' He looked critically at the row of graves.

'I don't expect so. But she might. Her mother hasn't decided yet. Although . . .' she remembered that Rosa and Juliet had belonged to a small church in their home village. 'I think it'll be closer to where they live. Lived.'

'In Laverton, yes,' he said, starting to unfold the map to find the village. 'I know where it is. I've been there.'

'Yes. Okay. Sorry, Adam, but I really have to go

now. You've got a phone, have you? To call Philip if you need him?'

He rolled his eyes. 'Broken,' he smiled. 'But I've got this.' He proffered a wrist, banded by an unfamiliar device. 'It's a tracker. Philip says everyone's going to have one soon. And dogs as well. Nobody will ever be lost again.'

Thea shuddered. 'What a ghastly idea.'

'No, no. It's *good*.' He leant down to give her his earnest assurances. 'It's really good.'

'If you say so,' she said, backing away from his large face. 'Well, stay as long as you want to. I'm pleased to have met you.' She considered holding out a hand for him to shake, but thought better of it. His grip might break a few metacarpals.

'Bye, then,' he said flatly.

Walking back with Hepzie, Thea reflected that there was at least a chance that she had just been speaking with Juliet's killer. Strong, big, unpredictable – the man might well have lashed out blindly and broken her neck. But she had seen *The Green Mile* and absorbed its message. Big silent men on the edge of society were as likely to be gentle giants, caring and protective, as they were to be casual killers. The story of the dog Gelert reinforced the message – as did *Frankenstein*, come to that. On the other hand, Adam Rogers had to be on the list of suspects, especially if he really had been Juliet's boyfriend. Volatile emotions, frustrations, misunderstandings were all entirely possible, and all of them recognised triggers for violence. And stories with messages very often bore little resemblance to the real world.

She ran through events of the past twenty-four hours or so. It was only a day since Anthony Spiller had found Juliet's body. The police must have worked fast to acquire every clue and angle already, and then clear away from the scene. Perhaps this had something to do with Gladwin's affection for Thea – trying to cause as little disruption to the burial business as possible. The idea was uncomfortable. Special treatment was close to the sort of corruption that Thea associated with Freemasonry and small-town politics. Drew had glimpsed some of it when working for a mainstream undertaker. It was, he had concluded, part of human nature – which did nothing to make it more acceptable.

The joint of pork was calling her. It needed two hours of cooking, at least, besides all the vegetables to prepare, table to lay, floor to sweep. Domestic stuff that she agreed was essential to the survival of the family, but which she still resented. Her own mother had often complained at the way social gatherings seemed to require a handsome meal at their core before they could properly function. 'Why is it that people only seem to communicate properly when sitting around a table with food in front of them?' she would say. Nobody ever offered a credible answer.

But it was still not quite eleven o'clock, which left her ample time. Her thoughts went back to the murder, with the central question nagging insistently at her: was it in any way connected to Drew and his burials? The location of Juliet's murder seemed to suggest so. There was a thread somewhere, linking the dead woman with one of the funerals, and therefore to her killer. The logic insisted that he or she – but surely *he* – was also known to Drew. A mourner, in fact. Rosa's theory about badger culling was appealing, but there was no shred of evidence to support it, as far as Thea knew. The additional fact that one of these very mourners had found the body made the link feel stronger. Had Anthony Spiller performed a classic double bluff, by being both the murderer and the discoverer? It wouldn't be the first time, if so. Did Gladwin think the same thing? How closely had Spiller been questioned? Frustration at not knowing the answers to such questions filled Thea's chest. She *needed* to know. It was visceral, this curiosity that always arose when she found herself close to a murder. She could not avoid or subdue it, however much Drew might want her to.

Neither could she avoid or subdue the ever-present image of Clovis Biddulph. His handsome face hovered inescapably behind every thought, superimposed on other faces that were there in the flesh. Embarrassment at this irrational reaction was every bit as strong as the other emotions going through her. What if *he* was the murderer? It was perfectly possible, even rather likely, although she could imagine no conceivable reason why he might be. He was just too good to be true. Strong-looking, intense, angry, and infinitely charismatic. He was a sort of Rasputin, she thought fancifully. Everything larger than life and imbued with a rare force. Probably, every woman he looked at melted shamefully, just as Thea had done.

She should tell Drew about it. If their relationship was as solid as she believed it to be, it could easily withstand a flurry of hormonal nonsense. But she could hear all her female friends and relations screaming *NO-O-O* at her. No marriage was as strong as that. It would undermine Drew's trust in her. It would taint her in his eyes. It would, at best, wound and worry him. Far better to remain silent and let the whole thing fade away, with Clovis never seen again.

She might, though, one day confess to another woman. Her sister Jocelyn, perhaps. Or even Gladwin. But probably *not* Gladwin. Certainly not if the awful thought that Clovis might be a killer turned into reality. She very strongly did not want that to happen.

She and Hepzie got back to the house without further incident. The Snowshill place would still not be admitting visitors even after all this time, but Drew and the others would have at least got into the garden, which was probably pretty enough to divert them for a while. The morning was yet young, and now she was in the kitchen, she found that her tasks were much less onerous than her mutinous thoughts had suggested. The hardest part was peeling a small mountain of potatoes and tracking down a roasting pan big enough to take them as well as the meat. She couldn't remember when she had last cooked for so many people. Christmas had never brought more than Jessica to her table – and more often, the Osbornes had joined another family for the large celebratory meal.

It was peaceful all alone in the house. The process of potato peeling was actually mildly soothing. There were broccoli, carrots and frozen peas to go with the meat. 'And apple sauce,' she muttered. Did they have any apple sauce, or apples with which to make it? By some miracle, there were two nice Bramleys in the wooden bowl she used for fruit. Drew must have got them at some point, bless his heart. And he'd never even said anything.

The phone and doorbell both remained silent, which felt rather like another miracle. By half past eleven, she had let all thoughts of Juliet Wilson's death slide into the back of her mind, to be replaced by more personal issues to do with the Peaceful Repose burial ground in Somerset. Given her natural inclination to assume that nothing truly terrible would happen, she focused on listing the various outcomes that might lead to wholesale happiness and well-being. The list was short. It basically boiled down to selling the whole North Staverton property, and enjoying an improved lifestyle in the Cotswolds as a result. In fact, the more closely she examined the situation, the more foolish it appeared for them to have retained ownership of the Somerset house in the first place. Maggs had been using the cool room and office in her operation of the business, but there had been no prospect of capitalising on the main house while it was an integral part of an undertaker's work. Who would want to be tenants under such circumstances? In retrospect, it seemed careless of Drew to allow such an entanglement between house and grounds, once he and his children had moved out. Thea had asked why Maggs and Den hadn't moved in, saving themselves time and money, only to receive the vague reply that they were too fond of their own little cottage, and Den was resistant to living so close to a field full of graves. 'I don't think it's actually that,' Drew had confided to Thea. 'It's more a case of not wanting to be any more committed to Peaceful Repose than they are already.' That assessment now seemed very persuasive in the light of Friday's announcement.

It would all work out happily, Thea assured herself now. The Broad Campden business would expand, with funds for better publicity and alterations to the access and parking arrangements. Without the ongoing responsibilities in Somerset, Drew could give all his attention to the Cotswolds. The more she thought about it, the more appealing it all seemed. She became impatient for Drew and Maggs to come back, so she could tell them that everything would be fine. They would put all matters regarding property on a more professional footing, too. Drew had been slack about maximising his assets and claiming refunds and rebates that he was almost certainly owed. He could give Andrew more secure employment, as well.

Feeling quite ridiculously optimistic, she went out into the garden to find a selection of flowers for a centrepiece. She gathered big white daisies, several sprays of greenery and an early pink rose, just on the brink of opening. It made a handsome display, when plonked into a big blue jug she'd bought fifteen years ago at a car boot sale.

Twelve o'clock saw almost all the work done. And still the others would only just be getting into the main attraction at Snowshill. Never having been inside the place herself, she had little idea of how long it would take to admire the whole collection. She knew she could trust Drew to get them all back by two, but she had a suspicion it would be sooner than that. The pork was making appetising smells and might well be ready early. Whatever happened, she had half an hour at her disposal, and she opted to use it selfishly, sitting in warm sunshine outside with a book.

But the gods had other ideas. Within three minutes of arranging herself comfortably on their only usable garden lounger, the doorbell rang, the dog barked, and a cloud drifted across the sun. Gritting her teeth, Thea got up again and tried to guess who the intruder might be. It was a long list of possibilities, including some wholly unknown newcomer wanting to arrange a funeral. That was the least likely by a long way, but still entirely feasible. Sudden death could make people forget all about protocols involving Sunday lunch, or advance phone calls.

The person on the doorstep had been somewhere on Thea's list, but she was still surprised.

'I am *so* sorry,' whined Lawrence Biddulph. 'But I really do have to speak to someone.'

Chapter Fourteen

Thea managed to be briskly polite, but far from friendly. She had no wish to listen to a spate of self-pity, and she had forgotten the exact details of the Biddulph family complications. There were things she was not supposed to say, she knew that much. 'Is it about the funeral?' she asked.

'Well, not really. My wife insists there's nothing to worry about, and my mother is behaving oddly because of the grief and so forth. Are you going to let me in?'

She did not answer directly, and made no move to invite him into the house. 'Drew isn't here. I can phone him if it's important, but it might be better if you just leave him a note, if there's anything he needs to know. It's Sunday lunchtime, you see,' she finished. 'So it's not entirely convenient.'

His face sagged, making it even longer than it had been before. He really was a very unprepossessing character. 'I see,' he mumbled. 'I should have known. It's nothing much, to be honest. Just a worry that things might go badly on Tuesday. My mother keeps saying it will all be fine.'

'Why wouldn't it be? My husband is very professional, you know.'

'I'm sure he is. And I don't have any real idea of what might happen. But people are being so *funny*. Peculiar. Evasive.' His eyes seemed to slide closer together, making him look sly and secretive. Thea assumed he was acting out the way he felt others were behaving. She had remembered that people really were withholding information from him, until after the funeral. They were treating this grown man as a child, and she thought she could understand their reasons. Or – not so much *their* as *her*. His mother was the only one who possessed all the facts in the family story, and she was the one trying to keep him in the dark for another few days.

'Just hang on until the burial's all done,' she advised. 'Things will calm down, then, and you'll have more time to talk it all through.'

Again he squinted at her. 'What things? You sound as if you know something, as well.'

She gave a minimal shrug. 'There's always loads of stuff – money, property, disposing of your father's things. Endless decisions to make. Thanking people for their cards . . .' She began to flounder. 'Look, I'm sorry I can't ask you in and have a proper talk. But

I'm in the middle of preparing a meal for seven people. It'll be ruined if I don't get back to it. You can phone Drew this afternoon, if you like. He'll be free from about three o'clock.'

'Oh.' The word erupted as frustration and impatience. 'I can't get any sense out of *anybody*.'

She waited in vain for an apology for disturbing her. Instead, he turned away, and began walking back along the lane. Where had he left his car, she wondered, as she nearly always did. Patterns were emerging, where people's good sense could be assessed purely on the basis of where they parked. Some defiantly squeezed their vehicles onto the side of the lane, crushing plants and impeding the movement of neighbours. These irritated even Drew, causing, as they did, bad feeling in the lane. 'We must get permission to put a sign up by the church, telling people they have to park there,' he said, repeatedly.

The lack of proper parking was a mark against the business, they both understood. In heavy rain, it was embarrassing to require people to walk a hundred yards or more down to the house. When Greta Simmonds had left her property to Drew, on condition he open a natural burial ground close by, she clearly had not thought through prosaic issues such as where people might leave their cars.

Lawrence Biddulph stomped out of sight like a mutinous four-year-old. *Funny*, thought Thea, *the way some people just never grow up*. You could still see their toddler-selves in their body language and sense of entitlement. To her jaded, middle-aged eye, there seemed to be increasing numbers of them.

She was forced to abandon her moments in the sun. The meat needed basting, the potatoes should get roasting, and she still hadn't made the fruit salad. The wine glasses could do with a wash, as well. They definitely weren't sparkling as they ought to.

Now she had another male face to join the procession through her imagination. Clovis remained dominant, but now his half-brother sidled up to him, the contrast in their features almost ludicrous. Plus Adam Rogers, Anthony Spiller and another shadowy Biddulph brother, whose name she'd forgotten. He was in a wheelchair – that was all she could recall. It was tempting to suspect that one of them was at least involved in the killing of Juliet Wilson – but nothing stronger could be said, given a complete absence of motive. Juliet's life had been full of projects and notions when Thea had first met her in Stanton. She roamed the countryside and made friends – and perhaps enemies. She walked uninvited into people's houses, and rebelled against her mother's efforts to contain her. But it sounded as if much of that had changed with the move to Blockley. She had a job, a boyfriend, and people similar to herself to share a home with. All that was new since the Stanton days.

But still, she had wandered off, and stayed undiscovered for three days or more. And still, nobody seemed to have any clear idea as to where she had been, or why. Even Rosa, with her badger-culling theories, had no actual evidence.

'Poor Juliet,' she sighed, yet again. 'What a dreadful thing.' She cut up fruit and made apple sauce, with her thoughts turning darker by the minute.

The others got back at one-forty, happy and hungry. The outing had gone even better than hoped, with Stephanie the most inspired by the weird things she had seen. 'The house was absolutely *full*,' she marvelled. 'Things hanging from the ceiling, and on hundreds of shelves, and squashed into corners. It's *fantastic*.'

'It certainly is unusual,' confirmed Den. 'I'm glad to have seen it.'

'We were first in the queue,' Timmy boasted. 'And we talked to lots of people.'

'That's good,' said Thea. 'Now, everybody go and wash hands or whatever, and be back here in five minutes. The meat's waiting for you.'

They obeyed with alacrity, and from then on, seven people enjoyed a classic Sunday roast, with only minor glitches. The gravy was too thin and the apple sauce tasted burnt. The fruit salad needed cream or something, which Thea was unable to provide. Meredith extruded most of the meat, after valiantly chewing it for a long time. Everybody laughed.

Once it was all finished, and the men were washing up, Maggs and the children went out into the garden for half an hour, before the Coopers had to depart. Thea followed them. It seemed to her that there was still a lot to resolve.

'I've been thinking,' she began. 'And it seems to me it wouldn't be such a disaster if we sold the North Staverton house, as well as the business – ideally all as a package. You'd be free of it, and we'd have a nice injection of cash.'

'That's what I said to Drew.' Maggs met Thea's eyes with an open, frank expression. 'But I don't think he likes the idea.'

'It would be a wrench for him, I know. But he must know he can't ever go back. I'm starting to think you've done us a favour. We needed a kick in the pants to make us realise we've been prevaricating.'

'He was so happy there, when I first knew him.' Maggs spoke in a low voice, not wanting Drew's children to hear her. 'So much has changed since then.'

'Yes,' said Thea.

'But it won't be easy.' Maggs seemed keen to emphasise the point. 'He hasn't any friends here, and it's not exactly his sort of place. In Somerset, people are much more on his wavelength. They don't care about the ethics of the business here, do they?'

'Some do.' Thea felt defensive. 'They're not all rich City traders using the Cotswolds as a playground, you know.'

'But there are enough of that type to create an atmosphere. It's lucky he's so easy-going. People like him, which is good. I'm not saying it's doomed to failure, but it looks fragile to me.'

'It's not. We've been here nearly a year now, and everything's gone pretty much as we hoped. The worst part is this house. It's completely wrong for the business. But we're working it out, and nobody's complained. They're all remarkably patient, in fact.' She shook her head. 'I don't understand your point. You've given us almost no choice but to stay here and concentrate on building it up as our sole source of income. Why are you trying to undermine it?'

'I'm not. I'm just having trouble letting go, I guess. It's as hard for me as it is for Drew. You don't really get it – how much we've come through together. Ten years, nearly. That Greta woman has a lot to answer for, leaving him this place.'

'I think that every day,' Thea agreed. 'But I must say I'm glad it was her and not me that's to blame. And without her, I never would have met him. She meant well.'

'Yeah. But she changed the course of history, just by dying when she did. I can't pretend to be glad about that.'

'Oh, Maggs.' Thea reached out a hand, and laid it on Maggs's bare forearm. 'It hasn't run smoothly, has it? And quite a bit of that really is my fault. We abandoned you, in reality. And you've done fantastically well, all on your own. It just came as such a shock to think of you giving it all up.'

'I know. I feel as if I've done something violent and scary. But exciting as well. We're lucky to have some options. We're in the perfect place for that, at least. It might not last – thousands of new houses are being built not far away, for one thing. It's going to be like Shaftesbury in Dorset. A very nice little town, wrecked by ghastly soulless new houses popping up on every field. That feels like a threat. Den's settled at the airport, and the money's reasonably good. My dad's got an annuity thing that's going to be better than he thought. He's promised to give me an allowance that would let me stay at home with another baby.'

'Wow! You never said anything about that.'

'It's a bit embarrassing, I suppose. Makes me feel like a dependent child. But my folks are very special people, and they're so thrilled to have grandchildren, they'll do anything to help.'

'You *are* lucky,' Thea agreed. 'I hope it works out for you.' Maggs had been adopted as a young baby by a Plymouth couple already over forty. They had made an excellent job of raising their dark-skinned daughter, and when Meredith was born, they uprooted themselves and moved to a nearby town in Somerset.

'And you,' said Maggs. 'It feels like a crisis now, but you've got the summer ahead and, as far as I can see, life isn't so very different for you than it was before.'

Thea bristled at that. What about all that shopping and cooking and listening to endless anecdotes about school, and having to be polite and forbearing with funeral people, and trying to get a footing in Broad Campden as permanent residents? 'As far as I can see, the only thing that's the same is Hepzie,' she said stiffly.

'What about all these murders, and that detective woman, and knowing your way around about fifty small villages? You're still in the middle of all the big events, being used as a sort of local spy or police informer. I mean – there you were, doing just that, when we arrived on Friday. Nothing had changed. Drew thinks the same,' she finished with a flash of triumph.

'He doesn't like it,' Thea acknowledged. 'But Den understands. He says I should try and get onto the payroll. With the police. As some sort of consultant. I *am* useful, if I say so myself.'

'I'm sure you are. So who killed this poor Juliet person, then?'

'I honestly have no idea. I still don't know exactly how it was done – whether it had to be someone very strong, or if anybody could have done it. It feels as if it must have been a man, but that's probably a dangerous assumption. The thing is, so many people knew her. Not that it was necessarily somebody she knew, of course. If she walked into some criminal goings-on, she might have been killed to keep her quiet. And then . . .'

'Stop!' Maggs ordered her. 'I don't want to hear all that. But I can see how involved you are. I bet it's all you've been thinking about since yesterday morning. I bet you're itching to go out there and ask all sorts of questions.' Maggs narrowed her eyes. 'What did you do this morning when we were out? You never said.'

'I went for a walk down to the burial field.'

'Aha! The scene of the crime, near enough. And did you talk to anybody?'

'Okay. Point taken,' said Thea, dodging that particular question. 'Now it must be time for you to start loading up the car.'

Stephanie and Timmy had taken Meredith to a corner of the small garden, and the three were sitting solemnly on the grass, searching for daisies. Stephanie had created a starry tiara, which she placed on the toddler's head. Meredith reached up and pulled at it, but Timmy restrained her. 'Oh Lord,' groaned Maggs. 'They've made her into a princess. After all I said, from the moment she was born – *no pink and no princesses*. And now look.'

Thea just laughed. A minute later they were all back in the house, Den carrying armfuls of baby equipment out to the car.

Thea was distracted by Maggs's accusations, which she had not been able to deny. It had not quite felt like a reproach, but she wondered whether Maggs believed that Drew was suffering in some way, as a result of his new wife's tendencies. Did Drew himself believe that?

She had said nothing about Adam Rogers or Lawrence Biddulph over lunch, and was unsure about telling Drew, even when the visitors had gone. He had enough to contend with, processing Maggs's announcement, and coming to the inevitable conclusion that Thea and Maggs had already reached. And Thea herself had some thinking to do, also thanks to their visitors. Maggs had put into stark words the essential facts as to where Thea's priorities lay. The truth could not be denied – she was at her happiest when helping Gladwin in a murder investigation. She understood that she had frequently acted as a link in a tenuous chain between the individuals centred on the crime and the forces of the law intent on unearthing the facts. Often it happened by accident, or coincidence, but it happened all the same. Everything Maggs had said was right – it was in Thea Slocombe's nature to be nosy, intrusive and sometimes outrageous. She said things you were not supposed to say, and thereby provoked a cascade of events that quite often helped the police identify their killer.

Drew had known this from the first. He had witnessed it at close quarters, when he himself was the object of police attention. But he had not willingly shared in it on subsequent occasions. Even when he was at Thea's side during the discovery of a victim, he had kept a large part of himself separate. Now he had his children here under the same roof, in the same part of the country, with no prospect of escape back to Somerset, even if only for a weekend. Because he was going to have to sell Peaceful Repose. And that might wreak some unwelcome changes.

Chapter Fifteen

The house seemed quiet and empty without the Coopers. 'Meredith is so *sweet*,' sighed Stephanie, more than once.

'I think Den's great,' enthused Timmy.

'They're good friends,' Drew agreed. 'Our best friends.'

Our only friends, thought Thea glumly. And that was likely to change, with the distance separating them, and Maggs's abandonment of the funeral business. 'We ought to make more effort to find friends here,' she said.

'That's right,' said Drew, far too heartily. 'Now, have you two got any homework that hasn't been done yet?'

He spent the next hour going through reading books; listening to Stephanie explain the latest system for dividing one large figure by another large figure; and congratulating Timmy on his amazing ability to list all the kings and queens of England, like any Victorian schoolboy. 'Where did you learn that?' Drew asked.

'*Horrible Histories*,' was the unexpected reply. 'They made a song of it, ages ago. Everybody knows it.'

'I'm impressed,' said Drew. 'The telly still has something to offer, then. Do you want to watch something now for a bit?'

They shrugged compliantly, so he left them to it, and joined Thea in the kitchen, where she was vaguely trying to restore some order.

'Hello,' she said, without really looking at him. 'All quiet in there?'

'Homework accomplished, and television on. Nobody's going to want much supper after that magnificent lunch.'

'Especially as it was so much later than usual.' She did look at him then, and was startled at the weariness on his face. 'Gosh, Drew! You look exhausted. I suppose it has been quite a long day.' She herself felt oddly fired up and energetic, restlessly wishing she could get out of the house for a while. It was still broad daylight, not much past five and pleasantly warm. 'Do you think we could go for a quick stroll down to the field with the dog, and leave the kids for ten minutes?'

'And risk having them taken into care?' He grinned to indicate a lack of seriousness. 'Why not?'

'We'd still have Hepzie. And we could probably visit them at weekends.'

'Come on, then. I'll go and tell them.'

'Great.' She heard him saying, with deliberate carelessness, 'Thea and I are popping out for a few minutes. Don't burn the house down, okay?' He came back to Thea. 'I'm not sure they even heard me. Timmy looks half-asleep.'

They turned right at the gate and were soon in the field at the end of the lane, where she had walked with Den the day before. 'Are you okay?' she asked. 'You've had a lot to deal with since Friday.'

'I don't know. I feel numb. And a bit scared. It's as if I accidentally climbed onto a rollercoaster that's much too adult for me, and now I can only cling on to the sides and hope for the best. I don't feel very grown-up, that's the trouble.' He gave her a shy little smile. 'I've always thought Maggs was infinitely more mature than me.'

'You're wrong. You're *completely* mature. Look how you deal with people so calmly and capably. If anybody's immature, it's me.'

'Oh, well, it's not a competition.' He sighed.

'There you are!' she said. 'That's a very grown-up thing to say.'

He was silent, as they walked to the corner and turned back. They could see part of the house from where they were. 'No sign of any smoke,' she reported.

'What?'

'The kids. They haven't set the house on fire yet.'

'Oh. Listen, Thea—' he burst out. 'We're going

to have to get serious, you know. This business with Maggs isn't going to go away. We've got to make some real decisions.'

'I know we have. But it doesn't have to be instant. And it might not be as hard as you think.' She bit back the blithe announcement as to the obvious solution that was on her tongue. She understood that it had to come from Drew himself, that he was the one it most affected. 'You haven't had time to think about it properly. But the fact is, we're here now, and it's going well enough, and everything's settled. You like it here, don't you?'

He stopped walking and turned to face her. 'Not as much as you do,' he said in a low voice. 'You *like* being on the rollercoaster. For me, it's mostly just scary.'

'Oh, *Drew*,' she said. Fear rose from the pit of her stomach to her throat. Fear that she had got everything wrong, that the future was dark and difficult, that nobody liked her and nothing at all was settled. 'Don't say that,' she pleaded. 'You didn't feel like this before Friday, did you? Not until Maggs threw a bomb at you. You're just shocked, that's all.'

'I don't know.' He sighed again. 'And it doesn't much matter, does it? I can't go back to before Friday, now everything's changed. I can't just sit back and let events take their course. I have to *decide* things. And that's what scares me.'

'And now you've got me scared as well.' She couldn't hide the hint of reproach. Somewhere she felt he was deliberately spoiling things, less than a year after they'd thought they'd got everything organised for the best.

'Sorry.' He took her hand. 'We'll be all right, though. Just so long as we can talk to each other properly, and say what we're really feeling and thinking. We're a team, my love, whatever happens.'

Guiltily, she remembered Clovis Biddulph and her wanton reaction to him. Would she ever succeed in telling Drew about that? And would it even be a good idea? 'That's right,' she agreed, with all the emphasis she could muster. 'You and me against the world. It's all going to turn out fine.'

They smiled into each other's eyes, and remembered the heady days of a year ago.

Two hours later, after a minimal evening meal, Thea supervised bath time and all the Sunday evening preparations for a new school week. She read stories and gave fond goodnight kisses, leaving Drew with a rare bottle of beer downstairs. When she joined him on the sofa, it was with flutters of anxiety still in her midriff.

'We ought to be thankful, you know,' she began. 'I met a man this morning who has far more reason to be gloomy than we have.'

He looked up, his head appearing almost too heavy for his neck. Every movement seemed imbued with effort. 'Did you?'

'His name is Adam Rogers, and he was Juliet

Wilson's boyfriend. Or so he said. I don't know how serious it was. He's obviously got some of the same learning difficulties as she had. He's big and soft.'

'And sad, presumably.'

'Sort of. I imagine it hadn't really hit him yet. He was in the burial field.'

Drew stiffened. 'What?'

'He'd gone to see the place where she died. He's got a kind of electronic tag so his house parents can keep track of him. He seemed to like it.' Her eyes grew wide. 'Isn't that awful!'

'I don't know. Is it?'

'It's demeaning. Treating him like a dog.'

'It sounds to me as if it gives him more freedom than he might have otherwise. Gives him an alibi as well,' he added casually. 'They'd know if he was the murderer, wouldn't they?'

She stared at him. 'That never even crossed my mind. At least—'

'I expect it did. You think more about Gladwin and her murders than anything else, after all.'

The fact that there was no hint of accusation in his tone made it all the harder to hear. 'I do not,' she protested. 'What a thing to say!'

'I don't mean *all* the time. But when there's been a death, and you get involved, it consumes your interest until it's resolved. That's how you've been since I met you. I'm not complaining. I'm glad you've got something to occupy you.'

'Den's been talking to you,' she realised. 'What did he say?'

'Nothing much. Just that you seemed to have a knack for detective work, and there was probably a place for you with the police, if they could get around all the bureaucracy. Which they probably can't, of course.'

'That's not new. We've talked about that already.' She had a sense of impending reproach, despite his claim to be pleased. 'I know you'd rather I was doing more with the funerals. I've let you down. I should probably try again, but I don't think I'll ever get it right.'

'You've done those visits to the hospice. That went well.'

'Mm. I don't mind when it's an old person who accepts that they're dying. I *like* them. It's the younger ones where I can't seem to strike the right note.'

'I'm not complaining,' he said again, more firmly. 'Stop rubbishing yourself. You're nowhere near as cold and callous as you seem to think. I *married* you, didn't I?' he ended impatiently. 'I still can't believe my luck. But let's not start analysing all that.'

'I wasn't going to,' she interrupted. 'You started it, anyway.' She gave him a playful smack, deliberately acting like a child.

'I didn't mean to. Have you said anything to Gladwin about this Rogers person?' He took a deep breath and sat up straighter. Thea had the impression that he was making a big effort to steer them into safer waters, entirely for her sake. She could not shake off the feeling that she had been letting him down for at least the past few days, if not for much longer.

'Not yet. I expect she knows all about him, anyway. And Rosa must have given her blessing, I suppose. I don't know what the rules are, if any. Would they ever have let Juliet get married, I wonder?'

'They'd have to, I think. If she was able to handle a job, she must have had quite a lot of autonomy. Did the boyfriend say anything about that?'

Thea shook her head. 'I don't really think he was a boyfriend in any serious sense of the word. It was probably just a sort of game between them.'

Drew frowned. 'Tricky business. What if he really did think he could marry her, and lashed out when she told him otherwise?'

'He didn't,' said Thea with conviction. 'Besides – what about the tracking thingy, giving him an alibi?'

'Ah yes.'

'And while we're at it, I forgot to mention that Lawrence Biddulph turned up this morning as well. He's got wind of something murky in the family broom cupboard and wanted me to enlighten him. I didn't even let him in, because I was cooking. He was quite annoying, actually. And I dare say he thought the same about me. He might complain.'

Drew passed a melodramatic hand across his brow. 'I don't want to know. The Biddulphs can all wait until Tuesday. They're not paying me enough to worry about them at a weekend.'

'That's the spirit,' she applauded.

They went quiet, Thea suspecting that Drew had been humouring her by engaging in talk about the murder case. She was grateful, as well as sorry that his interest was so shallow. After all, wasn't that normal for married couples – for each to devote attention to topics they had little real time for? It was part of the give and take of couplehood.

He was evidently reading her mind. 'I really am involved, you know,' he said. 'They found Juliet right next to my land. The graves are sure to be part of Gladwin's investigation. One of my people found the body.'

'And you might have been the last person to see her alive,' said Thea, without compunction. 'Don't forget that. You're more involved than me, when it comes down to it.'

'No need to remind me. It's not the first time, is it? Not by a long way. I'm surprised Maggs didn't say anything about the body we found in Peaceful Repose, before we were even open.'

'That's a long time ago now. She's probably forgotten.'

'And then again here. Right at the start, a bloke got killed just after Greta's burial.'

'And they thought you might have done it,' she finished for him. 'The first time I laid eyes on you, you were a murder suspect. Fate had designs on us from that moment on.'

'But I still don't find it exciting, or challenging, or something I want to get into. Which is where we're different, you and I.'

'And where we were half an hour ago,' she said. 'We've gone round in a big circle.'

He pulled her to him. 'That's okay. I like going round in circles with you, Mrs Slocombe. There's nothing else I'd rather be doing.'

She leant her head on his shoulder. 'Thank goodness for that,' she said, doing her utmost to believe him, and let it go at that. She managed it for two cosy minutes, before the mood cracked. 'Gladwin's sure to phone or visit tomorrow,' she murmured. 'I can tell her about Adam Rogers then.'

Drew simply made a whistling sound between his teeth.

Chapter Sixteen

Monday dawned early, with birdsong and a ringing telephone. Drew answered it sleepily, walking around the bedroom as he listened to what was clearly a long story, finding socks and a clean shirt. Then he became more focused, rummaging for a pad and pen that normally sat on his bedside table. Night-time calls were rare – certainly far rarer than for a mainstream undertaker, but they did happen. Nursing homes in particular favoured them, hoping for removal of their dead resident before the others woke up. Drew was still trying to educate some of them into accepting that he and Andrew did not remove bodies outside normal working hours.

But this was not a nursing home. Thea uncovered his notepad for him and handed him a pen. Then she watched as he wrote down a few words comprising a name and a phone number. 'Yes, that's right,' he said. 'Tell the hospital it's me doing the funeral, and come over to arrange the details as soon as you like . . . The end of the week would be perfectly feasible, yes . . . Thank you very much . . . Yes, please. There's only me, you see. We need to find a time when I'm not doing a burial. This afternoon or tomorrow after about two o'clock would be ideal . . . That's right. Thank you.'

'Anybody we know?' asked Thea, trying to read the name on the pad.

'Not the deceased, no. But that was Bernard Shipley, would you believe? His sister died and he wants one of our graves for her. Isn't that amazing?'

Bernard Shipley lived across the lane, and had become almost friendly towards them a few months earlier. The sister, however, was completely unknown to the Slocombes. 'How funny. And what a time to phone! Has the sister got a husband or anything?'

'Husband. Daughter. Another brother. She's in the John Radcliffe. She had an aortic aneurism a week ago, and they thought they'd saved her, but she'd lost too much blood. No need for a post-mortem, apparently. The daughter's got a long trip to Australia all booked for Saturday, and they couldn't find anybody to do the funeral this week.'

'Except you.'

'Except me. Bernard's been up most of the night trying to persuade the husband. He wanted a cremation, and there's a wait of nearly three weeks.'

'Scandalous.'

'Indeed.'

'Well, that's a good start to the week, isn't it?' she said cheerfully. 'That's three funerals booked.'

'Mm,' said Drew. 'Busy, busy. Miss Cotton needs to come back tomorrow at the latest. She's midday Thursday.' He was speaking mainly to himself, using undertaker's shorthand as he mentally reviewed his schedule for the week. Thea had just about learnt what it all meant.

'Which gives you Wednesday to recover from the Biddulphs. I expect you'll need it.'

'Don't.' He shuddered. 'It's just the sort of funeral I can do without. Family complications, ancient feuds, secrets and lies. It only needs another forgotten son to materialise, and we'll have civil war.'

'There sort of *is* another forgotten son,' said Thea slowly. 'Clovis has a brother, remember. The one in the wheelchair who had the accident. His name's Luc, I remember now – probably spelt the French way, given the granny's influence.'

Drew groaned. 'He'll get bounced around dreadfully between the car and the grave. We had such beautiful paths in North Staverton. Maggs made them. It's just bumpy grass here.'

'Andrew can make paths, if you ask him. He should have done that months ago.'

'We did mow it. It's fine for normal walking. But there's been a mole since then . . .' He sighed. 'Always something to worry about.'

There was no time for further chat. The school bus wouldn't wait; the dog needed to go out; the kitchen still wasn't very tidy. For the thousandth time, Thea asked herself how they could possibly cope if she had a proper job. People did, of course, and compared to most, the Slocombes were criminally idle. Drew routinely had a few hours each day where nothing had to be done. Thea fitted in a lot of reading, walking, gardening and other pursuits generally associated with elderly retired people. But there were plenty of busy times as well – and Monday morning topped the list.

It was all accomplished by half past eight, and Thea found herself with a mug of coffee, waiting for Drew to go into his office and leave her to her thoughts. She had no more to say to him for the time being. Instead, she wanted to think about Gladwin, Juliet and Clovis Biddulph, although not necessarily in that order. Where Clovis was concerned, she fully intended to give herself a very stern talking to, in light of the heart-to-heart she had enjoyed the previous day with Drew. She was married, and that demanded an exclusive devotion to her husband. To jeopardise their future together in any way at all would be extreme folly.

At least, she mentally amended, in any way that lay within her own control. She could not change her basic nature. She could not quell her inclination to get involved in murder investigations. And, if she had understood him correctly, Drew was never going to ask her to.

So where was Gladwin? How had they left it after the previous day's rushed visit? How was the investigation proceeding? Despite an assumption that she was useful to the police, she had to concede that she was far from the centre of whatever was going on. She did not even know exactly how Juliet had been killed. She knew almost no details of the woman's daily life, apart from a self-styled boyfriend and a devastated mother. If she simply let it go, would Gladwin leave her alone, excluding her completely? She had witnessed nothing, after all. Drew was closer to the action than she was – a realisation that she found irritating.

The doorbell came as a welcome interruption. Surely it was Gladwin, or one of her team, back in Broad Campden and wanting her input. She pulled open the door and started to treat the visitor to a wide smile, before observing that it was a woman who she realised was Linda Biddulph, after two or three seconds. Mother of Lawrence, stepmother of Clovis.

'Oh!' said Thea. The Biddulphs were not welcome. They were not on that day's agenda. They had nothing to do with anything and she didn't want to talk to any of them. 'You'll want Drew. Come in and I'll see if he's free.' She didn't know what Drew was doing, but she had heard him speaking on the phone. She reminded herself that it was perfectly normal for relatives to come and go in the days before a burial –

and sometimes they called in afterwards as well. 'Is it about tomorrow?' she added.

'Not exactly. Lawrence tells me he came here yesterday and you were very rude to him.' Her eyes were large, of a shade between brown and green. They fixed Thea with a very accusing gaze. 'Didn't I make it plain that he's not to be upset? That he's very vulnerable at the moment, and I'm doing my absolute best to protect him?'

'You did, yes. To Drew, anyway. He was out when Lawrence came here, and I was preparing a meal for seven people. It was Sunday morning. We saw him with his wife and daughter on Saturday as well. I'm sorry if I upset him. I didn't think I was being rude – but I honestly didn't have anything I could say to him. It's very inhibiting, you know, having to keep a secret from somebody like that. I hardly dared say anything at all.' She stepped back, inviting the woman into the house. 'Come and talk to Drew. He's the undertaker, not me.'

Mrs Biddulph was staring even more intently than before. 'Saturday? He was here on Saturday? What on earth for?'

Thea shook her head. 'I'm afraid I can't remember now. Just having a look at the field, I think. His wife seemed to want to show their little girl the place where your husband was to be buried. I expect Lawrence was a bit worried about the police being there, with the body and everything. We met them up by the church.

They'd been looking for us, but we were at the pub.'

'Police?' Linda blinked and frowned. 'What body?'

Thea was about to remark that surely Linda had seen it on the news, before remembering that a common part of grief following a death was a total lack of interest in the world outside. She found herself explaining patiently. 'It was found very early on Saturday. The police were here all day, looking for clues and all that. But they were doing their best not to interfere with the burial field. They kept right to the other end from the graves.'

'Who died? Some vagrant or something? And *where* was the body found?'

'On the edge of the woods, across another field, beyond ours. It wasn't a vagrant. Somebody we knew, in fact. And she was found by one of our mourners. Somebody who'd gone to sit by a grave. People do that a lot, you know.'

Linda Biddulph shook her head. 'This is dreadful. Poor Lawrence . . .' She paused, before saying, 'And Modestine was here as well, you say? What *on earth* were they thinking of? The child's far too young for this sort of thing.'

This woman had to be a control freak, Thea decided, despite having very scanty evidence. It felt as if nobody could make a move without her permission. So how had her precious son managed to marry and father a child, she wondered wickedly. The wife had seemed pretty assertive herself. Did the two women fight over the man? If so, the whole picture would start to resemble a cliché and become much less interesting.

The question addressed to her was not as rhetorical as she had first assumed. Linda Biddulph repeated it.

'Why did they come here without me on Saturday?'

'I told you. I think it was to show your granddaughter where her grandfather was to be buried. Rather sensible, in my opinion.'

'There's absolutely no question of the child being at the funeral,' asserted Linda. 'The idea's grotesque. She'll go to school as normal. And how did that woman die, anyway? What happened to her?'

'She was murdered,' said Thea recklessly. 'I don't know how exactly, but she was a very sweet and innocent person, and whoever did it has done a truly appalling thing, wrecking a lot of people's lives.' She spoke with force, letting her outrage spill out, regardless of how it might be perceived.

'And you know a good deal about murder, don't you,' muttered Linda.

Thea was distracted and failed to respond to this remark. She had noticed movement across the lane, behind the shrubs that grew around the house. It was Mr Shipley, whose sister had just died, doubtless coming to see Drew. She waited for him to emerge into full view, and then stepping around Linda Biddulph, she called to him, 'Are you coming here?'

He paused on the driveway, and then shook his head. His car was close by, which was unusual.

Normally he put it away in its garage after every trip. She couldn't see his face very clearly, but he looked bowed and slow. She could hardly yell, 'Sorry about your sister,' across the lane. It was bad enough that she'd called to him at all. Instead she just waved, and returned her attention to the woman. 'Busy morning,' she said. 'Sorry to keep you on the doorstep like this. You really ought to come in.'

'Seems it's a habit with you,' snapped Linda. 'Lawrence said you did the same to him.'

Thea silently counted to ten. 'I know – it's awful of me. People start talking and I just stand here letting them, instead of bringing them in. But you didn't seem to want to. And with Lawrence, I was just so *busy*.'

'Yes, you said. Cooking for seven people. Bully for you.' She cast a critical eye over Thea, and said, 'It strikes me you don't do a lot of that sort of thing. Cooking, housework, ironing. All that's a bit beneath you, isn't it?'

It was a direct attack, unprovoked and unfair. And it wasn't the first time. Looking at Linda, Thea understood that once again her reputation was well known. The house-sitter who repeatedly found herself at the heart of a murder. The newspapers loved her, and when she had married Drew and set up the alternative burial service, they had *really* loved her. Drew had borne it well, saying it was good for the business. His children had been less sure. It meant everyone at their new school was fully aware of what their father did for a living – and not everybody wanted to associate with the family of an undertaker.

'That's a beastly thing to say,' she defended. 'You don't know anything about my domestic life.' She swallowed back any further protests. The woman was a customer, after all. She was newly bereaved, so allowances had to be made. It felt as if everybody she met was newly bereaved, over the past few days – even Bernard Shipley. And she, Thea, was horribly prone to saying the wrong thing, treading on sensitivities and causing offence. 'But I admit I'm not terribly keen on housework,' she finished with a feeble smile.

'Right, then.' Linda seemed discomforted, perhaps regretting her outburst. 'I'd better go. I shouldn't have come. It was silly of me. I'm just so jittery about tomorrow, you see. And the next day, when I'm going to have to tell Lawrence the whole truth about his father. I can't leave it any longer. I have no idea how he'll react.' She fell silent, before looking up into the trees a short way down the lane. 'Listen to those birds,' she said. 'Aren't they wonderful?'

Thea thought at first she must have misheard, but decided it had to be real. 'Oh – yes. That's a blackbird. He's usually stopped by now. Then he starts again in the late afternoon. They're all over the place, and they answer each other across the woods and fields.'

'Lovely.'

Birdsong, it seemed, was getting to be something of a theme. There was the Spiller man and his deceased uncle, finding a body when he just wanted to hear the birds. Had Juliet been there for the same reason? The little patch of woods was home to collared doves, buzzards, and a whole range of tits and finches that chorused their daily greetings to the sun as it rose. Juliet had been a country girl, after all. And it was May – a time when people turned a little mad in their sudden awakening to the advent of summer and the existence of other species besides themselves.

'Yes. So . . . ?'

'Oh, I'm sorry. I don't need to talk to your husband. I know he'll do his best tomorrow. Whatever happens, he'll make sure it's properly dignified. The rest of it is my problem, not yours. I know that. But Lawrence doesn't understand. How could he? He's so – *fragile*. That wife of his is all wrong for him. Anybody can see that. She'll make everything so much worse. She's sure to try and turn him against me. It wouldn't be the first time, either. Well – I'm sorry. I'll go now. Perhaps I'll see you tomorrow.'

Do you want to? Thea felt moved to ask, but kept her mouth closed. Had she somehow earned Linda Biddulph's favour, after all? If so – how? She smiled and nodded and started to close the door. 'I hope it goes well,' she said vaguely, before leaving the woman to walk away.

'Who was at the door?' asked Drew, twenty minutes later, when he emerged from his office.

189

'Linda Biddulph.'

'What did she want? Why didn't she come in?' He looked alarmed and confused. 'What did you say to her?'

'Nothing much. She did most of the talking. Lawrence had complained to her about me not letting him in yesterday, and she came to remonstrate. But her heart wasn't in it, really. I think she's just killing time until tomorrow. She's going to tell him about his half-brothers on Wednesday. She must be terrified.'

'All that on the doorstep?'

'Well, yes. Where would I have taken her if she'd come in? Not the kitchen, surely. Or the sitting room. You were on the phone when I answered the door. And, actually, it was more me she wanted than you.'

'Well – thanks for fending her off, then. I'm sure you had better things to do.'

'Like waiting to see if Gladwin was going to call,' she nodded. 'And drinking too much coffee.'

'She didn't, I take it.'

'Not yet,' said Thea. 'They've probably got the killer already and she's forgotten to tell me. Why would she waste time doing that, anyway? I'm nothing to do with it, after all.'

'Yes you are. And so am I. We've established that. She'd make sure you knew if the investigation was over.'

'I suppose she would.' Thea thought about Rosa and Adam Rogers and poor Anthony Spiller who found the body. 'It's all such a mess,' she groaned. 'And I wasn't very nice to the Biddulph woman, because she was nothing to do with the main event. And that's bad, because funerals *are* the main event. I know that. Our livelihood depends on them.'

'Don't worry about it,' said Drew mildly. 'I find the Biddulphs pretty irritating myself, to be honest. I still can't understand how they've managed to keep Lawrence in the dark for all these years, anyway. Nor why they even wanted to. I was going through it all again just now, and I can't help thinking there's more to it. Some other reason than protecting his fragile ego, or whatever it was she said.'

'Well, maybe they thought he'd be crushed by low self-esteem if he met Clovis and had to match up to him. I mean – Clovis is everything Lawrence isn't. Handsome, good-natured, intelligent.'

Drew's eyebrows rose. 'Steady on! You sound as if you're getting a thing for him. Besides – how would Linda *know* he was like that? Has she even met him?'

'Good question.' Thea felt herself flush, and hoped he wouldn't notice. 'We have no idea, really, who knows who. Didn't somebody say that Clovis lives far enough away for them not to know each other at all?'

'I don't think we know where he lives,' said Drew. 'Linda has an idea it's Oxford way, but she's not sure.'

'Okay, but it's an unusual surname. There must have been a risk that Lawrence would find out the truth just by meeting somebody who knew them both and commented on the name.'

'I still don't get why it would *matter*?' said Drew again. 'Nobody can give a convincing explanation for it.'

'Money?' Thea suggested. 'Does Lawrence stand to inherit everything from his father, unless Clovis and the other one make a claim? Or could it be the other way around? Linda's more scared of *them* finding out that *Lawrence* exists?'

He shook his head. 'No, no. That can't be it. They've always known Stephen married again and had another son. The secret only works one way.'

'Of course it does. That was a daft idea. Well, it's not long now until it's all settled. Linda's scared about telling Lawrence, but it seems to me he's more than half-guessed it anyway. When he came yesterday, it felt as if he wanted me to confirm something he'd heard. It was really difficult to refuse to help him.' She pouted. 'If he wasn't such a whingeing idiot, I probably would have told him. But he's so childish and pathetic, I just lost patience with him.'

'Hmm,' was all Drew said.

'Oh, and I saw Mr Shipley just now, as well. He was going off somewhere. I assumed he was coming here to see you, but he wasn't.'

'It's not him making the arrangements, anyway. The sister's husband just phoned. He's coming on Wednesday. Funeral on Friday.'

'Cutting it fine,' Thea remarked.

'Not really. Andrew can dig the grave on Thursday,

and I can get the coffin put together then as well.' He'd talked her through the routine many times before, explaining that none of it took very long. The coffins mostly arrived as flat-packs, to be assembled like a very simple Ikea product. Only the more ornate or unusual ones were already put together before delivery. Drew had dropped just such a one on Hepzibah's leg, the previous Christmas, when unloading it from his van.

'Are you nervous about it?' she asked him. 'Seeing as how it's our neighbour's sister.'

'A bit. I certainly don't want to mess it up.'

Friday still seemed a long way off. Between now and then there was the hurdle of the Biddulph funeral, standing like a thorny hedge right in their faces. Nothing had really been resolved where that was concerned. Clovis could still cause trouble, and the discovery of a likely clash between Mrs Lawrence and her mother-in-law only heightened the tension.

'Well that won't happen,' she said with complete confidence.

Chapter Seventeen

It was just past eleven when Detective Superintendent Gladwin herself came to the door. Thea ran to greet her like a child. 'Hey!' she beamed. 'I didn't think I'd be seeing you. Come in. What's been happening? How's poor Rosa? Have you arrested anybody?'

Gladwin followed her into the kitchen, saying nothing. Thea produced coffee and waited.

'I can only stay a minute. It's not going well, I don't mind telling you. Juliet was known to just about everybody. She visited about fifty people between here and Stanton, via Snowshill and I don't-know-where. They all liked her and watched out for her, and let her play with their pets. She thought nothing of walking five miles along the paths, and back again, if she fancied visiting somebody. They're all desperately outraged by what's happened, and they all want to help.'

'So I'm just one in a long list, then.'

'Not exactly. Your husband was very possibly the

last person to see her alive, not counting her killer. We still have no idea what she was doing for three days.'

'Her mother thinks it might have something to do with the badger culling. But I've never seen that going on near here.'

Gladwin shook her head. 'No – they haven't been round this way for months now.'

'What about Adam Rogers – the one who says he was her boyfriend? I saw him yesterday.'

Gladwin's expression changed to a wary interest. 'Did you? How come?'

'He was in our field. Apparently, he wanted to see where she died. He's got some sort of tracking device, so he can go where he likes and his people can always find him.' Again she shuddered at this sinister method of supervision. 'I think that's awful, but he doesn't seem to mind.'

'He walked there, did he? From Blockley?'

'Apparently. I don't imagine he drives, does he?'

'No. But he's got a bike.' She hesitated. 'We interviewed him on Saturday afternoon. He wasn't really her boyfriend in the usual sense. They've got him on medication that keeps him damped down sexually.'

Thea reacted with even greater horror. 'No! Chemical castration, you mean? I thought they abandoned that in the 1950s. How can that be right?'

Gladwin made calming motions with her hands. 'It's really not so bad. He understands what it is, and seems happy enough to take it. It makes life easier all round. He is awfully *big*, you know. He could get into all kinds of trouble without these interventions.'

'Huh,' said Thea.

'It's the real world, whether you like it or not. Nothing's ever going to be perfect, is it? The man's as well integrated and contented as anyone could wish for. Well – he *was*, until this happened. Now he thinks everyone's suspecting him of being the killer. He's read the stories, the same as the rest of us. And it's not the first time. When he was sixteen, a girl was attacked, and he was in the frame for it. It was years before he got over it.'

'He didn't do it, obviously.'

'No, he didn't. But that doesn't prove anything now – one way or the other.'

'So tell me – *please* tell me, exactly how Juliet was killed.'

'We're still not a hundred per cent sure, but the way it looks is that she was hit on the side of the head, while standing close to a tree. That knocked her into the trunk, so that the other side of her head collided with it. And there's a place on her shoulder as well.'

'A place?'

'Where she'd been struck. But the head injuries caused her death.'

'Both of them?'

'Seemingly so. Neither one was enough on its own, but the double knock did awful things to her brain, and it swelled up inside the skull – fatally.'

Thea gave this explanation some thought. 'Does that make it murder or manslaughter, then? The knock against the tree was a sort of accident, wasn't it? So the actual blow was not bad enough to kill her?'

Gladwin gave a rueful smile. 'Wiser heads than mine will have to sort that one out. If it was down to me, I'd go for unpremeditated murder. But we just collect the evidence and present the case to the CPS. So far, the exact charge is academic. We've got to find the perpetrator first.'

'Could a woman have done it?'

'Just about. But she'd have to be tall, or have used a long implement, with a fair amount of strength behind it.'

'Can't think of anyone,' said Thea. The only tall people she'd met lately were the two Biddulph half-brothers, Clovis and Lawrence, and Adam Rogers. 'As tall as Juliet, you mean?'

'Within a few inches, yes. But that's probably a red herring. It entirely depends on the weapon. A wooden bat of some sort seems most likely, but it could have been a walking stick or even a random branch lying on the ground.'

'I thought forensics could work all that out these days.'

'They could if they had the resources. There were fragments of wood in both sides of her head – two different sorts. One was bark from a tree beside where she was found. The other was something else. Not likely to be a handy fallen branch, because that would be dead wood, and dead wood left outside goes soft and crumbly after a while. Not much use for hitting people with.'

'Well, thanks for telling me,' said Thea.

'I'm not supposed to, but it's not such a secret now as it was on Saturday. Too many people know the story, and some of my chaps are incapable of keeping quiet. They let things out when they're questioning someone, without realising they're doing it.'

'Hmm,' said Thea, thinking it was surely not so difficult to train them not to be so careless. But a clever interviewee would probably quickly work it out, however delicately the questions were worded.

'There's a big query over one of her housemates,' Gladwin disclosed. 'A woman called Tammy, who's on the autistic spectrum, but is very competent in a lot of ways. She's a bit older than the others, and has a job like Juliet had. But she's got a blind spot where other people's feelings are concerned, and manages to be extremely annoying much of the time. You don't know her, I suppose?'

'Sorry. Never heard of her. She sounds like a lot of people to me. How come she's living with Juliet and Adam?'

'Adam doesn't live there. He's in another supervised living place. Although she has a job, Tammy can't cope on her own, for various reasons. It's all very sensitive, as you can imagine. Social workers and so forth at every turn – and the jargon would send you mad all on its own. They can never call a spade a spade. In fact, I doubt if I'm even allowed to say the word "spade".'

'All part of the job,' said Thea absently. It had occurred to her that if she followed through with her idea of working officially with the police, the jargon might quickly send her mad, too.

'Right. What are you thinking?'

'Oh, nothing. You must be tempted to see one of these – what can I say? *Challenged*? – people as the most likely to have attacked Juliet. If only because anyone else would be disarmed by her vulnerability. She was so *sweet*. So innocent and trusting . . .' Her voice faded away and Gladwin met her eye.

'Exactly. There are people out there who find sweet innocence irresistible. It brings out the worst in them. And the fact is that the vast majority of people with learning difficulties are actually very non-violent. Either because they're on medication, or are scared of the world, or simply gentle by nature. The stereotypes are seriously wrong in that respect.'

'Is that true? So we're looking for somebody of full competence, then? But she wasn't raped or anything, was she?'

'Not a finger laid on her, that we can find. Nothing but two bangs on the head and a bruise on her shoulder.'

'Only two of which were inflicted deliberately.' It felt as if they were about to go around the same facts again, so Thea drained her coffee and then stood up. 'I mustn't keep you,' she said.

'No, you mustn't. I just wanted to check with you that there weren't some connections we were missing. I can't help feeling that Juliet knew one of your families – that she was close to your field for a reason. The birdsong man's the most likely, given the timing. That would throw suspicion on Mr Spiller who found her.'

'Oh dear. He seems so nice,' Thea protested. 'And very upset. Drew likes him, as well. He'd have to be a good actor.' She laughed at herself. 'And yes, I know the world is full of excellent actors. Even so . . .'

'I agree. It feels like too big a stretch. But so does everybody else. None of it feels right. And that makes me think we're missing a big part of the picture.'

'Hmm,' said Thea. 'Well, I'll call you if I think of anything.'

She started towards the hallway, but Gladwin stayed in place. 'Don't forget what I said about Mr Spiller,' she said. 'If you get the chance, have a little talk with him – see what you think.'

'I must admit his name does keep coming to mind. He phoned Drew on Saturday morning, apologising for being in the field. He seemed to think he might be getting us into some sort of trouble. Drew felt quite sorry for him.'

'He is quite sweet,' Gladwin nodded. 'Though I say so as shouldn't.' Her Geordie accent thickened. 'Everyone's like that in this one, though.'

Thea smiled. 'As you say – there must be a piece missing somewhere. Some absolute swine is out there, and we have no idea who it is.'

'Okay.' Gladwin smacked both palms down on the table. 'I can't stay another minute, much as I'd like to. Call me later on, if you like, and we'll bring it right up to date. There's more reports due in today, from the pathology people and forensics. It's still only forty-eight hours since we found her.'

Thea detected a hint of bravado. The apparent lack of any compelling line of enquiry must be bad news for the senior investigating officer. A high-profile murder, arousing vociferous outrage even in a half-deserted Cotswold village, needed to be solved. People would be imagining all kinds of monstrous threats behind their well-tamed hedgerows, bordering their renowned public footpaths. The murderer must be caught – that was axiomatic. And if Thea Slocombe could help with that, Gladwin for one was going to be more than happy to use her.

This busy Monday was proving to be quite a lot more stimulating than the weekend had been. Drew was in and out, making phone calls, taking Andrew down to the field to mark out the week's graves. At one point, he extracted a duster from the cupboard under the sink intending to spend five minutes running it over the shelves and woodwork in his office. 'Better clean the window later on, as well,' he muttered. 'Mike did a good job outside, but it's not so good inside.'

'I'll do it this evening,' Thea promised, far from certain that she would remember to fulfil the commitment. 'Maybe I should do all of them, and the mirrors.'

'Good idea,' said Drew neutrally.

'Gladwin thinks it might be helpful if I had a little talk with Anthony Spiller,' she said carefully. 'Have you got his address?'

Drew stopped in the doorway and gave her a long look. 'No. He didn't arrange the funeral. And I wouldn't tell you, even if I did have it. It's confidential. You know that.'

'Oh, yes, I know. But he did call you on Saturday, and I'm sure he'd be more than happy to chat. Don't you think?'

'Not if you're acting on behalf of the police, trying to get him to incriminate himself. I would think he'd feel profoundly betrayed. Is that what's going on?'

She flushed. 'Sort of. Not really. We both – me and Gladwin – think he's a sweetie. And he's been questioned already. They've got no reason to talk to him again. She just wanted me to . . . you know. See if I got any hunches. He might tell me something he'd forgotten. Some clue that would help them catch who did it. He's the only link between us and Juliet, when you think about it.'

'I'm trying *not* to think about it,' said Drew. 'And I'm sure you can find him without my help. Ask

Gladwin for his address. I'm surprised she hasn't given it to you already.'

Thea nodded. 'She should have done.' In her bag, hanging on the back of a chair, her phone burbled. She took it out, and laughed. 'And here it is, in a text. Fancy that!'

'So you won't be needing me,' said Drew, and went to do his dusting.

Chapter Eighteen

If she didn't bother with lunch, Thea had three hours and a bit to herself before the children got home from school. The arrangement was that she would always be there for them when they came in, since Drew's movements were so hard to predict. It made for a short day and gave rise to occasional flashes of resentment. It also pointed out the potential complications of Thea embarking on any kind of paid employment. If she was only to be available for about six hours a day, and less if much travelling were required, it hardly seemed worthwhile. At least to her. Most other people seemed to think that gave her a perfectly reasonable thirty-hour week, with all the benefits accruing from that. 'But what about the *dog*?' she protested. Not to mention all her other interests, which were hard to define, but suddenly felt important when threatened.

* * *

Anthony Spiller lived on the outskirts of Broadway – a village Thea seldom visited. It was over the border into Warwickshire, which had no significance other than creating a foolish psychological barrier. Deeper than that was her resistance to the level of self-consciousness the place manifested. It existed in a time warp, preserved for the delectation of American and Australian tourists, much too clean and tidy for her taste. But she freely acknowledged that this was her own prejudice. Most people thought the place was gorgeous. And real people did live there, obviously. Including Anthony Spiller.

The road was another deterrent. It swooped downhill in a series of wild curves that made her worry for the steering. Sandy spurs ran off to the left at intervals, designed for vehicles with failed brakes to take evasive action. There was something unnerving about that. The unusual width of the road probably had no direct link to the name 'Broadway', but it very much was a broad way, even so. It felt out of keeping with the more common narrow lanes and high hedges.

The Spiller house was of modest size and unarguably lovely. The biscuit-coloured stone was weathered, both in colour and texture. There were trees in the front garden, and a large bird-feeding station. Birds were clearly a strong interest throughout the family. She remembered a house-sitting job in Winchcombe, where the interest had become an obsession, with a hide, camera and assorted nuts and seeds to give them.

How many times had she walked up a strange garden path and knocked on the door? She did it repeatedly, very often impelled by nothing more worthy than curiosity. She always experienced a thrill at the prospect of seeing the interior of yet another home. She liked to examine their carpets and furniture and colour schemes – although more often disapproving than admiring. So many of them looked unlived-in, the cushions undented and the ornaments perfectly dusted.

She rang the bell and waited, rehearsing what she should say. Inside, there was the sound of footsteps, apparently coming down the stairs. When the door opened, it revealed a middle-aged woman in something Thea thought might be called a 'leisure suit'. Like pyjamas, only marginally more finished. There was elastic at the ankles and a pocket in the top. 'Hello?' she said.

'Hello. I'm Thea Slocombe. Is Anthony in?'

'Who?'

'Gosh! Have I got the wrong house? Isn't this Mayfield Cottage?'

'I meant – who are *you*? What do you want with my husband?'

'Oh. Sorry. My husband's the undertaker in Broad Campden. He buried your husband's uncle last week. Weren't you at the funeral?'

'Of course I was. But *you* weren't. And I can't be expected to remember the name of the undertaker, surely?'

'No.' The woman watched her struggle for something else to say. Mrs Spiller was definitely older and tougher than her husband. She was also careless of her appearance, and disinclined to be interrupted on what looked like a nice lazy day off. Thea found herself uncomfortably wrong-footed.

'So why do you want him?' the woman demanded.

'Um . . . well, he phoned Drew – my husband – on Saturday, after he found poor Juliet. He seemed upset, and we just thought maybe we should check that he's all right.'

'Poor Juliet?'

'Yes. That was her name. The dead woman in the woods close to the burial field. Anthony had gone to listen to the birds, and sit by the grave, and then he found her. It must have been a ghastly shock for him. Then the police asked a lot of questions, and that can't have been pleasant, either.'

The woman stood on her front step and stared at Thea in total incomprehension. 'I have no idea what you're talking about. Anthony isn't here. He hasn't been here since this time last week, and then he only stayed for half an hour. We separated six months ago. He's lodging with a friend in Chipping Campden.'

'Oh. Well, he gave this as his address to the police.'

She shrugged. 'I suppose it sounded better,' she said.

Thea laughed, despite a growing feeling that Anthony Spiller might not be quite the sweet innocent nephew she and Gladwin had taken him for. 'Surely that can't be it. Maybe he thinks he'll be coming back sometime soon?'

'I doubt it.' The woman hesitated. 'Look – do you want to come in and tell me the whole story? I can't make head or tail of it so far. Somebody called Juliet died in some woods and Anthony found her? Is that right?'

'More or less, yes.' Thea was already halfway into the house. She liked this estranged wife, she decided, and they definitely had quite a lot to say to each other.

'My name's Nancy, by the way,' the woman said as she led the way to a room at the back. Thea found herself in a room that could only be termed as 'snug'. It had bookshelves on three walls, a shaggy green rug on the floor and two elderly armchairs liberally filled with cushions. The fourth wall was mostly window, overlooking a patch of jungle that could hardly be called a garden. Tall grasses, shrubs, climbers and ramblers. 'They all produce berries or seeds,' Nancy explained wearily, having observed Thea's fascination. 'Attracts about fifty different sorts of bird.'

Thea's first thought was – *so how could Anthony bear to leave it?* Something rather serious must have gone wrong between him and his wife, which seemed a pity, since Thea was already liking the woman.

'I know,' said Nancy Spiller, as if reading her mind. 'It should have been me that left, not him. But Tony's a gentleman. Always has been. I think he must have been a very funny little boy. Uncle Dicky used to say he was born out of his time. He'd have been perfect as a Victorian clergyman.'

She sounded wistful and fond, and Thea felt sad, especially for Anthony. He'd lost uncle and wife, apparently, and then stumbled on a dead woman when he was trying to hear the dawn chorus. 'I'm sorry he's not here,' she said.

'I still don't understand why you want him. Are you with the police or something? How would you know his address otherwise?'

To the best of her recollection, Thea had never been asked that question before. Nancy had earned herself a gold star for quick thinking – and quick-thinking people automatically got themselves onto the list of suspects when a murder was being investigated. Uncle Dicky's funeral early on Thursday was starting to look like a highly significant point in the story. Both the Spillers had been there and, quite possibly, Juliet Wilson had been hiding amongst the trees. 'Did you know Juliet Wilson?' she asked, dodging the awkward question.

'Who? Is that "poor Juliet"? The one who died?'

'She was murdered, during the night between Friday and Saturday. Your husband found her when he went to listen to the birds and look at his uncle's grave. Then he phoned my husband after the police had questioned him, quite upset. We were busy, and worried we hadn't given him the space to say everything he wanted to. So I came here to see if I could offer anything—' She was going to say *like sympathy, or a listening ear*, but it sounded trite, and almost intrusive. Thea was often intrusive, according to a number of people.

'You provide a counselling service, do you? Isn't that rather American – chasing bereaved people in case they want to spill their misery all over you?'

Thea winced and wriggled in the soft chair. 'It wasn't meant like that,' she said feebly.

Nancy shook her large head, greying hair flipping from side to side. She was a big woman, at least fifty, with heavy eyebrows and a wide mouth. 'You obviously *are* with the police, or you'd have answered my question. Is Anthony a suspect, then? You think he killed this person?'

'No, no. I mean – I am friendly with the woman in charge of the investigation. And I knew Juliet, you see. And Drew might have been the last person to see her alive – before the one who killed her, of course. We're very much involved. I offered to come and talk to Anthony, that's all. I'm not authorised to take notes or anything like that. It's all completely informal.'

Nancy sniffed. 'That sounds highly irregular to me.'

'I know. It does, doesn't it?' Thea admitted. 'It's sort of evolved over a few years. I've found myself on the spot a few times, when a crime has been committed, and been useful to the police. And I've always had a lot of free time.'

'That makes you weird, for a start. Nobody has free time these days. Being busy is the greatest virtue, apparently.' Thea eyed the leisure suit meaningfully and Nancy laughed. 'Touché. I can't pretend to be fully occupied, can I? The thing is, I've had a pretty bad depression since Christmas. Couldn't get out of bed. Didn't wash my hair – all that stuff. But it's a lot better now. Uncle Dicky dying was the turning point, which sounds peculiar, I suppose. It was something to do with death being the worst thing that can happen, and I was just being self-indulgent. Wasting my life. I was getting into seriously bad habits.' She was speaking in jerky sentences, her face hardening. It was as if her words were battling with her inner workings. 'I've been going for CBT – you know, Cognitive Behavioural Therapy – which ought to have sorted me out. I'm the sort of person who told everybody to pull themselves together. Now I tell it to myself. It doesn't always work.'

Thea could find nothing helpful to say. Depression was not one of her areas of expertise. Grief, yes. Fear, sometimes. But on the whole she had a thick skin and a brisk outlook. World events often made her angry, but she never felt despair. 'Is that why Anthony left?' she asked, after a pause.

'What? Oh, no. Not really. I guess I was pretty poor company, but he was always very patient with me. I'm eight years older than him, you see. That's still quite unusual, and it brought us very close. Us against the world. Babes in the wood. That's a technical term amongst couple counsellors.'

Still the short sentences, and the tormented delivery. 'Uh-huh,' said Thea neutrally.

'He left because I asked him to. Simple as that. He was in my way. I couldn't manage both of us. It's not permanent – I hope. He's happy enough, as long as he thinks that. He's got a big family, and they're all very loving and close. Now Dicky's dead, they've all come together even more. His aunt adores him. Auntie Jenny. And there are cousins all over the place. Meanwhile I've been helped by going to the Paxford Centre. You know about that, I suppose?'

Thea frowned. 'Well, yes, actually. One or two people have mentioned it over the weekend. Juliet went there, so you must have known her.'

'Sorry. I never came across anybody called Juliet. I don't mix very much with people there. Just turn up for my appointments and come home again.'

'I'd never heard of it till a day or two ago. What does it do, exactly?'

'It's a funny mixture of Social Services and some private therapists. They've taken over a massive great manor house, and it's really taken off. Anybody with any sort of problem is free to go there. A lot of them just sit around and chat. There's a speech therapist and a physio, and a few others, funded by the state, as well as an osteopath and a couple of counsellors who you have to pay. And loads of volunteers, who mostly seem to be former patients – or "clients", as they call us. They read to people, push wheelchairs around, bring shopping for the handful of residents. It started as a day centre, but they've made a few rooms for people to stay. They have to pay for those, as well. But you don't want to know all that,' she finished abruptly. 'It's not remotely relevant. In fact, Anthony is definitely not relevant to your murder investigation, either. It sounds as if he was just unlucky to find that woman. In the wrong place at the wrong moment.'

'He didn't tell you about it?'

'Obviously not. I haven't seen him since Thursday. Nor phoned, emailed, skyped – no contact at all.'

'Right. Well . . .'

'You still want to talk to him, don't you?'

Thea wriggled her shoulders in overt embarrassment. 'I think I should,' she mumbled.

'Well, I'm not going to tell you where he is. What do you think about that?' She jutted out her chin in childlike defiance.

'I thought you might say that. I know when I'm beaten,' said Thea.

Nancy laughed again, as Thea had hoped she would. 'You're quite a one, aren't you?' she said, in admiration. 'I must say I rather like you.'

'Thanks. I like you, too.'

'But I'll kill you if you upset poor Tony. He's not your murderer. The idea's idiotic.'

'He's already upset,' said Thea. 'And nobody

seriously thinks he did it. He had perfectly good reasons to be where he was on Saturday morning. The police understand that. It's more the idea that he might have seen something important, without realising it.'

'Mm,' said Nancy.

It struck Thea that the woman was remarkably unconcerned by the fact of a murder. She had asked no questions at all about Juliet, or how she died, or what was going on in the investigation. Such a lack of curiosity felt bizarre. Almost, she realised, suspicious. Here was a big strong woman, who knew all about the alternative burial ground – had attended a funeral there two days before Juliet was killed. It was perfectly feasible that she knew Juliet herself, although quite how remained obscure. There was a tenuous theme developing around mental health, albeit of very different kinds. Depression bore no relation to learning disabilities. Even so, there could perhaps be professionals who dealt with them both – links that might usefully be traced.

'I'll go,' she said decisively. 'It was nice to meet you.'

'Come again,' said Nancy, as if she really meant it. 'I'll try to be dressed next time. Here – take my phone number, so you can warn me in advance. I could do with a new friend.'

'So could I,' said Thea, surprising herself. She took the scrap of paper with the phone number on it, noting with a smile that this was a transaction from the olden days. People keyed their numbers into each other's phones now. It was obviously a landline number. 'Haven't you got a mobile?' she asked.

'Somewhere, yes. But I've hidden it from myself. It had a lot to do with my depression, you see.'

Thea didn't see, but this was clearly an issue for another time. 'Okay,' she nodded. 'Bye, then.'

Chapter Nineteen

Two and three-quarter hours before she had to be back on duty at home, she calculated. She was hungry but pausing for a proper meal felt like wasted time. She was on the northern edge of the Cotswolds, with places like Snowshill, Stanton and Laverton only a few minutes' drive away. Laverton was where Rosa and Juliet had lived when Thea was in Stanton, two Christmases ago. She remembered seeing Juliet wandering ghostlike in a misty wood, claiming to be seeking out a suitable tree to take home and decorate. Now it was May, with new leaves and exuberant birds, and all the foolish anticipation of a decent summer for a change. At least there would be light evenings and flowers in the garden. Perhaps it was the improving season that had ameliorated Nancy Spiller's depression.

But there was still more than enough to be depressed about in Thea's own life: Maggs and Drew, Rosa Wilson, poor Adam Rogers. Even Mr Shipley's sister, who had probably been too young to die. And on a wider level, the endlessly startling Twitter-created world of politics, where anything seemed to be possible. No wonder Nancy Spiller had been overwhelmed by it.

All the places she'd mentally listed were to the west. Eastwards lay Paxford and Ebrington beyond her home village of Broad Campden. She had been to Paxford ages ago, but, as a rule, she seldom turned eastwards. She favoured Blockley and Moreton, and even Winchcombe, quite a long way to the south. And the thing was, she admitted to herself, she did not want to go home. Her dog had been left behind, having not walked anywhere that day. Walking Hepzie was a random business at best. There were few routines in the spaniel's life, which she appeared to cope with well enough. There would be enough time to let her have a little run in the field at the end of their lane once everyone was home and settled. It was light until nearly nine o'clock, after all.

She drove slowly away from Broadway, cogitating all the possible directions she might take. So many places in the area were associated with violent death and terrible behaviour. The list was oppressively long, tainting a lot of the beautiful villages. Knowledge of what the inhabitants were capable of added a dimension that no casual visitor could possibly even guess at. The nature of the Cotswolds region itself was still not quite defined in Thea's mind. There had been so many incarnations over the past thousand years and more. First, dense forest, mostly destroyed by the Saxons and their contemporaries. Then, the grassy uplands providing rich fodder for sheep, and rich wool profits for their owners. Huge churches, far too big for their communities, had been erected on this money. Railways had crossed the area, bringing tourists to admire the old stone buildings and increasingly ostentatious gardens. And still, to this day, money was evident in all its manifestations in almost every town and village. Big cars, hi-tech security systems, upmarket emporia and expensive pedigree dogs were inescapable. Not to mention horses, private planes and strange eccentric collections.

All of them potential motives for crime, of course. People valued their possessions above other people's lives, once in a while. They valued their own status and reputation every bit as highly. They exacted revenge, silenced those who knew too much, or simply lashed out when a particular psychological or emotional button was pushed. Which looked like the probable reason for Juliet Wilson's death.

Once more, she ran through the very short list of people who might lose their self-control badly enough to strike poor Juliet. The list comprised only two soft, nice, friendly men. Anthony Spiller and Adam Rogers were both impossible to imagine as killers. Nancy Spiller had not known Juliet – but then, she realised, that wasn't an essential qualification. If it was a simple act of sudden rage, anything might have sparked it off. Juliet could have seen something, heard something, made a noise just when a rare migrating bird came into sight, or have been mistaken for a threat of some sort. Perhaps she had loomed out of the early morning mist, terrifying some nervous birdwatcher, who blindly waved a stick in her face, thereby killing her. But wouldn't such a person immediately call ambulance and police and admit the whole tragic story? That's what anyone normal would do. And Anthony Spiller was apparently more or less normal. As normal as anybody could claim to be, anyway, she thought. A better word would be *conventional* or *conformist*, she supposed. Someone who abided by the rules of society without questioning them.

But then there was that same old fear of losing face. Of forever being known as the man who – even if by accident – had killed a beloved local figure. Even a conventional, conformist, *normal* person might quail at that prospect and run away from the scene of his own violence, lying and obfuscating his way out of the whole thing.

It could have been anyone, on that basis, she decided gloomily. Gladwin would never find him (or possibly her) because there would be no linkage, no fertile seams of investigation. No witnesses, motives or incriminating evidence.

Really, there was nowhere she wanted to drive to in the mood that gripped her. She might just as well go home and find something domestic to do. Or sit out in the watery sunshine and read a book.

The car was already heading towards Broad Campden. She took the smaller road, that went through Blockley, out of habit and a vague preference. It passed the burial ground before reaching her home village, and she liked to slow down and give it a quick inspection. Drew was sometimes there, in which case she might stop for a chat.

Instead, she was astonished to see a big white camper van parked inside the field. She braked hard, then reversed a little way for a better look. Trespassers! A whole new problem, which they had never considered, and which was sure to be awkward to deal with, or prevent in the future. The field had to be open for families to visit the graves, with one corner kept free for parking.

She stopped on the verge and got out. Full of righteous indignation, she marched towards the interlopers, wondering how long they'd been there. Had Drew or Andrew not seen them? She did not keep close track of their movements; they might not have gone to the field that day. 'Hey!' she shouted, when still twenty yards away. 'Hello?'

Nothing happened, but when she got closer, she could see movement through one of the windows. Then a door in the side opened, and a ramp dropped down, where there would normally be steps. She trotted up to it, and peered in. A man in a wheelchair was being delicately manoeuvred towards her by another man. The chair came down the ramp, with a brief rush at the end. Thea stepped back out of the way, and tried to understand what she was seeing.

'Mrs Slocombe,' said the man holding the handles of the wheelchair. 'We meet again.'

'Clovis Biddulph,' she squeaked. 'What on earth—?'

'I told you we'd camp out until my father's funeral took place. Well, here we are – all three of us. This is my brother Luc.'

She swallowed, her eyes glued to his face. It was just as lovely as before. Her bones went just as rubbery and her heart swelled and flipped idiotically. 'You *can't*,' she said. 'You really can't.'

'Sorry, but as you see, we absolutely can. We'll go as soon as the burial's done. We thought it might be today, but that seems to have been optimistic. There hasn't been a new grave dug, so now we're wondering if it's not even tomorrow, either.'

The brother was watching her. He had the same dark eyes and thick hair, but he was much less attractive than Clovis. His face was longer and thinner. A groove between his eyes made him look angry, and his lips were thin and tight. 'Three of you?' said Thea.

'That's right,' came a female voice from inside the camper. 'I'm the first Mrs Biddulph. Come to make trouble for the second one.' She laughed, as if at a very merry little joke. When she came into full view, Thea saw a slim, straight-backed woman of roughly seventy years old. She wore a dark-blue cotton shirt, open at a neck that was stringy and wrinkled with old tired skin. There were moles around her collarbones. Her tight jeans were grey, stopping short of slender ankles and bare feet. 'No, but seriously,' she went on, 'we do think it's time to stop all this nonsense about keeping us a secret. It's just so ridiculous. What are they afraid of, anyway? We're just people, the same as them.'

'Her, Ma. Not them. The son doesn't know about us, remember. It's him she's protecting. When he finds out we exist, it's going to sully his image of his dear old dad. How demeaning is that? It's disgracefully *rude*, when you think about it.' It was Luc who spoke, in a voice indistinguishable from that of his brother. He looked up at Thea. 'You probably can't even imagine it. He made it very clear to us, many years ago now, that he never wanted to see us or hear from us again.'

'And we did as he wanted,' added Clovis. 'We let his new son have him, and never did anything to rock the boat for them. I don't know what Linda's told you about us, but it won't have a word of truth in it. We behaved well and respected his wishes. But now . . .' He paused and looked at the other two. 'Now, we've had enough. We want to be here for his funeral, and I don't think anybody would regard that as unreasonable.'

'We've talked it all over, and we came to the conclusion that your very respectable husband is not going to do anything to have us removed, because it would make for very bad publicity, and serve no useful purpose whatever.' Again Luc was doing the talking. He smiled to soften the implied threat behind his words. 'Besides, by the time he could take out an injunction, we'd be gone anyway. We're not out to cause him any trouble. We're going to behave with absolute decorum. Your real problem is Linda. She's the unreasonable one in all this.'

Thea found nothing to say in disagreement. It fitted with her own observations – which she had voiced right at the very start, when Drew first told her the story. Except that then she had been sorry for Lawrence, and now she had almost forgotten he existed.

'It's a very nice place to be buried,' said the woman. 'Poor old Stephen! He really wouldn't want us to be here, you know. He did his best to wipe us out of his life. We hadn't heard a whisper from him for at least twenty years.' She gave a rueful shrug. 'So we reckoned this was our last chance to get anything close to our rights. I think we do have rights, don't you?'

'It's a lot more than twenty years, Ma,' said Clovis. 'That was when he told us we should leave him alone, for Lawrence's sake. I think I was about eighteen the last time any of us spoke to him – and then I had to pretend to be his insurance company before he'd come to the phone.'

'How did you know which company he used?' asked Thea, slowly returning to detective mode.

'I didn't. I just said I was calling to check his no claims

bonus. It usually works.' He grinned shamelessly, and her heart wobbled again.

'Stop it, Clo,' said his mother. 'You're making yourself sound like a petty criminal.'

Blood rushed to Thea's head. 'You do know there was a murder here, only three days ago?' she blurted. 'Don't you?'

'Not *here* exactly – was it?' asked Luc, looking at the grass and the tracks across it. 'Must have been through there, judging by all those ruts.'

'And we don't know anything about what happened, who died, what the police think about it. Nothing whatsoever to do with us,' said the woman.

'Maybe not, but the police are very likely to come back, and want to know what you're doing here.'

All three shrugged at the same time. 'So what?' said Clovis. 'We're not scared of the police.'

'We could start a trend,' added Luc. 'People could stay here overnight before their relation's funeral. You could charge them. It might be a nice little earner for you.'

Thea could not repress a smile. The man had wit, then. Perhaps he wasn't as bitter and twisted as she'd assumed. 'I don't think so,' she said.

'So, why don't we cut to the chase, and you tell us the exact time and date of our father's burial?' said Clovis. 'What do you have to lose, since we're here now? We had to do quite a bit of detective work to get this far.'

'Did you?' Thea was intrigued. 'I suppose it couldn't really have been so difficult.' A lateral thought entered her head. 'Did you know his child is called Modestine?'

Three faces expressed a range of humour, recognition, superiority. 'Keeping up the French connection, then,' said the mother. 'Stephen's old mum must have had a hand in it – again. She can't still be alive, can she?'

'She didn't keep in touch with you, then?' asked Thea.

'She did for ages. Last I heard was eight or nine years ago. She must have been well over ninety then. Funny old bird she was. Came from the primitive south, in the mountains, and never really learnt how to be civilised.'

Thea was irresistibly drawn in. 'How did Stephen's dad meet her?'

'It was in the war. He was doing something clandestine with the Resistance, and she was the daughter of the house where he was hiding out. A bit of a cliché, I suppose. I always thought it was a bit cruel to transplant her over here. She never did adapt. Had to have her *potager*, and kept goats in a garden that was too small for them. They used to eat the clothes off the washing line.'

The first Mrs Biddulph had gone misty with her memories – something that Thea had learnt was quite common after a death. Nostalgic reminiscences were a natural part of the mourning process. 'How bizarre, to get murdered beside a cemetery,' she murmured. 'It can't have been a coincidence.'

'I did hear a few seconds on the news about it,' said Clovis. 'Didn't sound as if they have much idea as to who did it.'

'That's right,' said Thea. 'Everybody loved her. It doesn't make any sense.'

'What was her name?' Clovis had wrinkled his brow. 'Something Shakespearean.'

'Juliet.'

'Nice,' said the woman. 'Unusual.'

'I know a Juliet,' said Luc, carelessly. 'It'd better not be her. She's a volunteer at the Paxford Centre, and we're all very fond of her. She likes to wheel me down to watch the ducks on the lake they've got there. It brightens everybody's day when she shows up.'

Chapter Twenty

Thea didn't have time to answer, partly because her breath had seized up at the implication that at least one Biddulph had known Juliet Wilson all along. She was still processing the significance of this when she heard Drew calling from the gateway into the road.

'Uh-oh,' said Clovis. 'Here comes the boss man.'

Drew came trotting across the field, looking from face to face in an effort to understand. Why was his wife so seemingly friendly with these trespassers? How had the wheelchair got there? What was he going to have to do about it?

'The Biddulph family,' said Thea in a rather airy introduction. 'Here for tomorrow's funeral.'

'Aha!' pounced Clovis. 'Tomorrow it is, then!'

'Oops,' said Thea, trying with some difficulty to take it seriously. Somewhere just below the surface there was an inescapable hilarity to these people – except perhaps for Luc, and even he was capable of cracking a joke. They were making a party of their father's funeral – and why not, she wondered. They were probably glad, if anything, that he was dead. He had done them no good for decades, treating them as a shameful secret. Why wouldn't they show up to celebrate?

'I should introduce myself properly,' said the woman. 'My name now is Kate Dalrymple. I was married to Stephen Biddulph, as you'll have realised. My present husband and I are living apart – otherwise he might have come along as well, just for the experience. He did know Stephen, briefly.'

Like the Spillers, thought Thea, wondering whether any marriages survived for long these days. Then she thought – *everybody knows each other, apparently*. She wanted some quiet, to process the startling discovery that Luc Biddulph had known Juliet Wilson – because it surely had to be the same Juliet. Did it mean anything important concerning the murder? So far, she could see no way in which it could. All it did was endorse the general feeling that there was nobody in the world who even mildly disliked Juliet, let alone hated her enough to kill her.

'You can't stay here overnight,' said Drew.

'I'm afraid we're going to,' said Clovis, with an awful courtesy. 'We're not doing you any harm, I promise. Nobody's even going to notice us.'

'Andrew's coming in a minute to dig the grave.' One of Drew's abiding taboos, inherited from working for a conventional undertaker, was that families should not witness the gravedigger at work.

'So?' Clovis cocked his head enquiringly.

Thea took Drew's arm. 'Why does that matter?' she asked.

'It just *does*,' he said, trying to smile. 'It's not . . . *right*.'

'We really don't mind. Does he use a digger?' asked Kate Dalrymple.

Drew flinched and nodded. Even that detail apparently had uncomfortable implications. There were mysteries surrounding the disposal of dead bodies that persisted even now. And the use of a mechanical digger somehow lacked dignity, needing to be kept away from general awareness. Thea had characterised this as stupid, sometime previously.

'Please don't worry about it,' begged Kate. 'I know we're breaking a whole lot of the usual protocols – but isn't that what you do here, anyway? No church service, no processions or eulogies or po-faced bearers. Who *are* the bearers, by the way?'

'We'll be using the trolley, and then Andrew and I will lower him,' said Drew.

'Doesn't that require four people?' Luc asked.

'Not the way we do it,' said Drew shortly.

'Hm.' said the man in the wheelchair.

Thea was still holding Drew by the arm. 'We can't very well force them to move,' she said. 'That would cause much worse disruption and trouble than letting them stay. Nobody can blame you for it, if you just leave them alone. You didn't tell them when the burial's going to be.'

'No. That was you,' he said crossly. 'Assuming it wasn't already on Facebook.'

'Not the actual day,' confirmed Clovis. 'Which is why we're here now – for fear of missing it.'

'Okay. All right. Have it your way.' His irritation clearly extended to his wife. 'But if there's any trouble tomorrow, don't expect me to take your side. My client is Linda Biddulph. I'm perfectly clear about that.'

The sound of Andrew arriving with the digger on a trailer behind his old Land Rover silenced them all. The digger did not belong to the business, but was hired on a special basis from a local garage, which had sidelines, including plant hire. It was their oldest piece of equipment, and Drew was regularly urged to just buy it outright. But they would not take less than a thousand pounds for it, and there was no obvious place to keep it, so things continued as they were. The garage got eighty pounds every time it was used – a cost added to the price of the funeral – and Andrew undertook to collect and return it after every grave was dug. Both he and Drew hated the thing, but it reduced the time required to prepare a grave by a factor of four or five, at least.

'I should go,' said Drew.

'And me. Not long till the kids get home,' said Thea. She wanted to add *I'll race you*, but she didn't think Drew was in that sort of mood. He was right, of course. The sight of the local undertaker and his wife sprinting through the quiet little village might arouse the sort of comment they really didn't need.

So, instead, they walked decorously home, side by side but not touching. 'I'll have to call Linda and tell her,' he said worriedly. 'I can't let her walk into the middle of that lot.'

'I suppose not. She'll be furious, won't she?'

'Probably. And she'll blame me.' He was quiet for a few strides. 'And you looked so pally with them,' he accused. 'Practically *encouraging* them.'

'I didn't mean to. We were talking about Juliet. I nearly forgot about the funeral. They're not very upset about Mr Biddulph dying, so they're not like the usual mourners.'

'And now they're just making mischief for the sake of it – is that what you mean?'

'I think they want to make a point. It can't be very nice when your father tries to pretend you don't exist. They want people to know the truth.'

'Well, a funeral is not the place for it.'

'No. Of course it isn't.' Thea's own thoughts remained more with the murder than the burial. 'Luc knew Juliet,' she burst out. 'Isn't that amazing? She was a volunteer at a centre in Paxford, and pushed his wheelchair. He said the same as everybody else – they all loved her.'

'Well, at least he didn't kill her,' said Drew, rather

absently. 'Did you say Paxford? Does one of them live there then? Surely they can't be as nearby as Paxford? They'd never have kept out of Lawrence's sight, if they were practically down the road.'

'I still don't know the answer to that. I get the feeling the centre's got a big catchment area. Nancy Spiller told me about it only this morning. That's a coincidence,' she noted. 'And it links everybody up alarmingly neatly.'

'I've heard about it,' he said. 'But I've never been there. It's not a nursing home. Nobody's ever died there, as far as I know.'

'You mean you've never had to remove a body from there.'

'Of course that's what I mean,' he said impatiently. 'What else?'

'I wonder whether Gladwin's been to talk to them about Juliet?'

'Who's Nancy Spiller?' he asked suddenly.

'Oh – wife of Anthony, who's the nephew of your Mr Fleming. The one who found Juliet's body.'

Drew groaned. 'Don't you get the feeling we're running on parallel tracks here? You can only think about the murder investigation, and I've got to focus on the burials. And never the twain shall meet.'

'You should be glad about that,' she teased him, refusing to worry about his tetchy mood. 'But they're coming dangerously close together, with one of your mourners finding Juliet, and you seeing her a day or

232

two before she died. And surely everybody's assuming she was there in the first place because of a funeral? Hovering around, waiting for a burial – or else wanting to commune with somebody already there. In a grave.' Her brain began whirring in a higher gear. 'If she knew Nancy Spiller, she might also have known the rest of the family – it might well have been Mr Fleming she was visiting. And that takes us back to the nephew as a person of interest. I suppose I should tell Gladwin,' she concluded. 'Just in case she's missed a step.'

'Lord help us,' sighed Drew, with affectionate exasperation. 'What's to become of us?'

'Although, Nancy didn't seem to know Juliet,' she mused, deliberately prolonging the source of Drew's complaint. Then she nudged him with her shoulder. 'You love it, really. Stop pretending you don't. If it bothered you that much, you'd never have got together with me. You can't say you weren't warned.'

'All my own fault, then,' he said lightly. They were twenty yards from home. 'Did you have any lunch?'

'Nope. Did you?'

'Leftovers.'

'Right.' It was nearly half past two, she realised. 'Time for tea and biscuits. I'll make it while you phone Linda Biddulph. You never know – she might be glad to get everything resolved. Clovis and his family seem perfectly civilised, after all. Once they've got Stephen out of the way, they might all end up the best of friends.'

'Ever the optimist,' he said. 'And I suppose you think Maggs is going to change her mind as well.'

She had forgotten about Maggs. The parallel lines analogy was looking more accurate than she had wanted to admit. Where she could think about little but Gladwin and the death of Juliet, Drew was obsessing about the future of his business. 'She might,' she said. 'Stranger things have happened.'

She waited until they'd had their tea and Drew had disappeared into his study for a second time. There remained roughly twenty minutes before the children came home. The dog was throwing reproachful spaniel glances her way, born of a day spent cooped up in the house for no good reason. 'Oh, stop it,' Thea told her. 'You can run about in the garden, like most dogs have to be happy with these days. Or get Stephanie to take you down to the field when she comes in.'

She turned her back on the animal and fished her phone out of her bag. Gladwin did not answer the summons, so Thea left a message. 'Just to tell you that I've met more people who knew Juliet. Well, one of them says she didn't, but she goes to the Paxford Centre, so she might know her by sight. They're two of our funeral people. Sounds as if it could explain a few connections.'

It was a mangled effort, she knew. And it was highly unlikely that the police had failed to already discover the significance of the Paxford Centre. Gladwin had sent somebody along to ask about

Juliet's involvement there, and might easily be making all sorts of connections, just as Thea was. But Thea's connections were special, in that they involved Drew and his funerals – families that Gladwin had not seen as relevant to the murder. Her investigations were likely to be more focused on Juliet's circle of friends in the care system.

The fact that Drew knew about the centre was irritating. It reminded her that he had talked to far more local people in the past year than she had herself. He had bedded himself in as the provider of an essential service, with all the personal attentions anyone could wish for. Linda Biddulph wasn't the only one to splurge the details of her family to him. His knack of asking the right questions, and then sitting back to listen to long convoluted responses, was indisputable.

Gladwin called back shortly before four o'clock. 'You think we should have another look at the place in Paxford?' she began. 'Okay, I'll go along with that. I've got more sense than to dismiss any suggestion made by Thea Osborne. Sorry – Slocombe. So, listen – I'm sending somebody round to talk to you. She's a new DS, called Caz Barkley. This is her first murder, and she's doing a great job so far. The thing is – and I absolutely shouldn't be telling you this – she's a product of the care system. She's got a special sensitivity about the victim here. That works both ways, of course. Helps and hinders. Don't tell her I told you. Just keep it in mind.'

'In case I say something crass,' Thea realised.

'You might say that. I couldn't possibly comment.'

'What time is she coming?'

'In about twenty minutes.'

Thea sighed. 'I'll take her out for a walk, then, with the dog. There won't be anywhere here that we can have a proper talk. Unless Drew lets me use his office.' She was far from sure that there was much prospect of that.

'The walk'll do her good,' laughed Gladwin, and left Thea to take it from there.

Caz Barkley arrived two minutes ahead of the predicted time. Thea opened the door to a young woman adorned with a nose ring and eyebrow studs. *What a stereotype*, was her instant reaction. The dark-brown hair was cut short, and there was no hint of any make-up. She wore a long yellow cotton top over brown leggings. Her trainers were black, and very clean. She was four inches taller and two or three stone heavier than Thea.

'Do you mind if we go for a walk and talk as we go?' Thea asked. 'My dog hasn't been out all day, and she needs a run. There's a field just down there.' She pointed.

The detective looked doubtful. 'Is it muddy?'

'Not at all. It hasn't rained for at least a week. It's really quite nice.'

'Okay, then.'

She appeared to be in her late twenties, with an accent that betrayed at least some years spent in Birmingham, but most likely the softer, southern edges. While not actually fat, she was well covered. There was no suggestion of any sort of fitness regime, no bulging muscles to be seen. There was a preoccupied look in her eyes, as if she was inwardly repeating protocols and instructions as to how to conduct an interview.

'We're supposed to be talking about the Paxford Centre, I think,' said Thea, trying to be helpful. She had whistled for Hepzie, who bounded joyfully ahead of them, as if liberated from a month of incarceration.

'I'm not sure I understand why,' said Barkley stiffly. 'We've talked to the people there. Juliet Wilson went as a volunteer, once a week at most. They all spoke highly of her. It's not at all like the place in Stow, which is only for people with learning difficulties.'

'Was it one of those situations where they helped her more than she helped them? I mean – did they let her think she was one of the carers, when really it was the other way around?'

This was met with a stony silence.

'Sorry – I probably worded that badly. I've never been to the place, so I've got no idea how it operates.'

'No,' said the DS with feeling.

'So tell me.'

'It's a converted mansion. Must have been a stately home, sort of place. A mile or more from the village. There's some NHS funding for three or four full-time health professionals, and a lot of individual units for different therapists. It works very well, I think. It feels like a community, all quite relaxed. Unusual in that way. Obviously, the volunteers all have their DBS checks, and they have to sign in and out, same as the visitors do.'

'What's a DBS?'

'It's the new CRB. They changed the name. Disclosure and Barring it is now.'

'Lord help us. Do visitors need to be checked as well?'

'Of course not.' The detective stopped walking and turned to face Thea. 'That's ridiculous.'

'The whole thing's ridiculous, if you ask me,' retorted Thea. 'Does this place cater for children as well?'

Caz shook her head. 'Adults only.'

'But they have people with all sorts of problems? Disabilities. Physical injuries like Luc Biddulph, and mental ones like Nancy Spiller.'

'Who are they?'

'Two people I met for the first time today, who probably don't know each other, but both attend this Paxford place. He was injured in a road accident, and she's had depression. Maybe they *do* know each other,' she finished thoughtfully. 'And they both knew Juliet.'

'Who are they?' repeated Caz.

238

'Oh – sorry. Both people we've done funerals for. Actually, one of the funerals isn't until tomorrow.' A sudden alarming thought hit her, which she definitely did not want to share. 'Isn't this field nice? Perfect for letting the dog run around. You'd think lots of people would use it, wouldn't you – but it's only us.'

'Yeah.' The detective did not even glance around. 'Grew up in the city, me. Not all that good with fields. Are there any cows?' She had only walked a few steps into the enclosure, before stopping and watching the spaniel quartering the whole field.

'Never seen any. I'm not sure what they do with it, to be honest. Maybe they'll cut the grass for hay.'

'Funny place. Haven't met a single farmer since I've been here, but there's all this *land* everywhere.'

Thea breathed more easily, hoping her distraction strategy had worked. 'They're mostly big tycoons with thousands of acres. Far less livestock than there used to be. This one's got a footpath running across it, that goes to Chipping Campden. It's the quickest way from us.'

'It can't be.'

'Well, I've never actually tested it. I'll race you sometime, and we'll see if you can get there quicker in a car.'

'Obviously, I can.'

Thea had a feeling she was coming across as teasing, and even a bit superior. 'Well, then,' she said. 'I hope I haven't brought you over here for nothing.

Gladwin always likes to know about connections, so I thought I should emphasise the significance of the Paxford place – but now I really think about it, it's probably not at all relevant. We already know that Juliet was a familiar figure all round the villages. Just about everybody knew her. It was only that I'd never heard of this centre, and then suddenly everybody was talking about it. But it's just me being ignorant. You've already been there for yourself.'

'I know a couple of people there,' Caz Barkley nodded. 'It's a really good place.' She turned to Thea. 'Has your dog run about enough now?'

'Well, not really. But then she'd stay out all day if she had the chance. We can go back if you like.'

'I'll need a note of the names of the people you're talking about. The ones who knew Juliet. If they've both had cause to use your burial service in the past few days, that makes them of interest to us. Where *is* the burial field, anyway? This isn't it, is it?'

'No. It's the other way.' Inwardly she slapped herself. Why hadn't she thought it all through more carefully before making that phone call? Nancy Spiller and Luc Biddulph were both liable to object to police attentions. 'But, honestly, I think it's a red herring. I was too quick to call Gladwin.'

'Not at all. It seems to us it might be very helpful.'

'But you've already got all the details for the Spillers,' Thea realised. 'He's the man who found Juliet's body. I went to see his wife this morning, and she mentioned the Paxford place. But she might not have known Juliet at all. She didn't seem to recognise the name.'

'What's *her* name again?' She had a pencil poised over a small notepad.

'Nancy. Nancy Spiller. She was having something called CBT. Or was it CTB?'

Barkley stared at her, wide-eyed. 'Don't you know what that is?'

Now who's being superior? Thea thought. 'Um . . . I do, if I think about it. She told me only this morning, but I'm not very good at that sort of thing,' she said.

'Cognitive behaviour therapy. Ring any bells?'

'Oh yes. Silly me. Sorry.'

'Where does this Nancy Spiller live, then?'

'Gladwin's got her address. She gave it to me in the first place. She's a very nice woman.'

Caz Barkley shrugged. 'And the other person? What's her name?'

'His. It's a man. He's called Luc Biddulph. I'm not sure, but I suspect it's spelt with a "C": L-U-C. The French way. Most of them have got French names. Except Lawrence.'

'Who is he? Luc, I mean.'

'The son of the man we're burying tomorrow. He's in a wheelchair, after a road accident not very long ago. Juliet pushed the chair around, apparently. I suppose he goes to Paxford for some sort of physiotherapy.' *And I do know what that is*, she wanted to add.

'And who's Lawrence?' She was writing quickly, noting more than mere names.

'Another son.' Thea was anxious to withhold as much Biddulph-related information as she could. Where she had initially been excited to discover a link between them and Juliet, she now wanted passionately to defend them from any police attention. 'The funeral's tomorrow,' she said again.

'Okay. Thanks. I'll take that back with me and see if it helps.'

'I don't think it will. The killer must have been a stranger – not somebody who knew Juliet. She was such a sweet person, nobody would deliberately kill her, knowing who she was.'

'We can't know that.' A shadow crossed the young face. 'There's no limit to what apparently normal people will do.'

Thea remembered Gladwin's unofficial disclosure about Caz's background. Had she been abused as a child – removed from feckless parents and consigned to a care home where the house-father was a secret paedophile? Did such things really happen? Nothing from Thea's own personal experience had ever come close to confirming the horror stories that filled the tabloids. A succession of Cotswold murders felt almost mundane by comparison. 'I guess so,' was all she said.

'I should go and have a look at your field,' Caz said. 'They tell me it's worth seeing.'

'Oh – well, it's not very interesting. Andrew's

digging a grave there at the moment. He doesn't really like being watched while he's doing that.'

'Your husband? But isn't he in the house with your kids?' The notion of unsupervised children was evidently very disconcerting.

'No, that's Drew. It is confusing, I know. Andrew works for us.'

Barkley glanced at her watch. 'I'd better get back, anyway. Some other time.'

'Where do you live?' Thea asked, in an impulsive attempt to forge a more personal link. 'Was it difficult to find somewhere?'

It was not a wise question. 'Why do you want to know that?' came the instant response.

'No reason. Just idle conversation. I got the idea you're new to the area, and prices are so high, it can't be easy.'

'I've got more in common with Juliet Wilson than you might think.' The tone was sour, almost bitter. 'I'm renting a place with two others in Cirencester. Satisfied?'

'Cirencester's nice,' said Thea faintly.

'Not a lot of nightlife, though.'

'Not like Gloucester.'

Caz Barkley gave a brief laugh. 'Some choice! I'll be thirty next birthday. I guess that means I'm in the right place. We'll see how it goes, anyway.'

'Are you all working overtime on this murder case?'

'Sort of. Not like on the telly, though. Do you

watch all those police dramas? Honestly,' she went on without waiting for an answer, 'they're ludicrous sometimes. There was a French one a while ago, where this woman detective doesn't sleep for about four days, and still goes running around a derelict industrial site by a beach, in bare feet. And she's pregnant. Ludicrous!'

'Why's she got bare feet?'

'That's another thing – she always wore these stupid shoes with heels. So, when she had to run over the pebbles, she fell over. So she took them off.' Caz looked down at her own sensible trainers. 'And then she had to run about a mile, half-carrying a girl who'd been shot, chased by a man with a gun.'

'Sounds exciting,' said Thea. 'I don't think anyone believes it's really like that.'

'I hope not, because it isn't.'

'So, you get a decent night's sleep, then. That's good.'

'Generally speaking, yes. We're not like junior doctors, anyway. And even they get more sleep than people think.'

They were back at the house, with Hepzie reluctantly trailing after them. 'It would be good to meet your husband,' said Caz hesitantly. 'I've heard such a lot about him. He's a bit of a local celebrity, according to the super.'

Thea laughed. 'He won't like that.'

'In a nice way. People like him.' She stopped, with a look of embarrassment.

244

Thea quickly grasped its import. 'More than they like me, I suppose. I'm the busybody who can't look after a house without letting a murder happen somewhere just down the road. Don't worry – I know all about my own reputation. That's mainly why I stopped doing the house-sitting.'

'That's not at all what I've heard.' Again she stopped. 'But if he's busy, I can leave it for now.'

'He might be. And I ought to be getting everybody some supper. There are funerals to arrange – always lots to do.' The words sounded corny and hollow in her own ears, but she sincerely hoped the woman would not hang around any longer. 'I'm sure we'll meet again soon,' she added.

Drew was tousled and unmistakably stressed when she went back indoors. 'Linda Biddulph's cancelled the burial,' he blurted, the moment he saw her. 'There is no way she's going to risk a confrontation at the graveside.'

Chapter Twenty-One

'She can't do that,' said Thea breathlessly. 'Didn't she sign an agreement or contract or something? What will she tell Lawrence?'

He shook his head. 'Nope. No contract. That's not the way it works. A funeral's too final – you have to get it right first time.'

She had heard him say this several times before. The logical implication had to be that families could change their minds right up to the last minute. Not that anybody ever did – until now. 'She's insane,' she said. 'What difference is it going to make? Lawrence has got to know eventually that he's got half-brothers. I still can't see why it matters so much.'

'No.' Drew was thoughtful. 'I think there must be more to it than she's told us. She sounded really scared at the very idea of seeing Clovis and his mother.'

'Not to mention Luc. Does Linda know he's in a wheelchair, I wonder? Did his father hear about his accident when it happened? The weirdest part is that Lawrence never knew there was another Biddulph family, not so far away. Surely somebody would have mentioned it? In a shop or bank or something – they'd say "Oh, I know a Biddulph, lives – wherever it is. Any relation I wonder?" Wouldn't that arouse his curiosity?'

'It might. But his mother would fob him off with some story about third cousins, or the "Stoke-on-Trent Biddulphs" who come from a completely different family.'

'I bet she and Stephen always made a big thing of him being the only son. Inheriting the house and any other stuff they might have. So now she's got to admit she told him a pack of lies all his life, and that frightens her. She probably thinks he'll never speak to her again.'

'She might be right.'

'With that wife of his, it's fairly likely, I guess.'

'So, what are we going to do?' She knew how concerned he must be at losing the funeral. If the news got out, it would reflect badly. But, of course, Linda Biddulph would do all in her power to prevent the news from getting out.

'She might think again, with any luck. She *liked* the place so much, when I took her to see it. She was in raptures about it – couldn't wait to tell Lawrence all about it.'

A thought rendered Thea silent. Other flimsy

floating notions were coming faintly into focus. 'When did you take her to see the field?'

'Oh – I don't know. The day she came to arrange the funeral, wasn't it? Oh, actually, no, it was the day before that. Wednesday. She didn't have time to come to the office, so I met her at the field so she could have a look at it first. We were only there ten minutes, at most. Then she drove off, and came back on Thursday to make the arrangements. That was when she told me about keeping it all secret.'

'And you had your moral dilemma,' Thea nodded. 'Seems a long time ago now.'

'It certainly does.'

'But that wasn't when you saw Juliet, was it? What time was Linda there? Did you go back again later that same day?'

'Steady on, officer. Don't I get to have my legal rights read to me first?'

'Shut up. Listen – do you think Juliet might have seen Linda? Maybe she knew her, as well. She knew Luc, after all.' She nibbled her lower lip in an effort to straighten her thoughts. 'No, that doesn't work. There's no reason why Linda should have anything to do with the Paxford Centre. For all we know, she's never even *met* Luc or Clovis.' She sighed. 'Sorry. I'm getting carried away, trying to connect everybody up.'

'There was no sign of Juliet when Linda was there. It was roughly two o'clock, at a guess. I came back here for a couple of hours, and then went down again to mark Mr Fleming's plot for Andrew. That was when I saw her. She came through that gate into the upper field, looking quite shy, and asked me if I liked being an undertaker. I've *told* you all this already.'

'You didn't tell me that bit,' she said mildly.

He shrugged and the stressed look intensified. 'What am I going to *do*? I've got Mr Biddulph here all coffined up. All the paperwork's done. I've never had a situation like this before.'

'I don't see why you have to do anything. It's all up to her and Lawrence, surely? She'll find another undertaker, who'll be happy to use your coffin, I imagine. You charge her for that and wasted time, and anything else you can think of, and wash your hands of the whole family.'

'Meanwhile, there are three people camping in my burial field,' he reminded her.

'Oh yes.' She was jolted into a new line of thought. 'I could go down and tell them, if you like.'

'They won't believe you. They'll think it's a ploy to get rid of them.'

'I'll convince them,' she said with groundless confidence. 'They seem to quite like me.'

'You mean you like them. But I can't imagine you can make anything worse, and we owe it to them to give it a try.'

'Do we? Why do we owe them anything?' She gave him a puzzled look.

'The sons, I mean. Doesn't it strike you that all three of them have been treated like pawns in some horrible adult game? The father and his two wives, fighting over something we don't understand, and keeping the brothers apart from each other all their lives?'

'Yes – but it's Lawrence who suffered most, not the others. Don't you think?'

'Not really. Seems to me it works both ways equally. If that'd been me, and my dad went off and had other kids, pretending I never existed, I'd have been . . . very upset.'

'You were going to say "devastated",' she teased him. They both regarded that particular word as forbidden, on the grounds of serious overuse.

'But I didn't. Anyway, the point remains. It's an outrageous thing to do.'

'I agree. But Stephen must have been the one to insist on it. It's all his fault, and now he's dead everybody has to try and make the best of it.'

'Which they're not really doing, are they? They're digging the hole deeper by the day. Or Linda is.'

Thea gave a little moan. 'Let me go and talk to them. Maybe they'll make me a cup of tea and explain the whole story.'

He waved an impatient hand in her direction, sweeping away the whole Biddulph family. 'Are we having any supper today?'

'Any other wife would tell you to answer your own question – but I'm far too nice for that.'

'It's my Achilles heel,' he said. 'Not only do I like to eat, but I like someone else to get it ready for me. So do my deplorable children. I realise this is desperately unfair.'

'It is. But I've got a really nice salad practically ready. Scotch eggs, cold chicken, pickled onions – everybody's favourites.'

'How?' he demanded. 'When you've been out all day?'

'Magic,' she told him. 'Go and see what they're doing, and say it'll be ready in fifteen minutes.'

Alone in the kitchen she ransacked the back of the fridge, and its thinly filled salad drawer. There were tomatoes and beetroot in there. The scotch eggs were about to achieve their sell-by date, and the cold chicken had been bought for the Coopers' visit and then somehow overlooked. There was also a small and rather dry remnant of the previous day's roast. 'Too much meat,' she muttered to herself, before she remembered that she and Stephanie had sown some lettuces in pots on the patio, and one at least had grown big enough to provide a few leaves.

'Home-grown lettuce,' she announced, when everyone turned up at the appointed moment.

Stephanie squealed in protest. 'You can't pick them *yet*.' Thea remembered that the child's mother had been an avid gardener, selling produce in a local market and knowing precisely when to sow and when to reap.

251

'It's just a few outer leaves,' she soothed. 'Not the whole plant.'

'Yummy,' said Drew, having nibbled one of the tiny offerings.

They ate dutifully, and Thea thought about the thousands of meals she was going to have to prepare in the coming years, until Timmy was eighteen and finally left home. She was completely determined that both children *would* leave home at or about eighteen, albeit only for about thirty weeks of each year for a while.

She remembered her own mother sighing about 'the endless bloody meals' that her life consisted of. Not given to swearing as a rule, the demands made on the mother of four children were never fully accepted. And then Jocelyn, her younger sister, had produced *five*, who presumably all wanted regular food. Even if they could cook and wash up, and make their own beds (did anyone actually make beds these days?), and feed the pet guinea pigs, somebody still had to buy the raw materials and pay for them, and generally keep track of it all.

'Okay,' she said, pushing back her chair. 'You won't be needing me for an hour or so, will you? I'll be back for bedtime.' She looked at Drew hopefully: he hadn't put them to bed for a few nights now.

'We'll be fine,' he said, with a smile that looked effortful. 'Good luck.'

'Where's she going?' asked Timmy of his father.

'To talk to some people. I should really be doing it, but Thea's probably going to make a better job of it.'

The little boy appeared to be considering a further string of questions, and then to change his mind. 'Oh,' he said.

'Did Maggs and Den get home all right?' asked Stephanie, who worried about road accidents.

'I'm sure they did,' said Drew.

'But you don't know for certain?'

'We'd have heard if they didn't. Maggs had some funeral work to see to today. If she hadn't shown up, the people would have phoned me to ask where she was.'

'Yes, but—'

'That's enough, Steph. You can get down now and go and finish that homework.'

As a last-minute thought, Thea invited her dog to go with her to the burial field. The brief run a couple of hours before had barely been enough. And the company would be nice. They set off together on the short walk that was becoming extremely familiar, and in only a few minutes were at the entrance to the field.

The camper van was still there, nestled into the hedge on the farthest side. Again, there was no sign of life until she got closer. Then she heard voices, and found the little family on camping chairs out of sight behind the vehicle. *At least they're being discreet*, she thought. Hepzie bounded up to them, tongue lolling, tail wagging.

'Hello, nice doggie,' came a female voice. 'And what's your name, then?'

'She's called Hepzibah,' said Thea, still fleetingly proud of the inspiration that had chosen something so distinctive, seven or eight years before. She looked at the three faces, noting how similar two of them were. Clovis Biddulph looked very like his mother. Something about the deep-set eyes and convex brow matched an instinctive aesthetic appreciation that conferred an impression of beauty on them both. Kate was grey-haired and weathered, but her bones would never change. Her long neck and well-defined jaw was also echoed in her son. 'Isn't he like you!' she breathed, in spite of herself.

'So they say.' She smiled, not at Clovis, but at her other son. 'And Luc's very like his dad.'

Clovis was giving Thea one of his looks, which she was doing her best to avoid. He stood up and took a step closer to her. 'We didn't expect to see you again this evening,' he said.

'No. Well . . . I've got something to tell you. Drew says you won't believe me, but—'

'Try us,' he invited.

'Drew called Linda and told her you were here. He had to, you see. She's his client. He's answerable to her. And he's worried about the funeral going wrong. Anyway,' she ploughed on as they all silently attended to her words, 'she said she's cancelling the whole thing in that case. The burial's off. Some other undertaker's going to have to do it. So your being here is for nothing. You might as well go.'

'I believe you,' said Kate. 'But I'm not sure I believe her. What if it's all bluff? She'll wait till your husband calls back to say we've gone, and then carry on as planned. Look – the grave's there now. She'll have to pay you for wasted time. And from what I know of young Linda, she's not one to waste anything, least of all money.'

'He's not going to call her back,' said Thea, not at all certain that this was true.

'She'll call him, then. They can't just leave it up in the air, can they? Stephen died nearly a week ago now, and I know you don't go in for embalming. To put it as delicately as I can – there's an issue here about time. I also know that undertakers in this country are nearly always booked up at least a week ahead – more often two weeks.'

'That's not quite right,' said Thea. 'There's always something early or late in the day that can be fitted in at short notice.'

'For their mates, maybe. Not some hysterical female who can't make up her mind.'

'Ma's right,' said Luc. 'And why does it matter so much to bloody Linda, anyway? What's she so scared of? That's the bit I can't understand. Never have been able to. What's so terrible about us, that we have to be kept such a secret, even now that our father's dead?'

'It's just a stupid sort of pride,' said Kate. 'Women as a rule don't like to be the second wife. They think it demeans them somehow. So she's always pretended to everybody that she was Stephen's one and only.'

'I'm a second wife,' said Thea. 'I can't say it bothers me.' But even as she spoke she knew it wasn't strictly true. She had never met Karen Slocombe, but never forgot that she had known and loved Drew for ten years or more, and was therefore both senior and superior in ways that could never be expunged.

'How do you know so much about Linda?' asked Clovis of his mother. 'You've never said any of this before.'

'I have my spies,' she said with a laugh. Then, when nobody even smiled, she elaborated. 'You probably don't remember your father's Aunt Etty? She died a couple of years ago, in her nineties. Until then, she often visited Steve and Linda. Well, she always liked me, and we'd get together every now and then for a gossip. She disapproved of Linda, especially keeping such a secret from her boy, but she blamed Stephen for it mostly. He doted on the boy, you know. Spoilt him, really. Kept telling him he was the best thing that ever happened to him, and how like himself he was. Not just in looks but interests and abilities – the whole package. So according to Etty, the very idea of other sons would have shaken Lawrence to the foundations.'

'So that's why Linda's so terrified of him finding out,' said Thea.

'Pretty poor show for me and Luc,' said Clovis. 'Disowned so completely by our father.'

'Probably healthier in the long run than being so overprotected, like Lawrence was,' said Kate.

'Was Etty the sister of the French grandmother?' asked Thea, trying to construct a family tree in her head.

'No, no. She was Stephen's father's sister. Henrietta, to be precise.'

'I do remember her, actually,' said Luc. 'Very frizzy hair and a long chin. Wasn't she my godmother?'

'Good God, I think she was,' said Kate. 'I'd quite forgotten that. You went to stay with her for a few days when you were twelve.'

'She let me sort out her stamp collection,' Luc reminisced. 'She said she'd leave them to me – but I suppose she never did.'

'Not to my knowledge,' Kate admitted. 'She probably sold them ages ago.'

'So,' said Thea, aiming for a decisive tone, 'what's going to happen now?'

'Nothing this evening,' said Clovis quickly. 'We can't up sticks now. We'll see what's what in the morning.'

'Lovely time of year for camping,' said Kate. 'Dawn chorus and all that. No sign of rain for days yet, apparently.'

Which sent Thea's thoughts rushing off to the

Spillers, Mr Fleming and his early morning burial. She wondered whether Luc Biddulph knew Nancy Spiller, and whether she dared ask him. A pattern or network was coming into focus, more all the time. Or, more accurately, it was as if a drawstring were being slowly closed, pulling all the disparate individuals together into a picture that really ought not to include them all. At the centre was Juliet Wilson, known to them all, and killed violently by somebody who could so easily be one of the people Thea had spoken with over the past few days.

'Drew won't want you here,' she said. 'There are more funerals this week. He'll get the police to move you.'

In a mutual accord, they all turned to look at the new grave, dug that afternoon by Andrew, waiting for Stephen Biddulph. 'Will they fill it in again or use it for someone else?' asked Clovis.

'Use it, I guess.' Miss Cotton would no doubt lie there instead. It felt wrong, unlucky, as if a cosmic plan had been overturned. 'Although I'm not at all sure.'

'We can't go while there's a risk that the burial will go ahead tomorrow,' said Kate. 'Not after all this.'

All this echoed in Thea's head. 'I must say, I still don't properly get why it matters so much to you,' she admitted. 'That sounds bad, I know. I can sort of see your point, obviously. But if Linda doesn't want you, don't you think you should respect her wishes, even if they offend you? It's all rather horrible, fighting over a dead man like this.' She was looking at Clovis, recalling his fury when he first telephoned, and noting how much he'd mellowed since then. 'She is wrong, I know. I said so to Drew last week. But she's lost her husband, and she knows she'll have to come clean to Lawrence about you three. Can't you give her some space – cut her some slack, as they say? It would be so much more dignified.'

'Which is what your precious husband values most of all, isn't it? Dignity and decorum.' Clovis was actually *sneering* at her, with his beautiful features.

'It is, actually. That's his job. That's what he does. It's extremely important, whether you realise it or not.' She met his eyes, and her heart fluttered. Fighting with him was insanely exhilarating. It made her feel alive and full of energy. Across the field she could see her dog racing after a squirrel, ears flying like wings. *That's how I feel*, she thought.

He looked down from his five foot eleven, and exhaled loudly. Now he was *scoffing*. 'Come on, Clo,' said his brother worriedly. 'Don't start on her. She's just the messenger.'

'We said all along we wouldn't cause any trouble,' said Kate. 'Maybe we should just pack up and go first thing tomorrow, after all.'

Clovis and Thea both looked at the waverers, something akin to disappointment in the air between them. He was relishing the spat as much as she was, Thea realised. There was no mistaking that look, as his eyes locked onto hers again. The wonder was that the others couldn't see it just as clearly.

'Definitely not,' he said. 'We're going to see it through to the end, now we've got this far.'

Chapter Twenty-Two

'I didn't get very far with them,' Thea reported back to Drew. 'It was pretty much as you said. They think Linda's bluffing.'

'What a mess,' he moaned. 'I'm not even sure what the right procedure is.'

'You mean, can you use that grave for somebody else?'

'What? Oh, no. That's not the issue at all. It's *money*, basically.'

'Right. Of course.' She was putting all her energy into appearing normal, getting the right level of concern for the business. He would expect her to have a reaction to the Biddulphs beyond ordinary interest, but not to an excessive degree. 'But *will* you use the same grave?'

'Why not?' He frowned at her. 'That's a minor point, surely?'

'Probably. I don't really know what to say. Kate's

a perfectly pleasant person, and both her sons seem very fond of her. There's a nice atmosphere, anyway. In fact, they're a lot nicer than Linda and Lawrence. You appear to be on the wrong side.'

'As if I had any choice. I'm not required to like all my families, am I? I still owe Linda a duty of care – and she's been very clear about what she wants me to do. I've failed her, basically.'

'You had no choice there, either. *You* didn't tell Clovis when the funeral was. Nobody did. Not until today, anyway.'

The children were upstairs, not quite in bed, and expecting stories. Yet again, Thea wondered at her own failure to anticipate the relentless evening routine of ensuring adequately brushed teeth and proper debriefing of the day's events, as well as a nightly story. With a bedroom each, this meant two different stories. Drew did his share, but there was no dodging it for Thea, who had bagged Timmy as the recipient of her readings. Surely, they were almost old enough for that particular ritual to stop? They could both read perfectly well enough to acquire the stories for themselves. But Drew was adamant. 'It's not just the story – it's the closeness. The attention. The relaxing conclusion to the day.'

'Of course it is,' Thea had sighed. When she agreed to marry Drew, so many of these domestic duties had failed to impinge on her imagination of how life would be. She loved him very much. She wanted to be married to him. She was well disposed towards his children, pitying them for the loss of their mother, and eager to earn their affection. The details would sort themselves out, she had supposed. And they had, with much less trouble than might have been expected. But there was a price to pay, which seemed to mount up with every passing week.

Now she set aside all thoughts of Clovis Biddulph and Juliet Wilson and Caz Barkley, and went upstairs to read another chapter of *Saddlebottom* by Dick King-Smith. They had bought a boxful of his books at a car boot sale, and Timmy loved them. Fortunately, Thea rather liked them as well.

She was just settled comfortably on the edge of the child's bed when the phone rang. 'I'll go,' shouted Drew, already halfway down the stairs. A minute later he was calling up, 'It's for you.'

'Ohhh,' whined Tim.

'Who is it?' Thea yelled.

'Gladwin.'

'Tell her to call back in fifteen minutes. She won't mind.' And evidently she didn't, because Drew was soon back in Stephanie's room, immersing them both in a story about Tracy Beaker.

Gladwin was punctual to the second, greeting Thea with a slightly snappy, 'Not used to being fobbed off, in my line of work.'

'Sorry. It was story time.'

'So I gather. Luckily, things have gone a bit quiet

for the moment. We're all taking the night off, fingers crossed.'

'So you're at home?'

'Right. Barkley filled me in on your little chat, by the way. That's why I'm phoning.'

'What did she say?'

'She thinks you're a creature from another planet. In her world, able-bodied women in their forties all have demanding full-time jobs. At first, she assumed you work with Drew, taking on a proper share of the funeral business. Then she thought you must have some sort of disability – or one of the kids did. I had to spell it out to her in short sentences. Now she doesn't know what to think.'

Thea winced at this perception of herself as an idle parasite. 'So, what about the murder? I don't think I was very helpful, was I?'

'That was my fault. I didn't brief her very well. It wasn't until she came back that I realised how unorthodox your position is. I'd forgotten, I guess.'

'You take me for granted.'

'Something like that. But she's keen to have a closer look at the Spillers. Seems he wasn't entirely straight with us, giving the Broadway address when he's not living there any more. It took us an hour to track him down in Chipping Campden. We'll be having another talk with him in the morning.'

'Oh dear,' said Thea. 'You can't really think he did it – can you?'

'That's not the point, as you very well know,' said Gladwin severely. 'What I think – in the way you mean – has nothing to do with anything.'

'I see.' And she did. Gladwin's tendency to let female intuitions and hunches direct her quest for evidence had been noted and criticised by someone above her in the police hierarchy. By employing Thea as an unofficial assistant, she was only increasing this deplorable habit. 'Well, I trust you to get to the truth of it all, eventually. You won't be charging an innocent man.'

'I'll do my best not to.'

'Is there anything else you want me to do, then?'

'Well . . . there's still Adam Rogers. Caz was supposed to talk to you about him, but I gather it got forgotten.'

'I'm not sure . . .' Thea began.

'No, I realise it's a lot to ask. He does need careful handling. What I thought was – maybe you could go to Blockley and have a look at Juliet's housemates at the same time? Adam's staying there for the time being, as well, for complicated reasons. He wants to be near her things, and the people who knew her. He's doing a kind of "grieving by numbers" exercise.'

'Say that again.'

'It's not as daft as it sounds. If you bear in mind he's stuck at the age of about six, it makes more sense. He understands what's happened, more or less, but isn't sure what he's meant to do about it. Somebody suggested he should find people to talk to about Juliet, and it all went from there.'

'He's not in her actual *room*, is he? Wouldn't that be rather too much?'

'I'm not actually sure. It could look a bit pervy, if so, if your mind worked in that sort of way.'

'You haven't closed it off, then? With police tape and all that?'

'Of course we haven't. Why would we? She wasn't killed there. We obviously searched it for anything that might give us some leads, but there wasn't anything. We couldn't find her phone, and she didn't keep a diary. Listen – Adam Rogers does look interesting on paper – if you just stick to the basic facts. But it's almost impossible to imagine him killing anybody. Plus, if that tracker he wears can be trusted, he was nowhere near the woods on Friday night or Saturday morning. Nor all that day. The thing isn't totally reliable, of course, but it would take more planning than he appears to be capable of.'

'So why do you want me to go and see him?'

'He might know something. He might have heard Juliet talking about somebody she was nervous about – or even throw more light on why the hell she was in those woods for three days in the first place.'

Something felt wrong in this. 'That sounds rather official,' she ventured. 'I'm not really sure I should be doing it. I mean – what if he suddenly bursts out with a confession? What do I do then?'

Gladwin was quiet for a moment. 'You're quite right. It is too much to ask of you.'

'The other thing is – who do I tell them I am, if I go to the house? They don't know me at all, and I can't pretend to be with the police, can I?'

'I'm not asking you to do that. But it wouldn't be entirely unorthodox. Civilians work for the police in all sorts of capacities these days.'

'Without any training? Or support? Isn't it more admin and filing and that sort of stuff?'

'You're welcome to come and do some filing, if that's what you prefer.'

'No, thanks.'

'Sorry. It's me. It's all getting a bit desperate, to be honest with you. And there's this other name Caz came back with. Biddulph? Is this something I need to know about, because if so, you can at least explain why. All Caz had grasped was that one of your funeral people turns out to have known Juliet in the Paxford place.'

Thea was strongly tempted by this opportunity to dismiss the whole Biddulph family as irrelevant to the police investigation. She had been hoping throughout the conversation that Caz had forgotten to pass on the name, or that Gladwin had deemed it of no interest. 'Oh, that's a bit of a red herring,' she said airily. 'There's been a glitch with the funeral, which has got Drew in a tizzy. Family feuds and all that.'

'But one of them did know Juliet? Luc with a "c" – is that right?'

'Yes. He's in a wheelchair, though – so he can hardly go onto your list of suspects. Even if he got Juliet to push him across two fields, so he could kill her, he'd never have got out again by himself.'

'He might have been with someone else,' murmured Gladwin. 'And this other person? Nancy Spiller? What about her?'

'Well, she's quite big and strong-looking. She had CBT at Paxford. Your Barkley girl had to remind me what that stood for – I got marked down for my ignorance. But Nancy didn't seem to know Juliet. She didn't react when I said the name, at least.'

'They called her "Big J" most of the time, not Juliet. We'll have to go and see her – the Spiller lady.' She sighed. 'I'm not happy about the Spillers, I must admit.'

They were back to where the conversation had started. 'So you said,' Thea remarked. 'Isn't "Big J" a bit rude?'

'Not really. Affectionate, as I understand it. Haven't we long since established that everybody loved the wretched woman?'

'So – I still don't know how I can best be useful to you. I will go to Blockley if you really want me to, but I don't much want to.'

'And I certainly can't order you to, can I? No, you're absolutely right. It looks as if your work is done for the time being. Go and help Drew with his glitch, and I'll keep you in mind. Okay?'

'Okay.'

'Look, Thea, you've given me new things to think about. New names and connections. That's great. And I shouldn't have asked you to see Adam Rogers. That was wrong of me. Well done for putting me right.'

Gladwin sounded tired, almost defeated. The murder of Juliet Wilson had been even more shocking than murder always is. People who might have looked the other way when a much less popular person got himself killed, had rallied in horrified outrage at the attack on Juliet. They probably phoned the police constantly, and tweeted about incompetence and lack of progress. The list of suspects comprised a thin unlikely set of avenues of enquiry. Nobody on it had any persuasive reason for wanting Juliet dead.

'Don't worry about it,' Thea said. 'It'll come right in the end.'

'Maybe. It doesn't always, you know. There are plenty of unsolved murders in the files.'

'Get an early night, anyway. It'll look different in the morning.' Not just for Gladwin, but herself and Drew and the Biddulphs, and perhaps even poor Rosa Wilson.

'Yeah, it will. It's going to rain, according to the forecast.'

Thea laughed and put the phone down.

It rang again almost immediately. Assuming it was Gladwin with another question, Thea said, 'Now what?'

'It's me. Maggs,' came the voice. 'Can I talk to Drew?'

'Oh, sorry. I thought you were someone else.'

'Obviously. Is he there?'

'Upstairs, I think.'

'No, I'm in here,' interrupted a voice on the line. There was an extension to the landline in the office at the back of the house, and Drew had picked it up. 'Hi, Maggs.'

Thea put her receiver down for the second time in two minutes, and drifted into the kitchen to make some coffee. She had almost forgotten Drew's crisis over Maggs, probably because it made her feel so helpless. 'Wherever thou goest, I will follow,' she muttered to herself, wondering whether it was true in her case. She had no special love for the Cotswolds in general. It had, after all, been the scene of so many horrible episodes. But in every case she had come through a shade stronger, braver and more confident in her own abilities. It had helped her over the loss of Carl, and shown her a part of England that was both separate and typical. It was a microcosm of the class system, the layers of history, the ebb and flow of human settlement. It was beautiful and quiet and sometimes quite friendly. She could not think of anywhere she would rather be. Which, she knew, was not the same as wanting passionately to stay there.

And where *was* that passion, she asked herself. Even her feelings for Drew had settled into a calm that made her restless at times. He was good and sweet and easy to be with. She had never doubted her good fortune in meeting him. He had a core of steel that gave her a focus and anchor that she had badly needed. She was glad to measure herself against him, knowing he was always going to be better than her. It was, she was discovering, oddly liberating. He could live with her restlessness, within certain limits. He was grateful for her domestic services most of the time. He found her intensely interesting. What did it matter if her family and small group of friends all thought he was too good for her? She and he knew better.

But she did not relish the prospect of the marriage being tested. Her lunatic response to Clovis Biddulph was terrifying enough. If Drew now decided to change course, thanks to Maggs, that would add pressure of a different kind. Then there was Gladwin's tepid offer of some sort of employment, which had been so exciting only a day or two before. Now it seemed there had been second thoughts – perhaps because those senior to the detective superintendent had other ideas.

Outside, clouds were rolling in, closing down the evening an hour earlier than usual. Rain tomorrow, Gladwin had said. Would that impel the Biddulphs to go home as requested? Would the empty grave, just dug by Andrew, fill with water? Would that mean Miss Cotton couldn't have it, after all? Was that why they were traditionally dug only hours before the interment was scheduled?

As if conjured by her thoughts, someone was heard

coming through their front gate, and ringing the doorbell. She thought she knew who it would be and, when she opened the door, she found she'd been right.

'Mr Biddulph,' she said formally. 'My husband's on the phone, but please come in. He won't be long.'

Chapter Twenty-Three

Lawrence Biddulph was even more tousled and blotchy than before. The past two days had not been kind to him, as anyone could see. He stumbled into the hallway, eyeing Hepzie nastily and waiting to be escorted into one of the rooms.

'I'll just tell him you're here,' said Thea. 'Hang on there a minute.'

Drew was still talking to Maggs, his hand flat against his brow, his head bent forward over his desk. 'You said that already,' he was saying. 'It doesn't help.'

Thea waved at him, mouthing *Visitor for you.*

'I've got to go,' he told the telephone. 'I'll call you back – tomorrow probably. Don't do anything until then, okay?'

He slotted the receiver into its rest and looked up at Thea. 'Who is it?'

'Lawrence Biddulph.' She cocked her head backwards to indicate that the caller was right behind her, preventing her from making any further comment.

'Okay,' said Drew wearily.

She couldn't help herself. When the two men were together in the office, she left the door slightly open and lingered just outside to listen. Somehow, she felt the family had become hers, every bit as much as Drew's, and she had a right to keep up with what was going on.

'I've just had a mega battle with my mother,' the man began. 'There is *no way* she can cancel the funeral. I can't even understand what she's talking about. She won't tell me, just cries and then shuts herself in her room. It's insane.'

'Sit down and let's look at it,' said Drew. 'Although I don't think there's much I can say that'll help. Your mother made the arrangements. I have to follow her instructions.'

'Not if she's off her rocker,' spat Lawrence. 'Which she has to be, the way she's carrying on.'

At this, Thea silently tiptoed back to the kitchen. How come neither of them had foreseen this turn of events? What did they think Linda would tell her son? The truth was, they had both forgotten about him, at least as far as the funeral was concerned. There was nothing Drew could do, unless he cut his losses and simply told the man the real reason for his mother's actions. In his place, Thea would have been very tempted to do just that. Wouldn't it be saving Linda a whole lot of bother? But Drew would never do such a thing. He would sit and take the ranting and pleading and even threats, doing nothing to defend himself. And Thea wasn't sure she wanted to listen to that.

Linda Biddulph was a fool, obviously. She was only making everything worse by withholding the facts from Lawrence. A fool or a coward. What was she so afraid of? The burial of her husband had already degenerated into an undignified mess, which had apparently been her worst fear a few days ago. Thea recalled Drew's moral anguish on Thursday when Linda asked him to lie to Clovis if he phoned. Now things had moved on, to the point where there seemed to be no hope of pleasing everyone. Was there something beyond the simple fact of another family coming to Lawrence's awareness? That question had arisen before, and now pressed more urgently on her. The most obvious answer involved inheritance. Did the first Biddulphs have a claim on Stephen's estate? Perhaps so, if he had failed to provide proper maintenance for his sons, or reneged on an agreement. But they had made no hint of that, and surely they would have demanded their dues while he was alive?

The image of Lawrence's wife floated into her mind. And the child, Modestine. They had all been in Broad Campden on Saturday, for reasons that remained murky. Thea's habit of making connections asserted itself, and she began to follow threads. Had Lawrence bumped into Anthony Spiller, for example? It appeared that they both visited the burial field that day. If Spiller had still been hanging around, trying to recover from the shock of finding a body, had they coincided? It seemed unlikely, and irrelevant, but the thought persisted. More than anything, it made her realise that events and encounters were going on the whole time, outside her awareness. And outside that of the police as well. *Who knew what?* And who knew who? Was there somebody else, still unnoticed, who knew everybody? Anthony Spiller had not been completely honest, when he gave the Broadway address to the police. Perhaps, then, Adam Rogers had also been untruthful. Perhaps his tracker device was often removed and left at home. There was no legal requirement for him to wear it, after all. It was just a convenience for his house-parents. He could easily give the impression that he was asleep in bed, when all the time he was out in Broad Campden, on the edge of a wood, committing murder.

And Clovis Biddulph, strong and angry, a law unto himself – he could just as easily have been exploring the village, trying to discover the date and time for his father's burial. He could have lashed out at a woman suddenly appearing to witness his clandestine behaviour.

No, she decided firmly. That was going too far. Beautiful Clovis could never kill anybody. Nor could his brother, or his mother. And why in the world would they, anyway?

She heard footsteps in the hall. 'Well, there it is,' Drew was saying. 'I've done the best I can.'

It sounded both firmer and more final than his usual manner of speaking. 'All I can suggest is you try to talk calmly to your mother and come to a decision between you.'

'As if *that's* going to happen,' came the sulky response. 'You can't reason with her when she gets like this. She's like a mad dog.'

Hmm, thought Thea. That made another one for the list, then. A woman in the first stages of grief, panicking about old secrets erupting – could she possibly have been Juliet's killer? It certainly didn't seem impossible, hearing her son's description of her. She could evidently be intimidating, and Thea herself had regarded her as a control freak.

She waited another minute while Lawrence was ushered out and Drew came into the kitchen, shoulders slumped in a parody of exhaustion. 'I give up,' he said. 'Everybody's mad.'

'You were brilliant with him,' she consoled. 'Heroic.'

'Were you listening?' He looked as if this might be a final straw.

'Only to the first bit. Then I came in here and sat thinking about it all. Again.'

'All what? The Biddulphs or the murder?'

'Both.'

'But they're not connected.'

'No. But somehow they got entangled inside my head.'

'Well, I wash my hands of all that. You might

remember that Maggs phoned, just before that lunatic showed up.'

'I do. But Lawrence isn't the lunatic. He's the injured party. He's only in a state because he knows something's been going on behind his back.'

'He doesn't really know even that. He's caught between his wife and mother, and hasn't the gumption to sort it all out.'

'Maggs,' she reminded him.

'Right. Yes. Let me make some coffee first. I need something to keep me awake. I've got some hard thinking to do before first thing tomorrow.'

'What? Why? I can make some proper coffee, if you like. I got some of those nice Brazilian coffee beans last week, in case Maggs or Den wanted the real thing.'

'The thing is,' he began. 'The thing, Thea, *is*—'

He never used her name when talking to her. It hit her between the eyes like a stone. He was going to say something terrible, give her an ultimatum, or accuse her of wrecking his life. 'What?' she demanded. 'What is it?'

'Maggs has been approached by a group of funeral directors. They want to buy Peaceful Repose, lock, stock and barrel. For a ridiculously huge sum of money.'

Chapter Twenty-Four

Her first unworthy thought was, *Thank goodness for that*. In her instant, selfish world, such a turn of events seemed to solve a whole lot of problems in one fell swoop. A lot of very welcome money, combined with the relief of not trying to juggle businesses in two different places. On the face of it, it had to be too good to be true.

Which it was, of course. Drew did not look the slightest bit happy about it. If anything, he looked rather angry.

'Gosh,' said Thea carefully. 'That was quick.'

'They're vultures,' he snapped. 'Maggs must have said something to someone, and it got back to them. It's an informal approach, apparently, testing out the water.'

'She's not in a position to negotiate with them anyway. They must know that.'

'Testing the water,' he said again. 'They'll know

how I feel about them, but also that I might not be able to refuse a tempting offer.'

'Who are "they", exactly?'

He looked at her as if she'd asked, 'Who is Boris Johnson?'. 'It's a large conglomerate of funeral directors who own the vast majority of the business across the country. In fact, there are only a few truly independent ones left. It's like book publishers. But I didn't expect them to want to take on alternative outfits like mine. They'd totally ruin it, of course.'

'Would they? How?'

'Tidy it all up, build fences round it, charge about five times what we've been doing. Honestly, they're only in it for the money. That was why I left Plants in the first place. It was all about the money.'

'Oh.' Privately, she thought he sounded more than a little paranoid about the so-called vultures. 'But couldn't you make them agree not to do any of that?'

'Of course not. I can't control what they charge, can I?'

'But nobody would use them if they were so expensive.'

'It'd be a gradual process. They'd pack the graves much closer together, as well. There's another four or five acres to go before that piece of land's full. That's at least two thousand burials, maybe twice as many. And I dare say they've got their eye on other patches in the area, for expansion.'

'But—' She wanted to say something about it showing how successful he'd been, and how the general trend was so much towards simpler and cheaper funerals now that such malevolent plans couldn't possibly work. 'How much are they offering, exactly?'

'They didn't say *exactly*, but the woman who phoned Maggs said something like "Double the market value of the house and land." That has to be well over half a million.'

'Oh God – Drew! We could put it straight in the bank. We've got no debts. You could build a lovely office down the road, and maybe see about getting another field – make a proper parking area. All sorts of things. And still have loads to spare.'

He put his hands on each side of his face and squeezed. 'I can't believe you're saying you think it's a good idea,' he choked. 'When you can see I think it's appalling. Outrageous. Insulting. You don't really think that, do you?'

'I don't think anything at the moment. Except it's entirely up to you, and whatever you decide is fine with me. But you have to admit that doing nothing isn't an option. Without Maggs, you've got a problem – which I suppose is what the vultures have realised.'

He moaned. 'It's all falling apart. I can feel it coming down on top of me.'

'Don't panic,' she advised him. 'It's a good problem to have, if you look at it objectively. Now you know there are people who would buy Peaceful Repose, you're in a stronger position. You've got options.' She wasn't at all sure of her ground, but a sense of relief persisted, despite Drew's misery.

'Maggs seems to agree with you.' He gave her a look so forlorn she moved closer and hugged him. 'What you're both telling me is – get real and grow up. Stop being so idealistic.'

'No, no. Your ideals are what everybody loves about you. Nobody's going to force you to sell out to some soulless corporation that won't care a hoot about ecology or birdsong or saving unnecessary expenditure. Those things are important.'

'They are. I was worried that you hadn't altogether understood that.'

'Of course I have. So has Maggs. How can you doubt it?'

'Money does terrible things to people. It's frightening.'

'Not me or Maggs. Not really.' She shivered at her own disgraceful instincts. The mere words 'half a million' had sent her wits flying in all directions. The same must have happened to Maggs – who might reasonably expect to receive a healthy proportion of the cash. In fact, once it was looked at calmly, the whole fantasy began to collapse. For Drew's beloved Peaceful Repose to be destroyed would be a wholesale tragedy. 'Whatever happens, we'll make sure it carries on just as it is now,' she promised. 'There'll be somebody just waiting to take it over, instead of Maggs, if we can just find them. What about Pandora? What's she going to do now?'

Pandora, rather like Andrew, had drifted into Drew's orbit and stayed to help out. Pandora was possibly the only female gravedigger in Britain, as well as a priceless stand-in for Maggs, who couldn't always manage to be in two places at once. Originally a babysitter for Stephanie and Tim, she was a quiet capable person who was very much taken for granted.

'Funny how none of us asked that before,' said Drew. 'I think she'll just do whatever she's asked to. She might go back to babysitting, or gardening, or something else entirely. Maggs didn't even mention her.'

'Pity she isn't rich enough to buy the business. She'd make sure it carried on as always.'

'Not rich or ambitious enough. She wouldn't want the responsibility. She'd never cope. And she's a bit old now to embark on something so demanding.'

'Pity,' said Thea again.

'Besides – I don't want to sell it,' he burst out, rather loudly. 'It's *mine*. I created it from nothing.'

'Yes, you did,' she said, tiredly. 'Nobody's forcing you to do anything. Maggs can tell these corporate people to get lost.'

'It's capitalism, isn't it? Big greedy outfits swallowing up all the little ones, making them outrageous offers they can't refuse. It happens all the time. And it's *wrong*.'

Thea didn't want to talk about it any more. It felt as if there was nothing she could usefully say, and quite a lot she might say by mistake that would only upset Drew even more. She had done her best to feel they were a single unit, that whatever he wanted was fine by her – and had pretty well succeeded. She had quashed any voices asking *What about me and MY life?* She had forfeited any claim to an independent life by marrying him, anyway. Her place was at his side and her ambitions were all bound up with his. His children were very nearly hers as well, now.

'Let's have an early night, then,' she said. 'It'll look easier in the morning.'

He huffed a brief laugh. 'Tomorrow we've got to tackle the Biddulphs, for a start. I can't see that going away without a battle. And it's going to rain.' He looked out of the window. 'In fact, it's raining already.'

'So it is. I'd better put the dog out before it gets too heavy.' Hepzie was stubbornly resistant to going out in the rain, as a general rule. Rather glad to have something to do, Thea pulled on her boots and opened the back door. 'Come on, you,' she said. 'Early night all round, okay?'

Outside there was a steady drizzle falling out of a black sky. The village lane was silent, but she could just catch the sound of a car swishing by on the road beyond the church. She thought of Clovis huddled in the camper van with his mother and brother, and hoped it didn't leak. Again, the thought occurred to her that the weather might send them home, giving up on their intention of disrupting Stephen Biddulph's funeral. If that happened, she was unlikely ever to see him again. She would forget that handsome face, with its expressive features and direct gaze. She would bury the disgraceful sensations his gaze created inside her. It was all foolish delusion anyway. She had no notion what sort of person he really was, or what sort of life he led. Why wasn't he married, for a start? A man as prepossessing as he was must surely have been captured long since. His mother appeared to be more or less normal, raising her sons, marrying again, capable of laughing at herself. So the stereotype of a man too damaged by maternal mismanagement to ever succeed in relationships did not appear to pertain.

But it hadn't been altogether normal for Kate to develop such a fixation on her first husband's funeral. In fact, wasn't there something a bit obsessive about all three of them? Linda, too, had got under Drew's skin, with her implacable refusal to disclose the truth to Lawrence – behaviour that was responsible for the whole tangled business, in fact. If she had told Lawrence a week ago, to give him time to absorb the shock and even perhaps to want to meet his brothers, everything would be resolved by now. The funeral might be awkward, with stilted conversation, but at least it wouldn't have been whipped away from Drew at the last minute.

She went in again, and made herself and Drew hot milky drinks, as if to compensate for the depressing weather and escalating crises. Then she tiptoed into each child's room and made sure they had all their school clothes laid out for the morning. The half-term holiday was only two weeks away, she remembered with relief. A whole week off from the relentless round of clothes, lunches, games kit, and anecdotes about misbehaving classmates. Instead, she would have to entertain them somehow. A different sort of obligation would be imposed on her. There was, effectively, no escape. They would mutate into adolescents, with hormones, and silences, and classmates that behaved even more appallingly. By the time Timmy left home, she, Thea, would be well into her fifties, and all ideas of romance or adventure or challenging occupation long since turned to dust.

But Drew was looking endearing and boyish in his blue pyjamas, the worried frown barely visible under his light-brown fringe. His hair was thick and straight and he disliked it cut too short, so it fell into his eyes at times. There were innumerable worse fates than being married to such a man. Other women might question her wisdom, or even her motives, in jumping so blindly into such a commitment, but Thea had always needed to be half of a couple. Losing Carl had set her adrift and removed much of her identity. She had filled the gap with Phil Hollis, for a year or so, before realising there was some fundamental lack in her feelings for him. Now Drew had claimed her, rescued her, understood and treasured her – and she hoped she was doing the same for him.

Chapter Twenty-Five

Waking on Tuesday, Thea realised she'd been waiting for this day to come, as some sort of culmination of recent events. Even without the Biddulph funeral, it still felt like the moment when everything came to a head, for reasons she couldn't properly explain, even to herself. There were no obvious deadlines or engagements to be aimed for. Then it hit her: it was the anniversary of Carl's death, 19th May. Five years ago, her young husband had been snatched away in a stupid road accident. She had not consciously noted the date over the past several weeks – and yet, subconsciously, it must have been sitting there waiting to be remembered. And along with the date, there was a sense of having moved into a world without Carl. Another year had passed, and here she was with a new partner. Somewhere lurked the idea that Carl was giving her his blessing on this day.

She went downstairs feeling weirdly buoyant. You

were not supposed to celebrate the day on which your husband died, and she was doing no such thing. Simply taking a larger step than usual into the future with Drew. 'Morning, all,' she trilled, looking round the kitchen with a smile.

'It's raining,' said Stephanie. 'I need my coat with a hood, and I can't find it.'

'There's a giant puddle just down the lane,' said Timmy. 'I saw it out of my window upstairs.'

'That grave's going to be half-full by now,' said Drew.

'It won't last much longer,' Thea promised them. 'You know the saying "Rain before seven, fine by eleven." It always works.'

'Yes, but it's only twenty to eight,' complained Stephanie. 'And it's raining *hard*.'

'The coat's in your cupboard. It'll be much too warm for this time of year. What about your anorak?'

Fifteen minutes later, they were all three huddled under an umbrella, waiting for the school bus. Timmy's puddle was indeed prodigious, and threatening to overflow into the front garden of the house next door. The movement of the water seemed unusual, causing Thea to wonder where it was all coming from. Looking round, she concluded that the slight downward slope from the church to their house was enough to start a spontaneous waterway during a prolonged downpour, which was augmented by small rivulets emerging from one or two gateways along its route.

The bus arrived five minutes late and, once the children were safely aboard, Thea grasped the umbrella firmly and set off down the Blockley road for a look at the burial field. She had offered to do so, telling Drew, 'I'll be wet anyway, so I might as well go now. You can stay in the dry, then.'

'That's very noble,' Drew had said. 'Just see whether that camper van's still there, and peep into the grave while you're at it. Andrew will have covered it up, but water is bound to have got in.'

A car slowed down beside her before she'd gone thirty yards, and a man leant across to speak to her, looking far from friendly. 'Hello? Mrs Slocombe? I'm Tony Spiller. Remember me?'

'Oh! Mr Spiller. What are you doing here?' Too late, she heard the rudeness in her words. This was Anthony Spiller, who she had wanted to see the previous morning. Who was staying with a friend in Chipping Campden, having left his nice wife Nancy in Broadway. 'Sorry,' she amended.

'I was coming to see you, actually. I gather you visited my wife yesterday. I wanted to find out why you did that. I can't begin to understand what you thought you were doing.'

She had stepped closer to the car, bending down to talk to him through the open passenger window. Her jaw dropped, and she could think of nothing to say. She could not even remember what story she'd told Nancy, now.

'How did you find my address?' he pressed on. 'There's no way your husband would have it. Did the police give it to you? If so, I'm going to issue a formal complaint.'

Her feet were getting wet, standing in a muddy rivulet, where water was flowing along the main village street. There was water everywhere, even in Anthony Spiller's car, where rain was getting in through the open window.

'Where are you going, anyway?' he asked her.

'Down to the field.'

'Get in and I'll drive you.'

She saw no reason to refuse, even if he was cross with her. People were often cross with her, after all, and none of them had ever done her physical harm. 'Okay,' she said, pulling down the umbrella with an effort. 'But I'll make everything horribly wet.'

He tossed this away with a twitch of his head.

'I hope this isn't silly of me,' she said as she got in. 'So many grim stories begin with an innocent female getting into a car with a strange man.'

'Am I strange? You've got a phone with you, haven't you? And somebody has probably seen us.'

'Yes to the phone,' she lied, patting her jacket pocket. 'And no, nobody's seen us.' There were no houses close to that stretch of road, and certainly no people strolling past in the rain. 'And I'm not sure whether you're strange or not. You seem to be in rather a bad mood.'

'I should be back at work today. I suppose I'll go in this afternoon, pleading emotional distress or something.'

'What do you do?' Before he could reply, she was mentally listing possibilities. Social worker. Vet. Insurance assessor. University tutor.

'Computers. Software design.'

Thea remembered the booklined snug in the Broadway house, and tried to reconcile that with a man who spent all day at a keyboard. 'Oh.'

'Boring, right? It's not, actually. And it's remarkably lucrative, even now.'

They were already at the field, and Thea could see the Biddulph camper van still in place. A sudden reluctance to confront the family yet again made her shrink down in her seat. 'Why are you coming here, anyway?' Anthony asked her.

'Oh, I told Drew I would have a look,' she said vaguely.

'Is that camper supposed to be there? Seems rather peculiar.'

'It's not, really. But I think they're leaving today. it's all a bit complicated.'

He turned and gave her a searching look. It felt like being in a private enclosed box, with rain streaming down the windows, and condensation rapidly fogging up the inside. He was a nice-looking man, in his mid-forties, mildly overweight and pale. 'Why did you go to Broadway, exactly?' he asked her again.

'I thought you might want to talk about finding Juliet. You were obviously upset, and we didn't really listen to you properly, did we? I was worried about you.' She thought back. 'You hadn't told Nancy about it, had you? She had no idea what had been going on here.'

'That's right. It didn't concern her. That's the whole point,' he said obscurely.

'Sorry? What is?'

'I need to see if I can live on my own, without her doing everything for me. I can't be a proper adult when she's around. She means well, and I know it isn't that simple. I just . . . felt suffocated.'

This account did not sit entirely consistently with Nancy's version of their separation, which Thea supposed was not very surprising. 'You haven't got children?'

'No. She never wanted any. We would have made very inadequate parents, so she's probably right.'

'It's a lovely house.'

'It is. We bought it ten years ago. I was on a contract that paid silly money and she was bringing in quite a lot at the time. We felt very grand, I remember.'

'Oh. Well, I should go. I'm sorry if I annoyed you. This business with poor Juliet has got everybody behaving strangely. And there's a whole lot else going on as well.' She peered through the murky windscreen at the camper van, with a sigh. 'Just one damned thing after another, in fact.'

He laughed at that. 'Life goes that way, don't you

293

find? My trouble is that I can't take anything seriously for long. Even finding that body – I mean, it was dreadful, and I was in a real panic for a bit, but now it seems unreal. Just a wild dream that can't properly concern me. Or Nancy. She didn't know Juliet any more than I did.'

'Well, she *might* have done, you know. They both went to that centre at Paxford, as it turns out. Nancy said she'd never come across a Juliet, but that was before I knew they called her Big J. It's starting to seem as if everybody knew everybody. Even the man in that camper van goes there sometimes. He probably knows Nancy.' All of a sudden, her head began to hurt with all these connections and suspicions. Something inside it was squeezing painfully. 'It's alarming,' she finished faintly.

'What is?'

'Well – if they all knew Juliet, they might all have had some reason to kill her. Some hidden grudge or dirty secret that made them want her out of the way.'

'Such drama!' he scoffed. 'That's not how it works in the real world, surely?'

'I'm afraid it is – sometimes, anyway. People do terrible things, you know. If you can imagine it, somebody somewhere's doing it. That's the truth of it.'

'Lucky for me I've got no imagination, then. I just tap the keyboard and work out algorithms. I can't even begin to grasp why anybody would want another person to be dead.'

'Not even if you had a rich aunt who was leaving you all her money, and was taking too long to die?'

'Definitely not. I love my aunts. And uncles. When Dicky died, I was consumed with sorrow. Don't you love that word – sorrow?' He diverged into savouring the sound. 'He was such a perfect man – he should have lived for ever.'

'Mm,' said Thea, lost for something to say.

'So – who's the main suspect, then? The police must have some sort of idea by now.'

'And you think they'd tell me, do you?'

'I think they might. You obviously got my address from them, which must mean you're working with them somehow. I might be unimaginative, but I'm not stupid,' he added.

She was having trouble keeping up with his erratic thinking. Was this the sort of logic required for a computer programmer? She very much doubted it. There was an inconsistency at the core of this man, more apparent with every passing moment. 'You didn't go to the Paxford Centre as well, did you?' she asked.

'No, I never did. Nancy went for her depression, that's all. She's better now.'

'Is she?'

'Why? Do you think she's not?'

'I can't say. Why were you here, really, on Saturday? You don't seem the sort of person to be interested in songbirds.'

Her own erratic processes were prompted by a sudden

sense of urgency. Gladwin had given up on her. Drew was wallowing in indecision. Clovis was a chimera. Juliet was dead. All that remained was this Anthony Spiller and his perplexing place in the whole business.

'Is there such a "sort of person"? I came to visit Uncle Dicky. It seemed mean to just leave him here all by himself. I wanted to be sure there was some life here – birds, or wild animals, or *something*. And then I found a dead person. It felt like a cruel joke.'

'I'll have to go,' she said again. 'The rain might be stopping – do you think?'

'Hard to say. But somebody over there seems to think so.' He indicated the camper van, where Kate Dalrymple was standing in the open doorway. 'You know her, I gather?'

'Not exactly. I know who she is, but I only met her yesterday.'

'Well, she looks nice enough. Off you go, then,' he said unchivalrously. 'I can't think of any more we might have to say to each other.'

Moments later she was standing by herself just inside the field, her umbrella open again and the rain still falling. Then, before she could start walking, a great brown wave sloshed against her legs, as a car braked violently in the puddle between Thea and the edge of the lane. 'Hey!' she shouted.

A woman pushed herself out of the driver's door, her gaze on the camper van. 'Is that them?' she demanded loudly. 'Still here, I see. Just let me talk to them.' She didn't even glance at Thea, who assumed the words were only peripherally aimed at her. She watched as Linda Biddulph marched across the grass in thin shoes and a hoodless jacket. Clearly, weather was of no concern to her at all.

It was sixty or seventy yards to the van, which was too far to hear normal conversation. So Thea automatically followed Linda as she yelled at the woman who had preceded her as wife to Stephen Biddulph. 'How dare you? What do you think you're doing? What did I ever do to you? Have you no hearts, any of you? Have you any idea of what you've done already?'

It was not entirely coherent, and the decibels rose as Kate simply watched, saying nothing. Then she shifted sideways to allow Clovis to emerge. He, it seemed, was much less dumbfounded than his mother. 'I take it you're my father's wife,' he said pleasantly.

Thea, now only fifteen yards distant, savoured his melodious voice, as he adopted the deceptively courteous tone. Why hadn't he talked to her like that? He'd been brusque, then businesslike, and finally faintly friendly. But he hadn't crooned or cajoled, as she expected him to do now.

'Couldn't you *wait*?' Linda snarled. 'What harm would that have done you? All I asked was a few more days, for Lawrence to say a dignified goodbye to his father. After that, I was going to tell him the whole story, and take whatever consequences there might be for myself.' She was calming down quickly in the face of the handsome man and his nice-looking mother. 'Couldn't you at least have done that?' she repeated.

'What about *our* need to say goodbye?' said Clovis. 'Did that never occur to you? We really can't see why we should respect your wishes, after all these years of pretending we didn't exist. Can you imagine what that feels like? Remember that time when our mother tried to visit you, twenty years ago now? He and I were waiting in the car, hoping you'd ask us in. You slammed the door in her face, and shut yourself in a back room, as if we were axe murderers. And all we wanted was to see our father and meet our little brother.'

'Stephen slammed the door, not me,' said Linda, suddenly on the defensive. 'It was Stephen who insisted we keep you away from Lawrence. It was his fear of the truth, not mine, that kept things as they were for so long.'

'Fear of the truth? Why? What did he think we were going to do?'

'Dilute his love for Lawrence,' she said. 'Shake the boy's faith in him as a father. Topple him from his pedestal. And it *would* have done. It still will. And I don't want that to happen yet. Can't you understand?' She was actually pleading. Kate and Thea exchanged glances, sharing their astonishment at this rapid change of balance.

'I don't understand what difference it makes whether or not he's been buried before Lawrence hears about us.' Clovis stood with folded arms, his features growing harder. 'You're going to have to accept that there's no good outcome here. Whatever happens, somebody's going to lose out.'

'Lawrence has already lost out,' said Kate quietly. 'You've kept him tied to your apron, protecting him against something that wasn't even any threat to him. I don't believe it was all Stephen's doing. He wasn't like that. You kept him away from my sons, because you didn't like the idea of being a second wife. Or a stepmother. It's you that this is all about, so stop pretending anything else.'

Linda wiped a hand down her face, sweeping away the rain. 'You don't understand. You've got no idea what it was like, when Lawrence was little. He was such a difficult child, with eczema and asthma, hopelessly faddy about food and frightened of everything. Stephen got him through it. He took him for long walks, told him stories, fed him a tiny bit at a time. He was the most dedicated parent in the world. You've got it all absolutely wrong if you think I tied him to me. I was the one on the outside. The real relationship was Stephen and Lawrence. All I could do was try to keep things as normal as I could.'

'But Lawrence has got a wife and child now,' Thea burst in, no longer able to remain on the sidelines. 'He's a fully grown man.'

'Yes, that's right. And it was all thanks to Stephen. He nurtured that boy through a thousand crisis points. Exams, girls, sport, teachers, jobs – everything was a huge challenge to him, but Stephen took him through them all, step by step. It was heroic. And all he asked in return was respect. And rightly or wrongly, he didn't think he'd get that if Lawrence knew he'd been married before and had two other sons.'

'The shame belongs to you both,' said Kate. 'You and Stephen equally. You stole my husband away like a woman in a trashy television sitcom. And he went willingly, I know that. But there are consequences, my dear, that keep on going through decades. My mother, for instance. She adored Stephen, and was utterly bereft when he went. It made her sad for the rest of her life. I actually think it killed her, years before she should have died. And much worse than that was my own loss. I lost the daughter I so desperately wanted.'

'What?' Linda's voice was strangled.

'I aborted her. I was seventeen weeks pregnant, so they knew it was a girl. How could I go through with a third child, when my husband had told me so emphatically that the marriage was dead and buried? I was thirty-eight, so I had no illusions about further chances with a new man. You did that, Linda. You killed my mother and my daughter. I hope you don't sleep easily at night, with so much on your conscience.'

'Hey, Mum, stop it,' Clovis cajoled. 'I never knew I might have had a little sister. How old was I?'

'You were ten and Luc was seven. You know that already. It was only a little while after your father left us.'

Thea understood that he had asked the question as a device to bring his mother back to earth, making her aware of her surroundings. But she herself was still sharing the anguish that Kate had just revealed. Loss was the unavoidable theme. The violence of a broken marriage had ripped the fabric of a wide circle of people. And Lawrence, product of the guilty couple, had perhaps never had much prospect of a normal life. Secrets, evasions, constant fear of exposure had gnawed away at the three of them, manifesting in the little boy's allergies and phobias that required such dedication from his father as atonement. 'Poor Lawrence,' she said softly.

Clovis looked at her. 'Poor everybody. Even Linda deserves some sympathy. She fell for a man who ought not to have been available. An old, old story.'

'A story that never ends happily,' came another voice from inside the van. 'You forget what I lost.' Kate and Clovis automatically stepped down onto the grass, leaving the way clear for Luc. He was not in his chair, but propped on crutches, his legs crumpled uselessly beneath him. 'You forget that we're here now because of me.'

Thea watched his face, taking a moment to realise that she was seeing something familiar. A lost little boy, seven years old, striving to understand why a parent had so abruptly disappeared. To her horror she felt tears gathering at the top of her nose. Here was Timmy Slocombe, over thirty years on, still dealing with the huge internal wound that life had dealt him. And another layer of connection pushed to the front of her mind: Luc bore a very strong resemblance to his younger brother Lawrence. Three small boys, then, with hopelessly damaged childhoods. And that wasn't counting Clovis, who seemed to have oddly detached himself from the proceedings.

'Because of you?' she repeated.

'It was me who wanted to be at my father's funeral. I had to see him finally put away. I had to see for myself that he had been somewhere, alive and happy all this time, when, for me, he had stopped existing when I was seven. The funeral would prove it – it would show me his whole life in a few minutes.' He snorted. 'I can't explain it properly, but it's very important. I worked it out last week, when I was at the centre. There was somebody there who helped me to understand.'

'Juliet,' said Thea, with a renewed stab of horror. 'Juliet Wilson.'

'That's right,' said Luc Biddulph.

Chapter Twenty-Six

It was still only nine-fifteen when Thea got back home. The rain had lessened, but not stopped, and she was wet to the skin everywhere but her head and shoulders. The first thing she did was to peel off her jeans and pants, rubbing the chilly flesh of her legs with a towel.

'You were a long time,' said Drew, who was still in the kitchen with a mug of coffee.

'It feels like hours. A lot's happened. I need to talk to Gladwin.'

'They're still there, then?'

'I'm afraid so. And Linda's shown up to confront them. That backfired spectacularly.' She shuddered at the images of high emotion and recriminations. 'There were tears,' she added.

'I'm not surprised. But how does it concern Gladwin?'

'I don't know for sure, but I've had a ghastly idea.'

'So have I.'

She looked at him more closely, reproaching herself for not having done so sooner. He was very pale, with grooves under his eyes. 'What's the matter?'

'I keep practising what I want to say to Maggs – and you. It comes out different each time. I think I'm going mad. I feel horribly out of control. It's as if some outside force is in charge of me. And that's idiotic. I know it's down to me, that I can make my own decisions. But somehow it all slides away when I try to force it.'

'Oh, God, Drew,' she moaned. 'Do we have to do this now? I've just had the most awful time with the Biddulphs, and here's you sounding just the same as they did. What's the matter with everybody?'

His face hardened. 'Perhaps it's not them, but you,' he said. 'You flitting from one crisis to the next, never getting properly involved, never hanging around to face the consequences. Well, life is real and earnest, and sometimes you just have to stand still and take what it throws at you.'

She flinched, the words like icy water in her face. 'I *am* taking it,' she protested. 'I'm here, aren't I?'

'Barely.'

The icy sensation spread further. 'I think you'd soon notice if I wasn't. There'd be no food, for a start. Nobody to hold everything together, in fifty different ways. You don't seem to understand about all that.'

'I did it before.'

And could do it again went unsaid, but hovered

terrifyingly in the air between them. What was happening, Thea asked herself desperately. How had it come to this in such a short time? Had Maggs flicked a switch and cast a dazzling light on the weaknesses in the Slocombe marriage?

'But you don't want to do that,' she said as lightly as she could, as if the awful words had actually been spoken.

'Do what?'

'Manage without me. Do you?'

'Of course not. Isn't that what I just said?'

'Not really, no. But it doesn't matter. You're absolutely right. My concerns for murder and the police and people acting crazily out there should definitely come second to your problems. I'm not being sarcastic or anything – I know that's the way it is. So tell me the whole thing, and we'll see if we can sort it out together. Okay?'

'I have told you the whole thing. There isn't anything new to say. Except I can't endure the thought of selling Peaceful Repose. I had a horrible dream . . .'

She put up a hand. 'No dreams,' she begged. 'Can we please skip the dream?'

He smiled then. It had been an early rediscovery that having someone to listen to your dreams being reported next morning was one of the major perks of couplehood. 'But they're always so desperately *boring*,' Thea had sighed.

'Doesn't matter. It's your duty to listen,' he had

said at that time, with mock severity. In more recent times he had relented and kept his nocturnal visions to himself.

'Linda Biddulph is at the field,' Thea told him, unable to restrain herself. 'She might come here, I suppose.'

'She's going to have to tell me what to do with her husband's body, and I'm going to tell her she's liable for the whole cost of the funeral, whatever happens next.'

'Good for you. Quite right too. Plus some for the added hassle.'

'Maybe not. Meanwhile, I've got Andrew standing by for the interment at eleven. And I've had a call from Hambling Grange. They've got someone for us. The family could show up at any moment – although it'll probably be tomorrow.'

'It's good to be busy,' said Thea, as she always did. 'Which one is Hambling Grange?'

'The expensive one near Cirencester. It's a man who died last night. I met his son ages ago in Somerset, apparently, and he decided then to use my services.'

'I hope he told his old dad?'

'I suspect not. I only got a few hints on the phone, but it sounds as if they never actually discussed it.'

Thea shrugged. It was a familiar scenario, though less so in the case of alternative woodland burials. It was only a minority of people who could be induced to meaningfully discuss their final resting places, with no real sign that this was ever going to change. While it was quite common for people to carelessly announce 'I want to be buried under an old oak tree', or something of the sort, they rarely thought it through in any detail. They left their relatives to make the practical decisions – which generally omitted oak trees altogether.

There was a frozen atmosphere in the house, as if neither of them could move or speak freely. Thea was aggrieved that her experiences of the morning were not getting a hearing, and she was fairly sure that Drew felt rather the same. Their efforts to overcome these feelings were making little headway, while the world outside was clamouring for attention. Except, just at that moment, it was doing no such thing. Linda Biddulph had yet to materialise with her final decision, and nobody else seemed to want the Slocombes for anything. Even the spaniel was in her basket quietly licking her feet.

'Well, we can't just stand here,' said Thea. 'This isn't getting us anywhere.'

'The trouble is, we don't seem to know where we want to get.'

'It's all Linda Biddulph's fault.' The line was intended to raise a smile, but failed. In Drew's mind the Biddulph funeral had receded into a hopeless cause in which he was powerless. It could therefore be set aside in favour of more urgent and personal matters. 'Well, all right then. Most of it's nothing to do with her,' Thea amended. 'Although—'

'Don't say it,' he snapped, more angrily than she

307

had ever seen him. 'It's obvious you just want to get right into the middle of it all and sort everybody out. Solving a murder one minute and reconciling warring families the next. Well, go on, then. I'm not stopping you. You don't have to hang around here offering misplaced sympathy for my worries when that's obviously the last thing you want to be doing.'

Fear silenced her. Drew's anger was so unexpected, so unfamiliar, that she found herself entirely defenceless before it. Always, he had confronted disagreements with calm reason, refusing to be provoked into saying anything hurtful. She had assumed that everything he said was sincerely meant, without sarcasm, or irony, or ulterior motives. The assumption still held good, so she carefully reran his words just as he'd uttered them. 'You think I'm more concerned with all that stuff than I am with the future of this business,' she summarised.

'Well, aren't you?'

'No. But it's not a fair comparison. I can't make your decision for you, but I can help the police catch a murderer. I think I can, anyway. And if I can sit down with you and really look at all the options, sensibly, then I might be useful. But it's not at all certain. If I say I want to stay here now we're settled, and I think it's time you let all the Somerset stuff go, that might come across as undue influence. It might just make everything more difficult for you.'

'Do you? Want to stay here and abandon everything else?'

'I don't want it badly enough to affect what you

decide. I'll go along with whatever that is.'

'Will you really? Even if I say I want to sell this house here and go back to the one in North Staverton?'

She went cold. 'Is that what you do want, then?'

'Answer the question.'

'All right then. Yes, I think so. It would be a horrible upheaval, and I don't much relish living in your old house, and I have no idea what I would do with myself. But yes, if it comes to that, I'd go. Of course I would.'

He did not look any happier. 'But you wouldn't want to, which means you'd martyr yourself for my sake. And that would make me feel guilty.'

'It'll work itself out,' she said bravely. 'We're big, grown-up people. We can do this – whatever it is.'

'I hope so. Now go away, there's a good wife. Go and do what you're best at, and leave me to wallow. I'll be better by lunchtime.'

Then his head lifted. 'Footsteps,' he identified. 'Right on cue.'

'I can't hear anything.' But half a second later the doorbell rang.

Two female police detectives stood shoulder-to-shoulder, one significantly taller and thinner than the other. 'Oh! Both of you,' said Thea. 'Do you want to come in?' Looking past them, she observed with relief that the rain had finally stopped.

Gladwin's smile was fleeting. 'Probably best not. We could do one of our walks instead.'

Caz Barkley gave an audible sigh, and both older women looked at her.

'We have to go down to your field, and either you or Drew should be with us.'

'Oh?' A sense of something ominous was growing.

'The thing is, we've had a complaint. Inappropriate use of a cemetery, disturbing the peace and jeopardising the graves. Words to that effect.'

'Good grief. I'll have to tell Drew, then. Who complained?'

'I'd better not say. Is Drew available?' Gladwin peered through the open door into the hallway. 'Has he got a funeral today?'

'He did have, but it's on hold. Complications.' Thea still felt a resistance to bringing the Biddulph family to Gladwin's attention. Even after the revelations and connections of the early morning, she wanted Juliet's death and Clovis's jumbled relations to remain separate. But now somebody else had done the deed instead. The police would find the camper van, and ask questions and get things confused. 'I can call him,' she offered reluctantly.

The sound of a ringing phone prevented her from doing any such thing. 'He *is* quite distracted just now,' she said. 'Do you think we could go without him?'

'No problem. But we should get a move on. You don't seem too worried. What if somebody's desecrating your graves, as we speak?'

'They won't be, but I'm happy to go with you and

see.' She started walking up the lane. Gladwin hurried after her, and began to increase the pace. 'You sound very sure,' she said.

Thea pulled a rueful face that Gladwin didn't see. 'It's all a fuss about nothing. I don't know who complained, but I can guess. And I don't think we need to fear for the graves. It's a family feud, basically. Not a police matter at all. I was there an hour or two ago. Nobody's going to do anything criminal.'

'Has this got anything to do with Juliet Wilson?' Caz asked breathlessly. 'I mean – it's right beside the place where she was killed, isn't it?' She was trotting behind them, finding the pace uncomfortable.

'It's a regularly used burial ground. People come and go all the time. They visit their dead relatives, leave flowers, plant trees – all the usual things. Not to mention new funerals happening every couple of days.'

'So Juliet Wilson might have been doing something like that as well – right? Your husband was the last known person to see her alive, right there in your field. She might have been there for two days or more before she died. What was she *doing* there?' The young detective looked from Gladwin to Thea and back, eyes wide and questioning. 'Where did she sleep? Who knew she was there?'

'She didn't sleep rough. We'd have found the place,' said Gladwin heavily. 'And she didn't have a car. She didn't go home. Nobody we've spoken to has the slightest idea. Not even her mother.'

'Are you sure you'd find the place in the woods?' queried Thea. 'Was she wearing a coat? Couldn't she just have curled up under a tree for the night? I got the impression she'd do something like that quite happily.'

'At least seven hours of darkness, temperatures about four or five centigrade? What about food and drink? What would she *do*?' Gladwin repeated the emphasis that Caz had used. 'I can't see it. I think she went to a house somewhere, at least for Wednesday and Thursday nights. Maybe in Chipping Campden, which is barely fifteen minutes' walk away.'

'A house? Whose house?' Thea frowned at this suggestion. 'Must be somebody we don't know about. Is it the person who killed her, then?' The idea that there was a whole unknown aspect to the case that rendered all her own speculations irrelevant was irksome.

'Could have been an empty house. Or a shed in a garden. Somewhere a bit warmer than the open air, anyway.'

They were within sight of the field in another minute. The camper van was concealed behind the hedge, and Thea entertained a wild hope that it would be gone. 'That makes more sense,' she said. 'And it fits with what Juliet was like. She didn't have much respect for private property.' She recalled the first time she had seen the woman in Stanton. Juliet had walked right into the house that Thea was in temporary charge of, without knocking or waiting for permission. Her apologetic mother had arrived soon after, trying to explain Juliet's diminished capacity.

'The crucial thing is that she came back here sometime in the early hours of Saturday, and somebody else was here at the same time, who killed her. Whether they came together, or met by accident, or what, is still obscure. The truth is, we're hardly any further forward than we were three days ago.'

'Who's that then?' asked Caz Barkley, seeing the camper van. 'Must be what the complaint was about.' She looked at Thea. 'You knew that was here?'

Thea sighed and nodded. 'I was hoping they might have gone by now. Are you going to force them to move?' she asked Gladwin.

'Only if you want me to. It's your land. You can allow anybody you like to be on it.'

'So – the person who complained hadn't got any real grounds. Is that right? Why are you here, then?' Thea was still addressing Gladwin, who was already heading for the van.

'Curiosity,' came the brief reply, thrown over her shoulder.

'No. Wait. Come back.' Thea's brain was suddenly working overtime. 'I need to tell you some things first. You don't know the full story. You'll get it all wrong if I don't explain.'

The wiry, dark-haired detective paused, then turned to give Thea a very stern look. 'Then why leave it till now?'

'I don't know. I've had a lot of other stuff to think about. You turned up at an awkward moment. I've been dashing round since eight o'clock this morning, one thing after another and I got soaking wet. But don't just barge in there – especially if you're not going to get them to move.' She was staring at the van, searching it for signs of life. 'Actually, it doesn't even look as if anybody's in there anyway.' But she observed that the van door was open, and the wheelchair ramp in place.

'Explain, then. Quickly.'

'It's a family called Biddulph. I did tell you a bit about them yesterday, remember? Drew was supposed to bury their father today. This is his first wife and two sons. There's a second wife and one son – Lawrence. He doesn't know his father was married before, and Linda, his mother, wanted to keep it that way until after the funeral. But Luc – one of the other sons – and his brother and mother, wanted to be here for the burial. It's all been terribly difficult for Drew. Now Linda's cancelled the whole thing because Clovis found out, and they've come to make sure they don't miss it.'

Gladwin digested this slowly. 'I think I get it,' she said. She looked at Caz. 'Can you take some notes? Family name Biddulph. Two wives, three sons, family secrets.'

'Where did they go?' Thea wondered aloud. 'I assume it was Linda who made the complaint? She must have hoped you'd move them. Pity, in a way, that you can't. We might still have the funeral, then. Gosh!' she suddenly realised. 'I wonder if people will start

314

showing up for it. She can't possibly have told them all that it's been cancelled.'

Caz was writing in her notebook. 'Linda – second wife?' she queried.

Before Thea could reply, Gladwin said, 'No, it wasn't her. It was the Spiller man. The one who found Juliet on Saturday. He said there was obviously going to be trouble, and he was worried about his uncle's grave.'

'Oh. How very peculiar of him. He drove me here this morning, when it was raining. He didn't seem especially worried then.'

'People,' said Caz, pointing with her pencil at the opening into the next field where the dead Juliet had been lying three days earlier.

Chapter Twenty-Seven

Luc's wheelchair was bumping awkwardly over the grass, followed by Clovis, whose face was rather red. Now and then, he helped the chair over a bump but, mostly, Luc was propelling it for himself. Kate came not far behind. Luc was talking urgently, turning his head to address his mother and brother. It was too far for the three women to hear his words, but his listeners were obviously paying close attention.

'That's them,' said Thea, watching the magnetic features of the older brother, and noting that there were no longer any internal flutterings as a result. Instead, she regarded him with suspicion, remembering her various encounters with him, and their effects on her. What exactly was he? A hollow sham? A genuinely engaged and concerned son and brother? An angry resentful son of a neglectful father? All and any seemed possible, along with several others. Was he, just possibly, a murderer? And why had they gone for a muddy walk in an empty field? Suspicion was slow to dawn, and uncomfortable to entertain, but she did her best not to dodge it.

'Them?' echoed Gladwin.

It was too late for muttered explanations. The small group gathered speed once they were in the well-mown burial field, and were soon only twenty feet away. 'Mrs Slocombe,' Clovis said, with a warm smile. 'Back again?'

'These are police detectives,' said Thea boldly. 'They're investigating the murder of Juliet Wilson.'

'Blimey, Thea,' snapped Gladwin. 'Think before you speak, will you?'

'Big J,' said Luc, with a downward glance to suggest sorrow. 'I still can't believe it.'

'What were you doing through there?' Gladwin asked. 'That's where the body was found. Did you – or one of you, at least – know that already?'

Thea had been silenced by the detective superintendent's reproach. She didn't see what she'd done wrong – police protocol required that officers make themselves known before speaking to anyone associated with an investigation. But there were probably plenty of exceptions, in practice. Much must depend on timing and context. Had she done it deliberately to warn Clovis, she asked herself.

'Could I have your names?' Gladwin went on, before anybody could answer her first question.

'I'm Kate Dalrymple, and these are my sons, Clovis and Luc Biddulph. Luc is spelt L-U-C. The French way.' She watched as Caz duly wrote in her notebook. 'We were just stretching our legs. And Luc knew Juliet Wilson, so he wanted to see where she died. We none of us know the exact spot, but Mrs Slocombe had given us a fair idea.'

'Why are you here?' Gladwin glanced warningly at Thea, whose instinct had been to repeat her earlier explanation.

'We learnt that this is the place where my first husband was to be buried, and that his current wife was anxious for us to stay away. We were not given the exact day and time for the burial, so chose to camp here until it happened.' Kate spoke with clear formality, her face betraying no emotion. 'The current Mrs Biddulph was informed of our presence and has cancelled the funeral as a result. Or so we're told. We decided to hang on until the end of today, in case that was a bluff.'

'But you did know Juliet Wilson?' Gladwin looked at Luc.

'She pushed me around the grounds at Paxford, and we chatted quite a lot. I was very fond of her. It came as a great shock to hear that she was dead.'

'Could you give any account of why she might have been here last week?'

'Not really. She knew my father had died, and she might have been curious to see where he was going to be buried. She never met him, of course. I haven't seen him myself for over thirty years. But I showed her a picture of him as he was then. She said I was exactly like him.'

'You are,' said Kate. 'It's uncanny.'

'So Lawrence must be as well, because he looks like you,' said Thea. 'You've got the same long cheeks and thick black eyebrows.'

'We've never seen him,' said Kate shortly.

Clovis gave her a look. 'He's no oil painting, if he's like Luc,' he said with a mock punch at his brother's shoulder.

'It's character that matters,' said Kate. 'Not that we know anything about Lawrence's character.'

Gladwin was observing all this with an expression of impatient disbelief. People did not normally behave in so relaxed a manner when in the presence of a senior police detective. Thea concluded that the Biddulphs, like her, could see no reason to associate themselves with the killing of Juliet Wilson. The image of Anthony Spiller came to mind – why had the idiot called the police that morning, anyway? Surely he couldn't seriously think there was any threat to his Uncle Dicky's grave?

'Nancy Spiller might have known Juliet as well,' she said aloud, following a thread that felt important. 'They called her "Big J" at Paxford, so when I talked about Juliet, it didn't ring any bells.'

'What?' Gladwin's impatience burgeoned. 'What are you talking about now?'

'Sorry. But don't you think the Paxford Centre must be

319

the key? All roads seem to lead to it, one way or another.'

'Do they?'

'It's possible that she met somebody else there, who lives hereabouts, which would explain where she was last week. I mean – if she stayed at their house without telling anybody.'

'A boyfriend, you mean?' It was Caz Barkley who voiced this question.

'I wasn't thinking that, actually, but it's feasible, I suppose. And we shouldn't forget Adam Rogers.' Little lights were going on inside her head. 'What if he found out that she was seeing somebody else and got jealous? He thinks *he's* her boyfriend.'

'We know he wasn't here on Saturday morning,' said Gladwin. 'Thanks to that tracker he wears.'

'Yes, but does he wear it all the time? He's not obliged to, after all. He could easily just take it off and leave it in his room, so people think that's where he is.'

'Oh,' said Gladwin. 'Silly me.' She glared at Barkley. 'Why didn't anybody think of that?'

Caz glared back, entirely unintimidated.

'Can we be excused, do you think?' Kate Dalrymple asked. 'It's nearly eleven, so if nothing happens in the next half-hour, we'll be on our way. It's been very nice to meet you,' she said to Thea, with an odd little smile. 'I think you've made rather a hit with Clovis.'

Thea felt herself flushing and could think of nothing to say.

'Stop it, Mama. You've embarrassed her. She's

married, don't forget.' Clovis was in full charm mode, giving Thea one of his most intense eye-to-eye gazes. 'Which, I agree, is rather a pity.'

'You ought to be married yourself,' Thea blurted, casting caution to the winds. 'I bet there's a girlfriend somewhere, at least.'

'Actually, no, there isn't. It's an awful cliché, but I still haven't met the right girl. I've left all that to Luc. He went in for the whole package, a while ago now. He's even got two grown-up kids to show for it.'

'Clovis likes his freedom,' said Luc, with a complicated glare at his brother. 'The land is littered with hearts he's broken. He might not look much like our French granny, but he's outrageously Gallic most of the time.'

Gladwin flapped a hand, demanding silence, again confounded by the irrelevant banter that ignored her presence. 'No, don't go yet,' she said, trying to sound authoritative. 'I need to know more about the place in Paxford. The main thing we gleaned from the people there is that everyone adored Juliet.'

Luc and Thea both nodded miserably as this oft-repeated remark.

Gladwin went on, 'Her mother said the same thing. She said she'd trust anybody from the centre, and had made sure she knew most of them personally.'

'Rosa went there as well?'

'Very much so. As a volunteer. Although not for the past six months or so. She's had a bothersome knee, which kept her indoors a lot over the winter.'

'I never saw anybody called Rosa,' said Luc. 'Who is she?'

'Juliet's mother,' said Thea.

'I see. Well, I wouldn't take her endorsement as gospel. A lot changes in six months. People come and go all the time. Did you say something about a Nancy Spiller?' he asked Thea.

'That's right. You know her as well?'

He was evidently uncomfortable in his chair, shifting his upper body increasingly and biting his lower lip. 'A bit,' he said, before looking up at Clovis. 'Clove – can we . . . you know?'

'Oops!' Clovis grabbed the handles of the chair and swivelled it round to face the camper van. 'Left that late, didn't we?'

'Damn it,' said Kate, throwing an angry look at Gladwin. 'Quick, boys. Lucky we left the ramp down.'

Enlightenment dawned slowly, with Caz the first to understand what was happening. 'Toilet issues,' she muttered, as Clovis hurtled his brother into the vehicle. 'Must be awkward in that little space.'

'Impossible, surely?' replied Gladwin, wide-eyed.

Kate had heard her. 'Rather public, certainly,' she said. 'No chance of closing the door, but they've got it to a fine art. Luc had a colostomy bag at first, but insisted on trying to get back to something like normal. It can get very messy, either way.' She was leading the threesome further away, towards the lines of graves.

322

'He's trained himself to a schedule, amazingly. But you've interrupted it.'

Gladwin said nothing, but Caz made a sympathetic sound, then said, 'I've got a cousin with the same sort of problem. He says it's the worst part of the whole business. He was in Afghanistan,' she elaborated. 'Got on the wrong side of a roadside bomb.'

Thea felt as if she was the only one actually concerned with the investigation into Juliet's murder. Gladwin had finally taken proper interest in the Paxford Centre, but seemed slow to draw any deductions about it. 'Well . . .' she began. 'I should go and see how Drew's doing. It looks as if Linda Biddulph was serious about cancelling the funeral. How silly of her.'

'Can you really cancel a funeral?' Gladwin asked. 'What happens to the body?'

'Good question. And there's an open grave over there, waiting for him.'

'That sounds like a safety hazard,' said Barkley. The other two threw her identical glances of exasperation. 'And won't it be full of water after all that rain?' the new detective went on, undaunted.

'Oh, stop,' said Thea. 'There's nothing I can do about it, is there?'

'I think I should arrange a formal interview with that Luc man,' worried Gladwin. 'He knew Juliet. He's here where she died. He knows other people that she knew. I can't let all that go unexamined, can I?'

'You should talk to him,' Thea agreed. 'I think he'd

be really pleased to be helpful. And there's no risk that you'll suspect him of being the killer.'

'Not so sure about his brother,' observed Barkley. 'Too good-looking to be real, if you ask me.'

'With no reason in the world to want Juliet dead,' snapped Thea. 'And he can't help his looks.'

'Oh no? That tan, for a start, can only have come from a lamp. Expensive haircut. Fancy shoes. And did you *smell* him? Who takes Tom Ford cologne on a camping trip? Have you any idea what it costs?'

Thea and Gladwin looked blank. 'Never heard of it,' said Thea.

'Nor me,' said Gladwin.

'Well it's about two hundred quid for a fifty mil bottle. What does that bloke do for a living?'

'No idea,' said Thea. 'And how come you know so much about male perfumes?'

'One of my foster dads was a buyer for Harrods, believe it or not. He used to bring the stuff home.'

'Unlikely job for a foster parent,' commented Thea.

'Don't see why. They get all sorts, you know. He had a very sensitive sense of smell, even when he was little. The story was, he applied for the job as a joke and was gobsmacked when they offered it him. Not as well paid as you might think, and he never got on too well with the rest of the staff, but now I can name about a hundred different scents. Tom Ford's one of the easy ones.'

'How long do you think they'll be?' Gladwin wondered, nodding towards the van.

'Ages, probably,' said Caz.

'Well, I ought to go,' said Thea. 'You don't need me any more.' She paused. 'Except . . .'

'What?' Gladwin seemed only marginally interested in further discussions.

'I had a wild idea, early this morning. It seems a bit daft now, and I'm not sure how it even arose, after everything else that's happened. But when I realised that there was a connection between the Biddulphs and Juliet, I started to wonder a bit about Lawrence and his mother. The way Lawrence looks so much like Luc, and lives quite near here, and has been kept so completely in the dark about his father. I mean – he's going to be really angry when he finds out the truth.'

'So?'

'I don't know – but maybe you ought to have a talk with his mother, at least.'

'I can't see the slightest grounds for doing that. I've been having much more focused thoughts about the Spiller man and his wife. He's altogether too *present*, if you know what I mean. He keeps showing up. And he wasn't honest with us, from the start.'

'You sound like me,' said Thea. 'Shouldn't you be searching for hard evidence, rather than speculating?'

'Watch it. The evidence is thin on the ground – literally. We've gathered everything we can think of, and it still doesn't point anywhere. Flash of temper seems the most likely scenario. No real motive, probably – just a moment of madness. Those are the hardest to catch, of course.'

'Go and talk to Lawrence Biddulph,' Thea advised. 'Tell him you're speaking to everybody who has recently had one of our funerals, or something.'

'Except he hasn't,' Gladwin pointed out.

'You could pretend you didn't know that.'

'Oh, Lord, Thea. I can never decide whether you're an awful impediment to due police procedure, or an inspired maverick that we'd never manage without. It usually feels as if you're somehow both those things at the same time.'

'Sorry,' said Thea insincerely.

'There's a car coming,' said Caz.

Initially Thea thought this an unnecessary warning, since they were well clear of the road and cars passed all the time. Then she realised it was slowing down. When it stopped in the entrance to the field, Thea gave the young detective another glance of admiration. This girl was really something, she was beginning to suspect. Acute senses, confident approach, interesting background. 'How did you know?' she asked. Caz merely shrugged.

'Bloody hell, it's Linda and Lawrence. And his missus, by the look of it.' Thea was peering unashamedly through the side windows of the car. 'Surely they can't think the funeral's still happening. No, that's impossible – she's the one who's giving the instructions.'

First out of the car was the younger Mrs Biddulph. Thea had only seen her once, and would have had difficulty in recognising her again, even if she hadn't been transformed into a screaming harridan. 'Come on,' she shouted. 'No more of this nonsense. Just come here with me and tell me what's been going on.'

At first it seemed that she was addressing her husband, but then it became clear that it was her mother-in-law she was yelling at. She pulled open the door behind the driver's seat and grabbed an arm. She seemed altogether oblivious of her audience of four women, twenty-five yards away.

Thea watched in horrified curiosity. The spectacle of the two Biddulph families coalescing for the first time was going to be highly dramatic. But Gladwin and Barkley had not yet grasped any of the implications, other than the expectation of a disturbance, during which their duties as police officers might well be required. Kate Dalrymple was staring at the car in silent fascination.

'Excuse me? Madam?' said Gladwin to the irate woman. 'What seems to be the trouble?'

Thea snorted with suppressed laughter at this stereotypical remark. And yet, what else could she say?

Lawrence now emerged from the car, standing tall and oddly defiant. The grooves on his face that Thea had noted on her first encounter with him were, if anything, deeper than ever. 'Is that them, then?' he asked his mother, who was vigorously trying to shake off her daughter-in-law's hold. 'Izzy – let her go, will you?' he added. 'Stop being so rough.'

At last, the occupants of the camper van became aware of something going on. Clovis came to the door and stepped down the ramp. The distance was, again, too great for conversation, but nobody moved to get closer. Thea felt herself to be the hub of a swirling wheel – the only person present who knew who everybody was. And even she had not known that Mrs Lawrence was called Izzy until that moment.

'Yes, that's them,' said Linda tightly. 'But there's one missing.'

'I didn't believe it,' Lawrence said. 'How *could* I believe such a thing of my father? How could *anybody* bear such a betrayal? *My* father. Only mine.' He was half-crying, his voice low.

'I was going to tell you after the funeral,' said Linda. 'I knew this would be your reaction. I knew you'd be shattered by it. I tried to tell them, make them understand.' She said this looking at Thea, not the people by the camper van. Izzy was hovering in front of her, more like a police officer than either of the actual ones.

'So many lies,' bleated Lawrence. 'Barefaced wicked lies, fed to me from a baby. My *whole life* has been a lie. I wasn't who I thought I was. *You* weren't, either. What did you do – steal him away from that woman over there? And her sons? You *robbed* them all. And you were so ashamed you kept it a secret all this time.'

Linda and Izzy both made soothing noises, while maintaining the hostility between the two of them. 'Izzy was very wrong to tell you,' said Linda. 'I don't know what she was thinking.'

'I keep telling you – I *didn't*,' shouted Izzy. 'It was someone else, not me.'

There was movement at the camper van, preparatory to Luc descending in his chair. He set off determinedly, rolling the wheels manually. Thea, watching him, was reminded of his claim that Juliet Wilson had been accustomed to pushing him around the grounds of the Paxford Centre. Had he *needed* pushing? Was there something more to that relationship than anybody had yet guessed?

'Good God, look at him,' said Izzy. 'He's the absolute image of you, Larry. You could be twins. Look at those eyebrows!'

'He's ten years older than me. He looks like Dad.' Lawrence was staring so hard his eyes were bulging. 'That's the thing, you see. That's what did it.'

This remark was so obscure that nobody made any attempt to follow it. Gladwin and Barkley were tense, watching each individual for signs of violence. Thea was wrestling with a new set of notions that linked back to earlier in the day and involved Juliet to a startling degree. 'This is going to be very interesting,' she said quietly. 'Pay close attention, you two.'

'What the hell do you think we're doing?' snapped Gladwin. 'I still don't understand what's going on.'

'First wife, second wife, sons who've never met each other. Plus one son's wife. Fight over the funeral of the father of all these men. Youngest son only just discovered he's got brothers. What's not to understand?' It was Caz Barkley who gave this succinct summary of the situation, and again Thea was deeply impressed. 'The question is – who spilt the beans and why? My money's on the Izzy woman.'

'I don't think so,' said Thea slowly.

Something in her voice alerted Gladwin. 'Uh-oh,' she said. 'What's this, then?'

'Juliet,' murmured Thea. 'Don't you think?'

Luc was now close enough for normal conversation, with Clovis and Kate hanging back nervously. Where was Clovis Biddulph's brave aggression now, wondered Thea. All that about not letting the funeral take place without him, and being so furious at the secrecy – all long since evaporated, it seemed. But then she realised that he had been nothing more than a mouthpiece for his brother all along. It was Luc's injured feelings and profound need that had impelled Clovis and Kate into coming here. Luc had been desperate to see his father's burial, as he had already explained. Luc, who resembled the man so closely, and had, like Lawrence, seen himself as a beloved son – until cruelly betrayed.

'Hello, brother,' he said now to Lawrence. 'Seems you and I have a lot in common.'

'Like what?'

'Let down by our old dad, basically. You got the

best of him, by the sound of it. Saw you through the teenage years, anyhow. Me – I was left to sort it out by myself.'

'Hang on.' Clovis stepped forward. 'What about me and Mama? We've always been there for you, haven't we?'

Luc turned awkwardly to look at his brother. 'In the beginning you were. But later you were always out with girls, drinking, partying. Not much time for me, as I remember it. And Mama had her new fella, didn't she? How old were we when she married again? Fifteen and seventeen? I'm not complaining about that, but I wouldn't say I had very much of her attention.'

Thea drank all this in, her mind still working overtime. Luc, of course, had been fully fit at the time he was talking about. His road accident was comparatively recent. But he had not forgotten or forgiven being abandoned by his father.

Lawrence, by contrast, was barely listening at all. He was watching Gladwin, a puzzled frown adding new grooves to his face. 'Who are you, anyway?' he finally asked.

'I thought you'd never ask. As it happens, I'm Detective Superintendent Sonia Gladwin, and this is Detective Sergeant Barkley. From the police,' she elaborated, for good measure.

'Why are you here?' Lawrence showed signs of alarm, bordering on panic. 'You finished with all the crime scene stuff days ago.'

Thea could not help but look from one brother to the other – Lawrence and Luc. So alike in appearance, and, it seemed, in their emotional states. Both harboured rage against their father – Luc for decades, and Lawrence for what? Two days? Two *hours*? 'Who told you?' she asked, before she could stop herself. The question had become burningly urgent – perhaps the key to everything.

'Who do you think?' said Caz Barkley.

Thea spun round and glared at her. 'There's such a thing as being too clever,' she warned. 'You can't possibly be sure,'

'Hey! Thea!' Gladwin uncharacteristically was pulling rank. 'You two – stop it. We're already about a thousand miles from due process. Don't make it any worse. And besides, I'm still not at all sure I know what anybody's talking about.'

'Are you police, then?' Izzy belatedly asked.

'Of course they are, you idiot,' said Lawrence. 'What did you think?'

The only response he got was a toss of her head.

'Police? Why?' demanded Linda, who had taken several steps away from Izzy and was obviously at rather a loss.

'Because a woman was murdered here three days ago,' said Luc loudly. 'A woman I knew personally, as it happens. The sweetest, kindest creature you could ever wish to meet.' He stared hard at Lawrence as he spoke the final words. 'Another loss, if anybody's interested.'

It was all swirling around, as Thea tried to monitor every exchange and shift in emphasis. Six people was too many for her to hope to catch everything, even though it was narrowing down to a confrontation between Luc and Lawrence. Clovis had become a mute observer, and Kate even more so. Her gaze was mainly fixed on Linda, her replacement in Stephen Biddulph's life. Linda was rubbing her arm where Izzy had grabbed her, and making small soothing noises directed at her son. The persistent question currently occupying Thea was *Who knows what?*

'What does that have to do with anything?' Izzy wanted to know. 'We're not here because of a murder, are we? Nobody here did it, did they?'

Barkley cleared her throat in an unmistakably meaningful manner. It spoke very much louder than words would have done. Almost everybody looked at her.

'Well, they didn't, did they?' challenged Izzy.

The comprehensive silence was unnerving. Thea found herself painstakingly following threads back to their sources. *Who knew what?* When nobody spoke, she felt emboldened to ask Kate a question. 'How did you know that Stephen had died? You must have found out very quickly. It was only a week ago, after all.'

'I want to know that too,' said Linda. 'We deliberately never put any notices anywhere.'

'It's a small world, pet,' said Kate, outrageously patronising and apparently less worried about the fact of a murder than most of the others. 'Your little granddaughter with the fatuous name has a best friend called Nevaeh – which I must say is even more fatuous. Anyway, be that as it may, the little friend has an older sister, who is a compulsive blogger with a particular interest in death and dying. By a series of minor coincidences, these blogs came to Luc's attention. He can tell you precisely how it all happened, if you like.'

'This is where Juliet comes in, isn't it?' Thea asked Luc.

He nodded. 'It was her friend Adam, initially. He loves reading blogs and getting involved in all kinds of forums, and so forth. He used to show them to Juliet, who always enjoyed that sort of thing as well. She recognised the name Biddulph and asked me all about it. She . . . well, you don't want to hear all that. Let's just say we talked about it for hours – that must have been last Monday.'

'Do you know where she was from Wednesday to Friday last week?' Gladwin asked this question before Thea could say anything more.

'I don't know for sure, but I think she was playing a sort of detective game, on my behalf. She was trying to find out where my father was going to be buried. We knew from the blogs that it was to be a natural burial, and this seemed the most likely place. She knew you, of course,' he looked at Thea. 'She was going to ask you outright, but she didn't know where you lived.'

'Yes, but where *was* she?' Gladwin repeated.

Luc shook his head. 'I don't know. I hope she wasn't sleeping rough, but I can't think of anywhere she'd go.'

'Adam might know,' suggested Kate. 'Or maybe her mother.'

'We've asked them,' said Gladwin with a hint of indignation. 'Obviously.'

'She died here early on Saturday morning,' said Thea. 'Most likely about five in the morning. She could have been here all night.' She was thinking aloud, groping for that final link in the chain of reasoning. Gladwin and Barkley looked as if they were doing the same. 'Anthony Spiller was here by six, for the birdsong. He says he found her dead not long after that.'

'Stop it!' shouted Izzy. 'This is nothing to do with me or Lawrence. If Modestine's friend accidentally started it all off, well good for her, I say. It should never have been kept such a secret. It was a wicked thing to do.' She pointed a finger at Linda. 'You – you're to blame for everything, right from the start. Selfish, stupid bitch that you are.'

'Why did you come here now?' Caz Barkley asked in a calm professional tone.

'Because we were supposed to be having a *funeral*, in case you've forgotten. The man was going to be buried here in this nice quiet place. We came to see it on Saturday, and even with all you police people over there, it was still lovely. Lawrence and Modestine both thought so – didn't you?' She appealed to her husband.

'You *did*, didn't you? Even if you could scarcely bear to look at it, you know it's perfect for him. And because of *her*, these others had to intrude and spoil it.' She frowned, hearing herself. 'Yes, that's right. Because she kept it all a secret, and they were insulted by that. Who wouldn't be?' She looked at Clovis, her features softening. 'And see what you've been missing all these years? They're *nice*, your brothers. Look at them! Who can blame them for wanting to see Stephen buried?'

It struck Thea that Izzy might have hidden virtues. She was certainly courageous, voicing feelings that were still reluctant to be drawn into the light. And she was genuinely concerned for those feelings to be recognised. And she had become aware of Clovis and his charms, which made her some sort of an ally.

Kate Dalrymple appeared to be thinking along similar lines. 'Thank you,' she said. 'Thank you very much.'

'It wasn't me, it was Stephen,' said Linda, chokingly. 'I always wanted to tell Lawrence the truth.'

'But it got to the stage where you didn't dare,' said Thea. 'Because he was so totally convinced that Stephen had been the perfect father, absolutely committed to his son, responsible for getting him through a difficult childhood. The idea that he'd had two other sons who he just walked away from would unbearably undermine of all that. Shattering a myth. Rocking his whole world.'

'So, when somebody told him he had a brother called Luc, who looked just like him, he lashed out because it was too much to bear,' said Caz Barkley, as if stating the obvious, turning from Linda to Gladwin, and then to Lawrence. 'He came here by himself very early that morning, and there was Juliet Wilson. They got talking and the name Biddulph perhaps came up, and she innocently chatted about Luc and his father dying, and this being the burial place – and you just couldn't stand it, could you? What did you hit her with?'

Afterwards, Thea wasn't sure whether there really had been a collective gasp, followed by a pattern of exchanged glances and slow comprehension. Barkley's unemotional accusation fitted so neatly with the previous revelations that not even Lawrence could argue with it. Linda and Izzy both went white as the truth sank in, Linda with a hand to her throat. Kate reached out for Clovis, who flew to her side and put an arm around her. Luc had a complacent expression, suggesting that he'd known the truth all along. Lawrence grew even more haggard, his whole body shaking.

Gladwin squared her shoulders. 'Lawrence Biddulph, I'm arresting you for the murder of Juliet Wilson.' She issued the usual caution, and then looked at Barkley. 'Well done,' she said. 'Very well done.'

'She's a genius,' said Thea.

And then Drew materialised, walking hesitantly into his field, gazing in bewilderment from face to face. 'There's a couple shown up for the funeral,' he said. 'They're waiting up the road. Brenda and Gilbert, I think they said.'

'Oh, God,' said Linda, with a near-hysterical giggle. 'Bloody Brenda and Gilbert, of all people.'

'Serves you right,' said Izzy faintly.

Nobody asked who the disappointed mourners were. It was a detail too many, thought Thea. She had gone to Drew, and was holding his arm possessively. 'Lawrence killed Juliet,' she said briefly.

'Surely not?'

'Afraid so.'

'Well you did say, right at the start, that he was going to be terribly angry.'

'So I did. And he was. But oh – poor Juliet! Poor, poor Juliet!'

'That's right,' came a voice. 'Of all the people involved, she was the one who least deserved even a slap, let alone to be killed.' He gazed up at his half-brother. 'And by the hand of such a weakling as him.'

'Enough,' said Gladwin. 'Come on – let's get back to the station, and see if we can construct a proper case for the prosecution out of all this chaos.'

'No problem,' said Caz, waving her notebook. 'I'm halfway there already.'

Chapter Twenty-Eight

Although Drew was suitably interested in Thea's account of how the murder had been solved, he was clearly also thinking of other things. He asked very few questions, and only said 'Poor Juliet,' once or twice, and 'What a miserable business.'

Thea kept going over it, regardless. 'Kate's a really nice person,' she said. 'And very witty. What an idiot Stephen Biddulph must have been to leave her for Linda.'

'He seems to have been rather an idiot altogether,' said Drew. 'And what's going to happen about his funeral?' he burst out. 'I can't keep him here indefinitely.'

'No idea,' said Thea.

'Well, I need to know. I've got a new person coming today, and that's going to be all I can take. Where am I going to put Mr Shipley's sister? They'll want her removed by tomorrow at the latest.' Drew's alternative operation was often an irritation to hospital mortuaries, with his dilatory habits. Space was so limited that he tended to collect bodies at the last possible moment.

'I feel rather sorry for Linda, all the same,' said Thea. 'She can't possibly have foreseen such terrible consequences when she seduced Stephen thirty years ago.'

'Was she pregnant with Lawrence at the time, do you think?'

'That never occurred to me.' She gave it some thought. 'It might explain a few things, if she was. The shame and secrecy, for a start. And the overcompensation towards Lawrence, as a result.'

'Psychology,' said Drew vaguely.

'Right. That Caz Barkley's a star, you know. She's going to be after Gladwin's job in a few years.'

'Yes, you said.' He was plainly running out of tolerance for any more debriefing. 'Now, I'm making a sandwich, and then I'll have to go and find Andrew to see if we can construct a proper schedule for the week. I've got to chase up a payment, as well.' He sighed.

Thea took her cue. 'I should be doing that for you. Who didn't pay?'

'The Tucker family. The burial was six weeks ago now.'

'Disgraceful! I'll put a bomb under them, if you like.'

'Don't upset them. Say we can take it in instalments, if that helps.'

'Mm. Phone or letter?'

'Letter's probably better. It can get awkward on the phone.'

Two hours later, with no contact from the police or any Biddulphs, Thea went out to post her letter to the Tuckers. Having missed the collection in the village, she decided to drive to Chipping Campden and catch up with some shopping at the same time. Her usual parking place was close to the church, where there was often enough space for one or two cars. While there was scant provision of ordinary food shops, it was still possible to buy vegetables and meat in the old-fashioned way – which she found infinitely preferable to the soulless supermarket routine.

As always, she paused to admire the handsome church, built with wool money, as was Northleach and several others. Unlike some, it was almost hyperactive with events, clubs, services and community doings. A woman was standing on the flight of shallow steps leading to it, with a little white dog on a lead. It took Thea half a minute to identify Rosa Wilson. Before she could think, she had waved and called her name. Rosa was slow to respond, and seemed to be in a daze. Not surprising, Thea realised. But she was committed to approaching and conversing. It was not an unwelcome prospect, she realised.

'Oh, Rosa. They'll have told you what happened? They know who killed Juliet.'

The woman nodded. 'Makes no sense at all,' she said. 'They say somebody's coming later on to explain it all.'

'So why—?' Thea nodded at the church.

'Juliet was sleeping here. I found a message on my phone from her. She said she was all right, and needed to stay here because she had a mystery to solve.'

This was too much to unpack in a hurry. 'Sleeping *here*? You mean, in the church?'

'Seemingly so.'

'But when did you get the message?'

'This morning. I've got two phones, you see, two different numbers. I only use this one for the car. Calling breakdown people, and so forth. I know, it's dotty of me, but that's how it is. One for the house and one for the car. Only little cheap things. Nothing fancy. So when the police asked to see my phone, I gave them the house one, and there was nothing from Juliet on it. I forgot all about this one.' She was holding out a small Nokia that resembled the one Thea had owned about seven years ago. 'Then today, I got it out to check the battery, and there was a voicemail from her.' She turned a grim face to Thea. 'If I'd had the sense to listen to it last week, she'd still be alive now.'

'But wouldn't the police have examined Juliet's phone, and discovered she'd made the call?'

'They never found it.'

'A mystery to solve?' Thea went on to the next startling fact. 'What did that mean?' Then she remembered. 'Oh – it must have been the Biddulph funeral. She was watching out for it, because Luc had told her the whole story, about how they wanted to be there, but Linda wouldn't tell them when it was.'

Rosa was obviously bemused. 'Biddulph? That's the man who killed her, is it?'

'No, no. His brother. She was watching our field from Wednesday to Saturday, for signs of a funeral. Then I suppose she'd phone Luc and tell him, so they could dash over in time for it.' She shook her head. 'Why didn't she just ask Drew on Wednesday when she saw him?'

Rosa was speechless with confusion. The church was open, and a small group of people who looked like tourists were strolling aimlessly around. Rosa and Thea hesitated, then began to look for discreet nooks where someone could hide. Rosa was holding back the dog, who was whining and tugging on his lead. 'Are dogs allowed in here?' Thea wondered.

'Probably not,' said Rosa carelessly. 'He wants to go over there, look.' She nodded towards a side chapel.

'Juliet. The funeral,' Thea prompted.

'What?'

Thea felt compelled to try to explain. 'Maybe she did ask Drew when Stephen Biddulph was going to be buried, and he wouldn't tell her. I'm not sure it had even been decided by then. But Luc – that's her friend at the Paxford Centre – can't have known what she was doing. His brother Clovis took charge, and they all showed up yesterday in a camper van.'

'I was going in to see if I could find where she was hiding,' said Rosa, cutting through this tangle of incomprehensible musings. 'Do you want to come with me or not? Look – Buster knows where to go.'

'All right, then.'

On one side of the church was a raised area on which stood a large memorial with pillars and a canopy resembling a four-poster bed, with a marble statue lying on it. Directed by the insistent dog, Rosa made for it, and moments later gave a muted cry of triumph. Buster was sniffing and wagging excitedly, and by the time Thea caught up, Rosa was bending over a discreetly hidden little nest. Folded neatly into the gap between the memorial and the furthest wall was a woollen blanket. When Rosa picked it up, a phone and a notepad fell out, along with a pen and a bundle of clothes. 'Oh!' moaned the woman. 'Look at these. Spare pants. She was always absolutely insistent on a new pair every morning.'

Thea knew that it was through such details as this that grief was very much deepened. 'Come on,' she said. 'We'll tell DS Gladwin what we've found. It completes the picture, just about.'

Rosa was sobbing unrestrainedly, and had to be supported back through the church, with curious gazes following their progress. 'Such a silly girl,' she mumbled. 'Getting the phones in a muddle. She should have called my other one.'

'Easy to do, though,' said Thea. 'If both the numbers were in hers.'

'And they were. It's my fault. I should have made sure . . .' Words failed her.

Thea silently sent malevolent curses to every mobile phone in existence. In her opinion they were a bad influence on the world, in ways too numerous to count. Timmy was clamouring for one of his own, repeatedly insisting that he was the only one in his class deprived of such an essential tool. Even Drew mildly pointed out that the lack of a phone made his son a freak, albeit at the tender age of eight.

'I'll be all right now,' Rosa sniffed, when they were in the street again, Juliet's possessions in her arms, and the dog jumping up at them. 'You get on with what you were doing. I'll go home, and wait for the police person. I can show them this stuff then.' She hugged the blanket to her chest. 'Thank you, dear,' she concluded.

Thea felt dismissed before she was ready. She would have liked to be there when every piece in the convoluted picture was assembled and explained. But she accepted that her presence was in no way required. 'All right, then,' she said. 'If you're sure.'

Thea's own phone was in her bag. She leant against a wall, and took it out. She wanted to hear Gladwin's voice, to tie up these final loose ends and share the sadness. At the end of the conversation, the detective said, 'Oh, while you're there, I've got something completely different to talk about.'

'Go on.'

'I've got an old school friend, who's just bought a property somewhere near Bibury. You know – east of here. Said to be the prettiest village in England.'

'Like five or six others,' said Thea.

'Very likely. Anyway, she's having alterations done to it, and can't be there to supervise. It's just for a week or so this summer. I know you don't do house-sitting any more, but I just thought I'd mention it.'

'Bibury,' said Thea. 'Not too far from here. If it was just for a week . . . could I take the kids as well, I wonder?'

'Absolutely not. The whole point would be to give you a break from the kids.'

'Oh. I see. Let me think about it, anyway. I'll let you know.'

She got home in good time to greet the returning children, and have drinks and biscuits waiting. Although her head was still full of Juliet, Lawrence, Clovis and Kate, she was valiantly trying to clear a space for more personal and domestic matters. There was every prospect of a gruelling evening with Drew, thrashing out the momentous decision he had already more than hinted was about to be taken. She had to be clear-thinking by then. Any reference to murders and police personnel would be strictly off limits. And she didn't think she would dare mention the prospect of house-sitting in Bibury without him or his children.

It seemed to take forever to get the children to bed, with the apprehension about the coming talk doing strange things to time. Before supper, Timmy had finally remembered to tell his father about the Oakhurst boy, who was said to have only weeks still to live. 'They want him to be buried in your field,' said the child hesitantly. 'Would that be all right?'

'Of course,' Drew smiled. 'I would see it as a privilege.'

Timmy was dubious as to the full meaning of this, but understood that his father was pleased. 'Oh,' he said.

'Really, Tim, that's fine. Should I call the family, do you think?'

The little boy had no answer to that, and Drew realised his mistake. 'If they talk to you about it again, just say I know about it, and will do everything I can for them. Can you do that?'

Timmy nodded, and Thea promised herself that she would not forget about the unhappy Oakhursts again.

Drew had been quiet all through supper, other than revealing that he had had a phone call from Clovis Biddulph, who was taking over arrangements for his father's burial and still wanted Drew to do it.

'With Linda's blessing, apparently,' he added.

'Gosh!' was the only response she permitted herself.

'He's hoping for this Friday. He has to go to Prague at the weekend, he says. He's a music publisher – did you know?'

'What does a music publisher do?' she wondered, after shaking her head. 'And why Prague?'

'Don't ask me. It sounds fairly lucrative, but beyond that I'm entirely ignorant.'

'Poor Linda,' she murmured, surprising herself. 'What's she going to do now?'

Drew merely shrugged.

And then, at last, it was eight-fifteen and they were sitting with coffee, television off and the dog warily eyeing them both.

'So,' said Drew heavily. 'Where were we?'

'Deciding what to do with the rest of our lives, that's all.'

'Except it's me that has to decide, isn't it? The whole thing is on me, and I'm not sure I'm competent to deal with it.'

'Don't be daft. Just work out what you really really want, and it'll all fall into place from there.'

'Rubbish,' he said, reaching for her hand. 'Twaddle, balderdash and nonsense.'

'Really?'

'Well, maybe not entirely. If I tell you what I want, that might be a start, but I can't quite believe it would get us very far on a practical level.'

'Try me.'

He sighed. 'Okay. Well – first off, I want you to be happy. Second, ditto the kids. Third, I want to be useful to people. I want to provide a service that's hard to get anywhere else. It doesn't matter much where that happens. We're here now, so it may as well be here.'

Hope flared. 'That's all good,' she encouraged. 'Can't see any problems so far.'

He faced her and squeezed her hand. 'I think we might have overstated the problems. Things have a habit of working themselves out, if you keep your nerve.'

'Do they?' She thought of Maggs, Gladwin and Rosa Wilson, in a jumble of melancholy and low-level satisfaction that there had, at least, been answers to most of the questions.

'There are a few truths I had to remind myself of. One is: you can never go back. That thing about not stepping into the same river twice. It would be crazy to go back to North Staverton. So, I'll sell it. I'll advertise for an ethical undertaker to carry it on as it is now. I'll do all I can to keep it independent, which means taking much less money than what Maggs was offered. She won't be surprised. We're staying here, Thea. We'll spend the money on expanding, publicising, promoting what we do here. I'll get it more businesslike in some ways – but the personal touch is crucial.'

349

'Yes,' she whispered, hardly able to believe her ears.

'And you can make your own arrangements with Gladwin – whatever works best. It's absolutely fine with me. And I promise to do more of the cooking.'

'Do you?' she smiled. 'Then I think we can safely say the crisis has been resolved to the satisfaction of all parties.'

'Good,' said Drew.

REBECCA TOPE is the author of three bestselling crime series, set in the stunning Cotswolds, Lake District and West Country. She lives on a smallholding in rural Herefordshire, where she enjoys the silence and plants a lot of trees, but also manages to travel the world and enjoy civilisation from time to time. Most of her varied experiences and activities find their way into her books, sooner or later.

rebeccatope.com